FOUL PLAY

SQUEAKY CLEAN MYSTERIES, BOOK 8

CHRISTY BARRITT

COPYRIGHT:

"PAULETTE ZOLLIN." I shook my head as I soaked in my former classmate. She hadn't changed a bit, other than aging gracefully. "It's been years. Years."

My old middle school friend smiled and reached out her lithe arms to give me a hug. "Gabby, you look great. Time has been good to you."

I bounced my head from side to side, pondering the truth—or absolute fallacy—in her words. The years had actually been both hard and rewarding. Lately, that seemed more apparent than ever. "I don't know if I'd say that, but I try not to complain. What are you doing now?"

Paulette's father was filthy rich, and I imagined her spending her days drinking cocktails on the beach while being fanned by bronzed, shirtless men. If I closed my eyes and tried really hard, I might be able to imagine her working. But it was so much of a stretch that it required too much effort at the moment.

Paulette hooked a silky blonde hair behind her ear and smiled demurely. She unlocked the door and we stepped inside the former Oceanside Middle School. "I'm actually working for my father. This place is my big project."

She spread her arms out to display the building before us.

My gaze traveled beyond her as my mind voyaged back in time. Had it really been seventeen years since I was a middle schooler here at Oceanside? It just didn't seem possible. The school had long since closed, replaced by a newer, more modern building about three miles away.

"Look at this place," I muttered.

The school hadn't looked great back when I was a student. It had been rather old and worn down and well used by the students who scurried from class to class. Now, after being abandoned for the past six years, the building seemed to have withered without students inside to keep it alive.

Gone were the posters advertising extra curricular activities and after school clubs. The sports trophies had been cleared from the showcase display. There were no art projects. Instead, the hallway was bare, with no signs of life. All I saw was a light hanging haphazardly from the ceiling, a ladder propped against the wall, and a toolbox resting in the middle of the floor. In the distance, I spotted some graffiti spray-painted on the wall across from the offices.

Paulette's gaze followed mine. "My father decided to take on the renovations. I'm just over-seeing the project."

Paulette was actually working and not just living off her family's money? I would have never guessed it.

My old friend had come a long way since middle school, when she seemed incompetent at doing anything except looking pretty. I'd always liked Paulette, and we'd helped each other out back in our tween days. I'd stuck up for her; she'd been a loyal friend. It had been an unlikely relationship that worked for both of us.

"Tell me about this project."

"We're turning this place into the Cultural Arts Center of Virginia Beach," Paulette started. "The old classrooms will be used for community meetings, art classes, and galleries. The cafeteria will be redone and made into a restaurant. We're going about all of this in phases. Two hallways here at the school are blocked off because we're not even sure if we'll use them again. At this point, there's no need to heat and run electricity throughout the entire place."

We kept walking, past the principal's office and the stinky bathrooms and my old English classroom. We paused at a set of double doors and Paulette opened one. I slipped inside and caught my breath.

This room, I mused, was the crowning glory of the place.

The auditorium, also known as the place where my career in theater had been made.

Okay, my career really hadn't been *made* here. I mean, I was a crime scene cleaner today. But I'd acted in every performance I could during my seventh and eighth grade years, and I'd *felt* like a star, even if I'd just been an extra.

Being in theater had helped me have a place to belong, something I desperately needed at the time. The adolescent years were turbulent for most, but add to that the fact that my brother had vanished on my watch and my family had become the living, breathing definition of dysfunctional shortly after, and that time in my life had almost been torture.

"This is what will kick off everything," Paulette continued. "Our big opening for the entire center will be a musical done by local talent. It's called *The Music of the Specter*. It was written just for us."

Just the thought of a musical taking place here made something wiggle through my blood.

Excitement—that's what it was. I couldn't get my love for musical theater out of my system.

"I'm sure you're curious about why I asked you here." Paulette rubbed her manicured hands together . . . nervously?

"I have been curious."

Since she'd called yesterday, my mind had run through a million scenarios, including a possible middle school reunion or a flash mob organizational meeting she needed me to oversee. I'd even considered that maybe it was for no good reason at all except to relive the not-so-glorious days of old.

I stared at Paulette a moment. She was beautiful —stunning, actually. She had pale, porcelain skin and glossy blonde hair cut in an expensive bob that reached her jawline. She was probably 5' 8" and model thin. Her blue eyes were striking but troubled at the moment.

Her father was one of the wealthiest men in the area. Growing up, kids had either made fun of her for being a bit of an airhead or they'd used her because of her family's money. Even as a thirteen year old, I couldn't stand for people mistreating others, so I'd taken her under my wing.

Right now, as I waited for her to gather her thoughts, I shoved my hands down into my jean pockets, feeling rather frumpy next to my cultured friend. Most of my fingernails had been broken, and I never bothered to paint them. Working as a crime scene cleaner, I literally had to get my hands dirty. Plus, I'd just come from one job and could possibly have sawdust in my hair.

"As I mentioned, we're working on a production of *The Music of the Specter*. It's really the highlight of this whole center. It's what we're going to be known for." Paulette leaned against one of the seats, still frowning. "We started rehearsal two weeks ago and, since then, everything under the sun has gone wrong."

I tensed, remembering the stage production of *Oklahoma* that we'd done here in seventh grade. Someone had tried to sabotage the play back then. In fact, figuring out the person behind the acts of vandalism had been one of the first mysteries I'd solved. I'd been hooked ever since.

"What's happened?" I asked.

Her frown deepened. "It's been a lot like that play in middle school. We've had falling spotlights. A section of the stage collapsed. One of the curtains fell and nearly clobbered the man playing the Specter. I'm afraid that if we don't figure out what's going on soon, this whole production is going to be shut down before it's really even started."

"So *Specter* has its very own specter?" The

thought amused me in a strange way, but I had a twisted sense of humor. I had to or I wouldn't survive in my grim profession.

She nodded. "Ironic, isn't it? I mean, since Zollin Industries bought this place, we've been in the process of updating everything in the building to bring it up to standard. I know that these things have happened because someone *made* them happen. Someone wants to ruin this production."

We started walking together toward the stage. I suddenly remembered the smell of greasy fries in the cafeteria and dirty socks in the gym. I remembered the taunts of my nemesis, Donabell Bullock. I remembered the sweet conversations I'd had with my best friend Becca while sitting in these very seats. Mostly, we'd talked about boys.

Now here I was again, this time with Paulette. I hadn't seen this coming.

"I'm sorry to hear about what's been happening," I started. "But that still doesn't explain why I'm here. To reminisce about old times?"

Paulette cast a rueful smile my way. "No, I wish. It's actually because I'd like for you to consider investigating for me."

"Really?" My pulse spiked.

She nodded. "Really. I realize we haven't spoken in years, but I've kept tabs on you. You're like an urban legend among the old middle school gang—

and my father. Every time your name shows up in the newspaper, he chuckles and says, 'Hey Paulette, take a look at this. It's our old friend Gabby.' I think you'd be a great one to look into these disturbances."

"I'm honored." For someone as successful as Mr. Zollin to even remember me gave me a thrill.

Paulette's eyes locked on mine. "I'd like for you to go undercover, Gabby. I'd give you a minor role in the play and, in the meantime, you would snoop around and try to figure out what's going on. My father's already approved the expense, and I think you'll agree the compensation he's offering is generous."

I paused by the stage. "Tell me about the play. Who's in it. How'd you find the actors. When's opening night, etc."

Something flashed in her gaze. "You'll never believe this. Guess who's directing?"

I shrugged, not even having a good guess. "Who?"

"Mrs. Baker."

My eyes widened. "Our old drama teacher? No way."

Paulette smiled. "It's true. She stopped teaching when her baby was born, but now her daughter is in middle school and she has more time on her hands. As soon as Mrs. Baker heard about what we were doing, she volunteered to help."

"I'd love to see her again." Mrs. Baker had been a huge influence in my life during a time when I'd been unsure about so many things.

Paulette crossed her arms, turning to look back at the stage. "So, we had auditions about a month ago. Everything seemed flawless for the week after the cast was announced. We have a great cast, a wonderful set designer, and an experienced stage manager. All the pieces were in place to make this a successful play."

"That's good news."

"It was at the first practice that things started going wrong. That's when the curtain fell and nearly clobbered Jerome, who plays the Specter. The incidents have continued since then." She pressed her lips together. "I'm afraid this whole play will be ruined, Gabby. I can't afford it—not personally and not professionally."

I wondered exactly what she meant, but I didn't ask.

"Did you have anyone check out the incidents? The curtain, for example. Did anyone inspect it to see if it was properly installed? Can you be sure it wasn't an accident?"

"Our maintenance man checked it out. He said he didn't see any signs of foul play. It looked like the track holding the curtain in place separated from the plaster."

"Did you check out the company that installed everything? Maybe they didn't know what they were doing."

"They're professionals. They design auditoriums and stages for theaters across the country. I verified they were reputable by calling their references. I didn't find anything suspicious."

"What happened next?"

"Next a spotlight fell. Thankfully, no one was on stage at the time. After that, one of the actresses got locked in her dressing room. The door was totally jammed, and I didn't think we were ever going to get her out. She was absolutely hysterical. Another night, all the lights went out in the auditorium. It was pitch black in here." She shook her head. "It's all been very strange."

"Strange is a good word for it."

"Now do you see what I'm saying? All these things can't be a coincidence. There's something going on." She turned to me, a hopeful look in her eyes. "So, what do you say? Will you take the case?"

Will you take the case? I liked the sound of that. Despite the rush of pride, I had to think about the offer for a moment.

I still had a big workload with the business I co-owned. We'd called it Trauma Care for years but had recently renamed it Squeaky Clean when we'd expanded to do more than crime scene cleaning.

I had to make sure I didn't leave my business partner Chad holding the bag—or the mop, for that matter. I had to shoulder my part of the responsibility.

"Practices are just in the evenings, right?" I mentally ran through my schedule.

"That's correct."

"So I can still work at my day job." Day job was a bit of an understatement. The job consumed most of my time, especially when you considered I was on call 24-7. It had gotten a little easier in recent months since we'd hired a couple of part-timers to help carry the workload.

"Of course."

I smiled wider than I had in a long time. The past couple of months had been relatively uneventful. I told myself that was a good thing, that I needed things to slow down. But I was itching to dive into an investigation again. "I'll do it then."

She grinned widely. "Great! You have no idea how much I was hoping you'd say that." She took my arm and pulled me toward the steps. "Come on, let me show you the stage and give you an overview of the play."

As I followed her, a strange lump formed in my throat. I reached the center of the stage and, at once, I felt like a thirteen year old again. I clearly remembered making my debut. I remembered seeing my mom and dad in the audience. I heard the applause, felt the rush of excitement that came after a performance.

Beyond the stage experience, I was taken back in time to middle school. I remembered trying to straighten my curly red hair so I'd fit in with everyone else. I remembered the taunts from the resident school diva. I remembered my first crush. My first boyfriend. My first mystery.

All those things, in some way, shaped me into the person I was today.

Paulette cleared her throat. "So, the musical we're doing is an original written by a woman named Arie Berry."

"Should I know who she is?" I asked, feeling a touch uncultured for a moment. The woman's name didn't ring any bells, however. With a rhyming, sing-songy name like that, certainly I'd remember it.

Paulette shook her head. "Arie actually found me online and pitched the idea to me. I read the script and heard the music, and I was on board. It's a fascinating storyline. I just knew that this was the play we had to do to launch our theater and introduce it to the world."

I couldn't wait to see the production. I adored the theater, and it had been a long time since I'd immersed myself in that world. I routinely listened to show tunes and my friend Garrett had taken me to see *Wicked* when it came into town at Christmastime.

Paulette walked behind the curtain—not the old dusty one we used to have. No, this one was black and shiny and didn't make me sneeze when I got too close.

Apparently, the broken one had been repaired.

"Doesn't all of this bring back memories?" Paulette tugged at the curtain.

I tensed for a moment, waiting for the drape to fall again. Thankfully, it didn't. "Does it ever."

"The woman I found for the lead part is really phenomenal." She turned to me, and I saw the worry in her eyes. "Gabby, a lot is depending on this. It's my chance to prove to my father that I'm able to do more than ride his coat tails. I want to show everyone that I can stand on my own two feet, that I can be a success at something."

Something about her words clutched my heart. I'd always wanted to see Paulette succeed. It was obvious this was really important to her, as well. "I'll do whatever I can."

"You were always such a good friend, Gabby."

We turned the corner toward the dressing rooms and stopped in our tracks.

I looked down and gasped. I spotted some shoes. Attached to legs. Did they lead to . . . a body? A curtain blocked my view.

I shoved the drape aside and felt the blood drain from my face.

I knew a dead body when I spotted one. And, unless this was some elaborate prop, there was one behind the stage.

CHAPTER
TWO

THE LIFELESS FACE of a young brunette stared zombie-like at the ceiling. Dried blood formed a crusty river from her nose. Her chest was morbidly still, absent the rise and fall of breath.

"Scarlet," Paulette whispered, her hand flying over her mouth. A half gasp/half cry escaped from her.

"Who's Scarlet?"

"She's Scarlet." She pointed at the dead body.

I gathered that. I kept those words silent.

"But *who* is she?" I asked instead. "Stage manager? Actress? Custodian?"

"The lead." Paulette shook her head, her skin even paler than usual. "The one reason I knew this play was going to be a success. Oh my goodness. What happened to her?"

Despair invaded my friend's voice and she looked like she might pass out. Her gaze fixated on the corpse in front of us, and her hand traveled to her stomach.

I squeezed her arm, trying to take her focus off Scarlet. "Paulette, I need you to go call the police. I'm going to stay here with Scarlet until the officers get here. Okay?"

She nodded stiffly, pulled her gaze from the body, and hurried off the stage.

As soon as she disappeared, I squatted down beside Scarlet. I didn't have to feel her neck for a pulse to know she was dead.

It was obvious from her absolute stillness.

I looked down at her and shook my head.

Scarlet had been beautiful, probably in her mid-twenties with a slim build and flawless skin. She wore colorful striped socks and black shoes with curled toes. Part of her costume? I didn't know. Based on the expensive looking highlights in her hair, her French tipped fingernails, and the sparkling ring on her finger, I imagined her as the type to always go out wearing her best.

The only blood I saw trickled from the corner of her nose. I didn't see any gunshot wounds. There were no visible bruises. Her clothes didn't look especially tousled.

What had happened to her?

I glanced around, trying to use my time quickly and wisely. As soon as the police arrived, I'd be whisked away from the crime scene. This was my only chance to gather any clues.

Behind me, there were two chairs, still upright and facing the stage. There was a table with some empty water bottles and a couple of copies of what was probably the script.

Nothing appeared out of place.

I glanced up. The catwalk was directly above me.

And part of the railing dangled.

Scarlet had fallen from up there, I realized. But why in the world would she have been on the catwalk? In heels, at that.

I still had a million questions, but just then I heard voices in the auditorium. I stepped from behind the stage and saw Paulette leading two uniformed cops toward me. Her skin still looked pale and her hands trembled as she pointed toward me.

"We found Scarlet back there," she whispered.

The cops took one look at Scarlet and called the homicide squad. While the two officers secured the scene, I pulled Paulette away to ask her some questions.

"When was the last time you saw Scarlet?" I asked.

"Last night at rehearsal."

"Was that what she was wearing?"

She blinked several times. "What was she wearing last night? I—I don't . . . I don't know. I wasn't paying attention."

"Sweatpants? A sweatshirt?" I prompted her. "Striped, multicolored socks with strange-looking black heels?"

Her eyes manically darted back and forth. "No. No. Scarlet wasn't that type. She was wearing a gray Ralph Lauren sweater and some 7 jeans."

Paulette had always known fashion.

"Good. That's what I needed to know. That means she changed clothes sometime between practice and the time she died. Paulette, were you the last one to leave after rehearsal?"

"I was. I always am. I didn't want to chance anything happening . . . and now look what's happened." She muffled her cry with hands over her face.

I placed a hand on her arm. "Paulette, I want to help. Stick with me here for a minute, though, okay?"

She pulled her hands down. Her action may have been affirmative, but her gaze was still riddled with uncertainty. "Whatever I can do."

"Okay, think carefully. What time did you leave?" I kept my voice even and calm, trying not to upset her even more.

"Around eleven." She dipped her head down in a slow nod as if to confirm her words.

"Anyone leave with you?"

"I walked out with Anthony. He's the stage manager."

"Does anyone else have a key to the place?" I asked.

"Yes, Anthony has a key. So does the manager of the entire Cultural Arts Center. Her name is Ms. Maggie. Oh . . . and Mrs. Baker has a key, also." She looked at me with worry in her gaze. "Was I too trusting? Did I give too many people keys? What's my father going to think?"

I laid a hand on her arm. "It's okay, Paulette. You did just fine. I'm just trying to ascertain how Scarlet may have gotten in here after hours."

"I have no idea," she whispered. "I know I locked up behind myself. If there's one thing I'm careful about it's safety. I had a break in at my house a few months ago, and I've been paranoid ever since."

I had more questions, but before I could say anything, I heard a voice in the distance.

"If it isn't Gabby St. Claire."

I turned and spotted Detective Charlie Henderson walking down the center aisle toward the stage. She wore a grey pants suit that emphasized her long legs, and I could see the edge of her gun peeking out from beneath her jacket. Her honey blonde hair was swept up in a neat bun

My, my, my. Wasn't this a grand reunion? And not just of the middle school variety.

Charlie was my ex-boyfriend's current girlfriend. The one he'd essentially started dating while I was dating him. Despite what might seem like bad blood, I'd always liked Charlie, and I thought she and Parker were good for each other. Not many people could put up with someone as arrogant as my ex.

"I see you're back to work," I said.

Charlie had had a baby not terribly long ago. Maybe five months? I couldn't remember for sure. As the distance between us lessened, I noticed the dark circles under her eyes.

She frowned ever-so-slightly. "My mom moved to the area, just to help me take care of George. She's been a big help. I don't think I could have gone back to work if she hadn't moved here."

"I know your schedule and Parker's are both full."

She scowled. "I guess you haven't talked to Parker in a while."

I didn't even want to ask. But I did. "What's going on?"

"We split. He split, I should say. He warned me he wasn't the settling down type. I thought I'd reformed him." She shrugged stiffly. "You know the story."

Yeah, I knew the story. And I knew Parker. I'd

really hoped that he'd grown up. "I'm sorry, Charlie. I thought he was different, too."

She let out a sigh and evened her features into a professional expression. "Anyway, I hear there's a dead body?"

I nodded. "Let me show you where."

Three hours later, the crime scene was finally cleared, Scarlet's body was carried away to the Medical Examiner's Office, and Paulette and I stood alone in the auditorium.

The standing part didn't last long.

As soon as the door closed and the authorities left, she sank into one of the wooden chairs carved with "Mitch Hearts Laura" and uncountable pieces of ABC gum stuck around the arms.

"I can't believe Scarlet is dead. She was so young. She had so much potential." Paulette ran a tissue under her eyes, wiping away the moisture there.

I sat down beside her and squeezed her arm. "I'm sorry, Paulette. I know this must be hard for you, not only because you lost a friend, but because you put so much work into the play."

She sucked in a quick breath and her wide eyes fixated on me. "What do you mean?"

I chomped down, trying to figure out how I'd just

put my foot in my mouth without even realizing it. Certainly she realized the implications of a dead lead actress . . . right?

I softened my voice. "I mean, your lead is dead. Unless you have an understudy, I'm guessing you'll pull the plug on *The Spector*."

She moaned. "I didn't even think about that! We've put thousands of dollars into this auditorium. I can't just cancel everything."

"At least it looks like her death was an accident," I tried to offer some comforting words. But even as the consolation left my lips, I doubted its truth. There was more to this story, and I wanted to know what.

Charlie and a couple of crime scene techs had gone up to the catwalk and essentially proven my original theory: that was the place from where Scarlet had fallen. According to them, there were no signs of foul play. They were still going to do some tests and run the evidence. I imagined they'd talk to Scarlet's friends and family. They'd try to figure out why she came back to the school, if she was meeting anyone, and all the normal stuff.

In the meantime, no one was allowed to go on the catwalk or stage until it was determined if any safety protocols had been broken.

"Accidents like that will make it so no one wants to go near this place. It was bad enough with all the small incidents of vandalism. But someone dying?"

She moaned. "What am I going to do? All those people who said I'd never be anything more than a spoiled rich girl with rocks for brains? They're going to be right."

Oh no. I couldn't let my friend go here.

"Paulette, you and I both know that isn't true."

She looked at me and sniffled. "Did you hear about that new dinner cruise ship that was all set to depart from Norfolk, Destiny's Edge?"

I nodded slowly. "I vaguely remember something."

"It was a multi-million dollar project. State of the art, luxurious, small but spacious. It was going to revolutionize the dinner cruise industry."

"Sounds nice."

She frowned. "Then everything went wrong. There wasn't enough staff, everyone got food poisoning, the entertainment backed out at the last minute. Destiny's Edge made its maiden voyage and that was it. The whole company was sunk. Sure, it held on for three more months, but it was a disaster of Titanic proportions—only no one died."

"That sounds awful." But why was she telling me this?

Her gaze met mine. "I was in charge of that project. It was the first big thing that Daddy trusted me with."

Ouch! "That stinks."

"It took me four years to convince him to let me take on this project. And now look! It's like a replay of Destiny's Edge." She let out a sob.

I patted her shoulder again, trying to think of something compassionate, sensitive, and true to say. "We're going to figure this out. One way or another."

She looked up at me and sniffled. "Oh, Gabby. You were always a lifesaver. Some things never change."

"I'll help you figure out what happened."

"I know the perfect way you can do it!" Her eyes suddenly brightened. "You can take Scarlet's part in the play! You can be Elsa McGoverness!"

A mix of horror and elation rushed through me with enough force to make me dizzy.

"Me?" I squeaked.

She nodded, her eyes suddenly bright again. "You've always been a great actress. You'd be perfect!"

I swallowed hard, uncertainty making my stomach flutter. "I don't know . . ."

"There's nothing to know. You're in!"

I sucked on my bottom lip a moment, unsure how to break the news to her that I wasn't exactly lead performer material. Looking at Paulette's hopeful eyes now, I wasn't sure she could even handle the news.

Instead, I nodded. "Sounds like a plan."

CHAPTER THREE

"EVERYONE, I'd like to introduce you to our newest cast member," Paulette started, looking amazingly pulled together considering what we'd discovered only five hours earlier. "This is Gabby St. Claire."

Everyone stared at me. I hadn't expected a rousing round of applause. After all, one of their own had just died. Paulette had announced the news, the cast had spent about an hour crying and mourning—as they should—and now she was addressing the practical side of the loss.

We all sat in the chorus room, which had three elevated levels with chairs. Paulette stood at the front, where a teacher might have given instruction, while the rest of the cast sat in a semi-circle on the risers, sniffling with tissues in hand and an unwelcoming air about them.

She called me up to the front with her. The reception, not surprisingly, seemed a little cold. I would have probably handled things differently myself, if I'd had a choice in the matter. But Paulette had gotten the crazy idea in her head that I would take the lead part, and there was no changing her mind.

I wished Mrs. Baker could have been here. My former teacher had a way of smoothing over bad situations. Things might have gone better if I'd had her in my corner, but apparently she had an awards ceremony to attend with her daughter.

I couldn't wait to see her.

I realized Paulette was staring at me, waiting for me to say something. I cleared my throat, trying to figure out the best approach to take in the midst of the glares from the cast. There really wasn't one, I decided.

"I'm glad to be here but very sorry for the reason behind my addition," I started, thinking I sounded rather graceful.

Of course, a new person getting the lead role might not go over so well with some of the folks here, and I guessed I couldn't blame them.

After the cops left and before rehearsal, I'd reviewed the script. The play was such an odd little production—not that I'd told Paulette that. It was a mixture of *Phantom of the Opera*, *Les Miserables*, and *The Sound of Music*. It was hard for me to wrap my mind around.

In the play, a nun was sent to star in a musical where mysterious things were happening on set. Meanwhile, a man who'd been wrongly accused of a crime he never committed had escaped prison and now lived between the walls of the old theater, hoping that the detective after him wouldn't find him until he redeemed his life. People called him the Specter.

This was the script that Paulette had thought was brilliant? It was practically a knockoff—a parody minus the cleverness. Add to that the fact that the songs were in abnormally high keys, the range was difficult, and the background tracks all sounded synthesized, reminding me slightly of carnival music. It seemed a recipe for disaster, on more than one level.

I kept my mouth shut.

Paulette had given me a CD of the songs I needed to learn: Yes, I'd have to sing.

And, don't get me wrong—I loved singing. But that didn't mean I was any good at it.

My mind jumped back to the present.

"Even though we don't have access to the stage right now, we're going to run through Act One," Paulette continued. "Everyone in place."

Still feeling self conscious because of the veiled hostility of the other actors, I vowed to remain low key. Paulette remained firm that we shouldn't tell anyone I was investigating this case. She thought I'd do better undercover—as the lead, the most vied for position.

So now I looked like the girl with connections, the actor who only had this role because of who I knew. Which, in reality, was true.

I had no idea where to go to "get in place," so I wandered to the middle of the makeshift stage.

"You're over there." One of the male actors pointed stage left and cast another scowl my way.

I thanked him, trying not to freeze in panic when I realized all the other actors would take one look at me and realize I was a total and complete amateur. It wouldn't take a detective to figure that out.

I comforted myself with the thought that this *was* community theater; I supposed most of the people up here were officially amateurs. Still, I'd bet they had more experience than me. Based on the daggers some were shooting my way, they may even be rooting for me to fail.

Just as I reached center stage, a shrill voice cut through the air. "My play is going to be ruined!"

I glanced over at the door and saw an incredibly tall woman with sleek dark hair push into the room, waving a stack of papers in her hands.

Paulette shrank back. "Arie. I didn't realize you were going to be here tonight."

"Not even a call?" Arie demanded as she reached Paulette. "You didn't have the *courtesy* to let me know *yourself* that the lead *actress* in *my* play *died*?"

Based on the woman's histrionics, she should have been an actress. She was certainly dramatic enough.

"Arie, it's been a long day." Paulette tucked a hair behind her ear, her shoulders slumping slightly. "I was going to call you."

"I had to get a text from a cast member!" Arie's nostrils flared and her hand went to her hip.

Paulette glanced back at the cast. I followed her gaze and noticed a slight smile curled the lips of the actor who'd grumbled at me earlier about where to stand.

Interesting. If I remembered correctly, he was Jerome—my costar.

"We're all in shock over this," Paulette tried to explain.

My old friend was going to be eaten alive, I realized.

I felt the need to jump back into my old middle school role—the need to try and protect her. But Paulette was a woman now. Certainly she could stand up for herself . . . right?

"I personally handpicked Scarlet to play the role

of Elsa McGoverness in this musical. Now, it's all going to be ruined! And it's your fault!" Her icy glare temporarily froze Paulette.

Paulette opened her mouth and then shut it again. She took a step back, her hand fluttering through the air.

Meanwhile, Arie inched closer. "I *trusted* you with this script. It was going to be my *big break*! I'd be smart to pull out now and find a *new* theater troupe for the production."

"But . . . I—you can't. We—"

"I *can*, and I *might*!" Arie insisted. "It's bad enough that a *ghost* is haunting this auditorium, but now *this*!"

"Enough!" I yelled.

My head was going to explode if I heard any more of this.

Everyone turned to look at me.

So much for staying low key.

"Who do *you* think you *are* charging in here and insulting *the producer* who took a *chance* on you and your work? You're out of line." I took a page from her book and overly emphasized all the important words in my sentence. That seemed to be her language.

Arie stared at me, her gaze cold enough to ice over the sun. "*Who* are *you*?"

I held my chin up, fully aware that I was about to

drop a bombshell. "I'm the new Elsa McGoverness."

Her mouth gaped open in anger as she turned back to Paulette. "You cast someone *new* without even *consulting* with me?"

"Arie—" I started.

"It's not *Airie*. It's Arie—pronounced *R-E*. No rhyming involved! How many times do I have to say that to you people around here?" She spewed before turning back to Paulette. "I'm calling my lawyer. That's all there is to it! I will not have my name ruined like this."

Before anyone could say anything else, Arie stormed out the door.

I looked at Paulette. The poor girl looked like she might have a breakdown. She did her nervous little tugging her hair behind her ear gesture and offered a feeble smile.

"The show must go on," she said, a little too softly for the words to have their full effect. When everyone stared at her a moment, she finally clapped her hands. "You heard me. Chop chop!"

Good for her. I was glad she'd pulled it together enough to get through practice. Otherwise, I feared too many people in this room might smell blood and see Paulette as someone they could eat alive.

I'd seen it happen with Paulette one too many times in the past.

Maybe, finally, things had changed.

CHAPTER
FOUR

I WALKED out of the Cultural Arts Center with Paulette at 11 and watched her lock the door behind us. Before we'd left, I'd confirmed there was no one in the building. Tomorrow morning there shouldn't be any surprises waiting for anyone.

Unless someone with a key, for some reason, went inside during the night. Paulette insisted that all her key keepers were trustworthy, though. She'd even given me one, which made me wonder just how many other people had keys.

I pulled my coat closer as a winter wind swept through the parking lot. It was mid-January and a cold snap had claimed the area. The air was brittle and, with the brisk wind, the bite was painful.

"So, tell me about the ghost haunting this place," I prodded as we headed toward our vehicles—mine an old white work van and hers a Land Rover. In the heat of the moment, I'd let Arie's words slip right on by me, but they'd come back to . . . well, come back to haunt me now.

Paulette shook her head. "At our second rehearsal, Arie stormed in one night—she has a habit of doing that—and she had all these old news articles with her. They were about this teacher who'd died at the school back in the 70s."

"What?" I would have heard about that, right? I mean, there'd always been this rumor that a ghost haunted the place, but I thought it was all just a story someone made up to scare us measly middle schoolers. I had no idea there was actually any truth to it. I was still skeptical.

"She found the newspaper articles to prove it," Paulette continued, pulling her white wool coat tighter around her neck. "I guess the school administration tried to bury it. They didn't want students freaking out."

"Tell me about the articles."

We walked toward the parking lot at the other side of the building.

"The woman's name was Rose Hines. She'd just started teaching here. Drama, for that matter. One day, a custodian found Rose in the orchestra pit. Apparently, she'd stayed late trying to prep some of the props, and she fell, hit her head, and died."

Curiosity—and suspicion—clawed at me. "Was there ever an investigation into it?"

Paulette shrugged. "I think so, but there were no signs of a crime. It just appeared to be a tragic accident. So now Arie thinks that the ghost of Rose is coming back to haunt us."

"I don't believe in ghosts," I stated, just to get my opinion out there.

"I don't know if I do or not. I went to a psychic once and some of the things she told me came true. Maybe there is a supernatural element alive and well in this world."

"I believe in the supernatural, but I don't put my faith in ghosts or psychics."

"Then who?"

"I put my faith in God," I told her. "I'd love to tell you about Him sometime."

I swallowed hard. I was a new Christian and whenever it came to talking to people about my faith, I started to feel like a little child, for some reason. I guess I was a baby Christian. Still, I had great news to share about how Christ had changed my life and given me hope. Why would I want to keep that to myself?

"Sometime," Paulette said with a nod as we reached the end of the sidewalk

I paused at the edge of the parking lot. A man was leaning against my van.

"You good?" Paulette asked nervously. She was probably still thinking of Scarlet's demise and wondering if the man was trustworthy. Everyone in the cast seemed to be on edge, and rightfully so. Whispers had run rampant during practice. Cast members had insisted on walking each other to cars. I'd noticed several looking over their shoulders while on stage.

All of them except Jerome. He seemed content to glare at me. What was his problem? And what about that glance I'd seen him and Arie exchange?

I remembered Paulette's question and nodded. "Yeah, I'm fine. I'll see you tomorrow for rehearsal."

I watched her walk away before turning back to my van. I smiled at the man there. He leaned against my door, his ankles crossed, and wearing clothing that cost more than my monthly rent. An overhead streetlight illuminated his grin.

"Garrett Mercer," I murmured. "Fancy seeing you here."

"I quite enjoy hanging out in dark parking lots, waiting for beautiful women until the wee hours of the night."

I playfully jabbed him in the chest. "If you weren't so cute, that would sound creepy."

He stood and straightened his sleeves. "It does, doesn't it?" His British accent had a way of sounding self-deprecating and adorable. "I didn't think you were ever going to get out of there."

"It's been quite the day, to say the least."

"You still up for dinner?" he asked.

"I totally forgot to call! I'm sorry." I'd even texted him right before practice to tell him I was at the school and running late. I was supposed to call when I knew when we'd be done.

"No apologies necessary, Love. I know you're a busy lady."

"How long have you been waiting?"

"Only three hours."

"Three hours!"

"I jest. I jest." He chuckled, the moon reflecting in his gaze and making his eyes glimmer. "I actually tried to call about an hour ago. When you didn't answer, I decided to swing by. I saw your van was still here. You hungry?"

I glanced at my watch. "At this hour? Isn't it late to eat?"

He shrugged. "You can think of it as late or you can consider it romantic. I know what I choose."

I smiled. "Why not then?"

"Great. I found this cozy little place. It's only about a mile from here. Want to give it a try?"

"Why not?"

We bypassed my van—which smelled like cleaning fluids anyway—and climbed into his hybrid. I let myself melt into the soft leather seat. It had been a long day, and I was tired. I wished I could hop in the shower, change into something more respectable—something that would make me feel pretty. But Garrett seemed to like me just as I was. He never complained, at least.

Usually, his companionship had a way of cheering me up. The two of us had a bit of a complicated relationship that wavered somewhere between friendship and romance.

I first met him when I was trying to figure out who'd shot my then fiancé, Riley Thomas. Garrett had later hired me to work a cold case involving the murder of his family. During that time, my fiancé and I had decided to take some steps back—way back. Riley was recovering from a brain injury, and he'd moved back up to D.C., a good three hours from here, in order to let his family help with his grueling therapy.

Riley and I still talked every so often. It had started weekly, then moved to every other week, and eventually less than that. Every time I heard his voice, my heart panged with sadness.

Initially, I'd hoped he might come down for a visit or that he might fight to keep me in his life. He hadn't. He'd all but disappeared.

I'd gone up to visit him twice. After the second time, his mother had kindly told me that he seemed upset every time he talked to me. She'd hinted that I was hampering his recovery.

At that moment I'd realized that, more than anything else, Riley needed time and if I truly loved him that's exactly what I should give him. I knew that things might never return to the way they'd been. All the dreaming and wishing in the world wouldn't do a thing to change those possibilities.

So now I left the ball in his court. I didn't like it, but I accepted it.

All of that said, I wasn't ready to jump into another relationship. Garrett knew that. We were just hanging out, talking almost every day, and enjoying each other's company.

In all honesty, I was surprised that he'd stuck around this long. He was a hot commodity in the area and could date anyone he wanted. He owned a successful coffee business, he was interested in giving back to the community, he was rich, handsome, and he had a killer accent. He'd even warned me a couple of months ago that he wouldn't wait forever.

That had been in November. It was now mid-January, and he was still hanging around. For all I knew, he could be dating other people. But I had a feeling he wasn't.

My friends all liked Garrett. There was really nothing not to like about him.

Except that he wasn't Riley.

We pulled up to a restaurant off Shore Drive in Virginia Beach. The eatery was a little shack that sat on the Chesapeake Bay and, despite its rustic appearance, it had five star prices.

Garrett didn't even have to say anything to the waiter. As soon as he spotted Garrett, he nodded toward the back, motioning for us to follow him. He led us to a covered deck overlooking the water. Party lights hung overhead, and the Mamas and the Papas played from somewhere overhead. Most of the people around us had had too much to drink, evidenced by both the bottles and glasses on their tables and the volume of their laughter.

But I tuned all of that out. Garrett and I had a corner table. Glass covered the sides of the deck, but I guessed it was removed in warm weather so patrons could enjoy the balmy breezes off the water. The place was nice, and it had great views.

"You like?" Garrett asked, that charming smile on his face.

I'd always said he reminded me of Gerard Butler, only more handsome—if that was possible.

I nodded. "I like."

His smile widened. "Great. Now, I have to recommend the tuna—grilled with the mango salsa—or the scallop cakes. Both are wickedly wonderful."

"Sounds like you've eaten here quite a bit before."

Maybe he *was* seeing other women. My heart ached a little at the thought, though I knew I had no right to feel that way. Everything was way too complicated right now.

"Business meetings," he corrected, almost as if he could read my thoughts. "I love bringing board members here for lunch. Wild caught local fish. Vegetables grown through sustainable, clean farming. Fresh air off the bay. It gives them just a taste for the area without being too overwhelming. Don't you think?"

I nodded and stared out at the black water outside for a moment. "I do."

I loved his enthusiasm for his job. He was passionate and innovative and he'd pulled his life together in the face of tragedy. What was there not to admire about that?

"So, how was the meeting with your friend?" Garrett closed his menu and took a sip of his water. He knew I wasn't a fan of alcohol—my dad had been a drunk for most of my childhood —so he respectfully refrained when he was around me.

"We found a dead body behind the stage," I blurted.

Garrett stared at me. "What?"

"It's true." I explained what happened.

"You don't have to look for mysteries, do you?

They just find you. You're like a magnet, and crimes are like the anvil that's always being drawn closer."

"An anvil that's bound to start coming at me so fast that it knocks me smack in the forehead?"

He chuckled. Even the way he held his water goblet, raised suspended in the air, made him seem affluent. So different from me.

"Now, I didn't say that," he started. "I'm sure you'd still look charming, even if you had a big red welt on your face."

"You're kind." I straightened the napkin in my lap. "Anyway, Paulette asked me to investigate."

"And you said?"

I shrugged. "I said yes."

"Good girl. You're in your element when you're investigating."

I felt myself beaming. "Thank you."

The waitress interrupted to take our orders. I got tuna, cooked medium, with a cucumber salad and rice pilaf. Garrett ordered oysters and some she crab soup.

As soon as the waitress wandered away, I leaned toward Garrett, my thoughts still on my eventful evening. "I guess Paulette has a lot riding on this whole musical. Yet, despite that, she gave me the lead role. I'm taking the place of the woman who died."

The pit in my stomach grew as I said the words aloud.

Garrett seemed a little too amused as he bent toward me. "Now, that is something I wouldn't miss for the world. Gabby St. Claire, on stage, star of the show."

"Singing and dancing," I finished.

"Even better."

"It's going to be humiliating."

He waved his hand in the air, as if swatting away the negative thoughts. "Don't be silly. You'll be great."

"That's kind of you, but you've never seen me sing or dance."

"We've danced together. Remember—at the gala you attended with me."

Believe me, I hadn't forgotten. Hadn't forgotten his closeness, his warmth, the way my skin tingled at his touch. But I didn't want him to know that. "You've never seen my jazz hands."

He pulled his head back as his eyebrows shot up. "They sound a little scary. You couldn't pay me to miss it. Maybe I'll give everyone at the company free tickets. I'll bet your friend would like that. It would be my way of supporting the arts."

I held a hand up. "Let's slow down. You need to check your definition of 'the arts.'"

He grinned. "You know, a friend of mine wanted to buy that property the school was located on. He thought it could be great for one of the neighborhoods he develops. Small world, isn't it?"

"I think it's fascinating that they've turned it into the Cultural Arts Center. I'm glad it's still standing. I have a lot of memories of that place."

"My friend's wife—the friend who wanted to buy the property—used to go to school there, but she didn't seem all that inclined to hold on to the building."

"She probably had money staked in it, so of course not."

"Donabell definitely likes her money."

My lips parted. "Did you say Donabell?"

He nodded. "I did. She's my friend's wife."

"Donabell Bullock?"

"Donabell Castlerock. Not sure what her maiden name was." He shrugged and took another sip of water.

"How many people named Donabell could there be around here?"

He raised his eyebrows again in wry amusement. "I'm getting the sense that you know her?"

I stopped myself from snorting—thank goodness. "If it's the same Donabell, then she was my middle school nemesis. She thrived on making my life miserable."

He shrugged. "Are you going to hold it against me that I'm friends with her husband?"

"Of course not. That would be silly."

"Good. Because people do grow up. You might be surprised." The corner of his lips curled up.

I raised an eyebrow. I had a hard time thinking about Donabell ever changing. How strange was it that two of my old middle school classmates were suddenly making appearances in my present day life? It almost seemed surreal.

"I'll have to arrange a reunion."

"No thank you." My words sounded harsher than I intended.

His grin faded and he leaned closer. "I have a question for you, Gabby."

Before he could start, the waitress appeared with our food. Apparently, Garrett must have been their VIP customer because I'd never known a kitchen staff to put meals together this quickly.

Anxiety churned in my stomach as I anticipated his question. Was this the moment when he would make me decide if I wanted to date him or not? If I said no, would we still be friends?

I had to admit, Garrett had been there for me these past couple of months. With Riley gone and Sierra being married now, I'd felt a little alone at times. Garrett had filled up those lonely minutes. He hadn't even complained—okay, maybe he had once or twice—but overall, he'd seemed content to simply hang out.

Garrett shoved his plate forward, ignoring it for a moment.

"So," he started. He leaned toward me, tugging at his crisp sleeves. His gaze looked serious. "I have a proposition for you."

That didn't sound good. I remained silent and waited for him to continue.

"I'm heading to Africa next month. I'm going to tour the area and see some of the wells that GCI has built for residents there."

I nodded, having no idea what that had to do with me. "Sounds fascinating."

Garrett's company, Global Coffee Initiative, donated money per bag of coffee sold to people living in third world countries. It was a great business model that had really set Garrett apart from other companies out there. It had even landed him on some magazine covers, for both his business sense and his drop dead good looks.

"I want you to go with me, Gabby."

I blinked, certain I hadn't heard him correctly. "What?"

He nodded. "You could come a little later if the play runs over, of course. But I'd like for you to join me on my tour. You've got to know that I adore you, Gabby." He lowered his voice in a way that made me blush.

And I almost never blushed.

"I . . . I don't know what to say."

"Say yes."

The thought of traveling internationally made my heart race. At my core, I longed for some adventure, a change of scenery, maybe even a way to avoid the muck in my life.

But there was also reality. I had a business to run, bills to pay, and obligations to keep. Leaving would be irresponsible on so many different levels.

"I'm flattered, but I can't see how I could do that." I flaked off a piece of my tuna. "I have too many other things to think about, starting with money."

"The trip would be on me, of course."

I shook my head, the answer suddenly very clear. "I don't like handouts."

"I know. That's why you can come as my bodyguard."

This time I did snort at the ludicrous idea. I fully expected Garrett to follow suit. He didn't.

I quickly sobered. "You're serious?"

He nodded. "You've saved my life before, Gabby. You're observant. You can handle yourself in tense situations."

Maybe Garrett didn't know me that well because I'd handled myself very poorly in some very sticky situations before. Should I burst his bubble? I decided not to, at least not completely.

"I don't know, Garrett. That may have simply been dumb luck in the past."

His gaze didn't break from mine. "It wasn't."

Suddenly feeling flustered, I stabbed a piece of tuna and tried to buy some time. "I need to think about it."

My words surprised even me. Think about it? I couldn't seriously consider his request.

But he'd offered me a legitimate job. I wasn't just arm candy. I would be earning my keep while seeing the world. It wasn't like people were knocking down my door to hire me in the forensic field. I'd had some interviews, but nothing had panned out. Certainly being a bodyguard was a step up from being a crime scene cleaner . . . right?

"All right. Think about it, then. I'll need an answer in a couple of weeks, though."

I nodded. And for the rest of dinner, my thoughts volleyed back and forth between the dead body I'd found and the possibility of expanding my horizons.

I had a lot to think about.

"WHAT IN THE world are you listening to?" Clarice asked. "It's hurting my ears."

Clarice was a college student whom Chad and I had hired to work for us part-time. Right now, the two of us, along with Chad, were at the scene of a shooting at one of the housing projects in downtown Norfolk. There'd been a gun battle, apparently, because the walls and furniture were littered with bullet holes.

The residents here couldn't afford to pay me, but their landlord's insurance could. The unfortunate part was that it always took a long time to get paid when our clients used insurance—there was a lot of red tape.

Chad, the co-owner of the business, had decided to set up all these projections for the company. He'd also set monthly finance goals and deadlines to buy more equipment and hire new workers. He'd jumped in with both feet. He had more business sense than I'd thought he would and that made us a good balance. I had to stop thinking like a mom and pop business owner and start thinking big. Otherwise, we were going to get caught in the same cycles. That's what Chad had said, at least.

Right now, we had plaster to patch and some blood to scrub off the wall, ceiling, and carpet. I took a break from scouring and pushed my safety glasses to the top of my head. Clarice had asked about the music blaring through the room. "It's for the play I'm now starring in."

Clarice blanched. She was a prissy girl I never imagined would be helping me with this job right now. She'd traded in her new designer clothes for her old designer clothes. But when she fixed up, she looked like a million bucks. She was a pop culture diva, she still almost fainted at the sight of blood, and she made me laugh.

In some ways, she reminded me of Paulette. They were both pretty and came off as airheads sometimes. Clarice had confided once that she acted like an airhead on occasion because that's who people assumed she was. She'd grown up a lot since I'd known her. Being abducted by a serial killer could do that.

As a new song blared on, Clarice shook her head. "I'm sorry, but this is awful. I expect someone to come out juggling on a unicycle—and wearing a red, bulbous nose."

I squirmed. I'd been thinking the exact same thing. Still, I didn't want to overreact. I mean, Paulette had raved about this musical. "Isn't awful a strong word?"

"I'm no musical connoisseur, but I think I'd purposely burst my eardrums if I had to listen to this," Chad quipped. "Paying to listen to it? I'd demand my money back."

I actually did consider myself somewhat of a musical connoisseur. I had soundtracks running through my head constantly. This music all sounded canned, like amateur knock offs of real musical numbers. Even worse was that all the lyrics were reminiscent of actual hit musicals. Song titles like, "The Sound of the Music of the Night" and "Do You Hear the People Dream." I suppose if someone wanted to imitate those musicals on purpose, almost like a parody, then this would be brilliant. But this musical was no parody.

"Well, I'm going undercover. Part of my assignment is to learn this music." I sounded so legit when I said it like that. "This sad part is that this play is both a comedy and a tragedy, yet it's meant to be neither."

"It gives new meaning to 'foul play.'" Clarice laughed at her own joke.

I couldn't help but smile. She was so right.

"Did you say undercover?" Chad raised his eyebrows as he measured a section of drywall. "Well, look at you."

"I'm scrambling to try to learn this music, as well as my lines. It's only two weeks until opening night. As Elsa McGovernness, I have a lot of work to do."

"Sign me up. Sierra and I will be there for your big debut."

"Me too!" Clarice added.

"My big debut actually came in middle school. I was an extra in *Oklahoma*, thank you very much."

"We have a pro on our hands," Chad said with a grin. He stood, wiping some dust from his pants, and held up the drywall square. "This is all ready to install. You remember how, right?"

"Of course." I'd done one bad patch job and now he doubted my competence. Men . . .

"Great. I need to get to our second job site and make sure Braxton is okay."

Braxton was a new guy Chad had just hired. I'd only met him once, and I'd made Chad promise that he'd never make me work with him. The man was a regular know-it-all who talked nonstop. He drove me crazy.

However, he was better than the other guy Chad

had hired during the holidays. Thank goodness he was out of the picture now. I'd had no idea how complicated expanding the business would be.

"We're good," I told him.

He grabbed his toolbox, waved goodbye, and left.

As soon as the door closed, I glanced over at Clarice. She was considering pursuing a degree in criminal justice herself and always seemed eager to help with any type of investigation that I had going on. Plus, it was good for her to keep her mind occupied.

"Clarice, when you have a chance, could you do me a favor?"

"Sure, whatever you need."

"I need someone to research a woman named Rose Hines. She was apparently a drama teacher who died at the former Oceanside Middle School."

"Sounds intriguing." She raised her eyebrows comically.

"It might be. I'd never heard about it before, but the woman who wrote *The Music of the Specter* is making a big deal out of it. I'd like to find out some more information."

"I'm on it." Clarice rocked back on her heels. "So, I have a date tonight."

I'd started to pull my goggles back on but stopped. "A date? Really?"

I hadn't known her to date anyone. The girl was

pretty enough to date whoever she wanted. But after the ordeal she'd been through, she'd been cautious about whom she hung out with. She was still in therapy.

Truth be told, I should probably be in therapy still too. I told myself that crime scene cleaning was all the therapy I needed, but deep down I knew that was just an excuse. I had issues. There was no doubt about that. But I figured time would work everything out. A small voice inside kept whispering, "Ignorance is bliss—until the truth finally hits and you crack." I ignored it.

"So, tell me about this date. How'd you meet him?"

"Yeah, it's so crazy." Her eyes gleamed. But there was something else there. Hesitation? I couldn't be sure. "I can't wait—"

My phone rang, and I saw it was Paulette.

"Hold that thought. I've got to take this." I stepped away from the living room, into a dingy kitchen for some privacy. "Hey, Paulette. What's up?"

A sniffle sounded on the line. "Oh, Gabby. It's awful."

"What's awful?" I tensed.

"The police just called me. They said that Scarlet's death wasn't an accident. They said that catwalk was rigged and, based on some bruises or something, they think she was pushed."

My pulse spiked. "They really think she was murdered?"

Another sniffle. "That's right. What am I going to do?"

"Calm down. Where are you?"

"At home."

I glanced around the house I was cleaning, trying to determine how much longer I'd be here. "I can be there in an hour, an hour and a half tops. Does that work?"

"Thank you, Gabby. That's perfect."

I got her address and hung up. Life really was starting to get interesting again.

An hour later, I finished the job with Clarice. Even better—the drywall patch looked great. We'd had to replace that section because it looked like someone or something had rammed into it and left a huge indention. Previously, we'd subcontracted out work like that. But Chad crunched the numbers and realized how much we'd save doing it ourselves.

I had one more scene to clean today before rehearsal started, but I needed to squeeze in my meeting with Paulette. I'd told Clarice to meet me at the second job site in a few hours.

If it were anyone else, I would have sent him or her to the job site alone. But I had this need to take Clarice under my wing. Because of her affiliation with me, a serial killer had targeted her. I didn't know if there was anything I could ever do to ease my guilt about that entire situation. I guess I felt like her guardian now, in some ways.

An automated voice from my phone told me to turn left and, like a mindless robot, I did. I normally fought tooth and nail not to use GPS, but I hadn't had time to go home and get directions, so I was relying on my phone. I'd just upgraded, using some of the money I'd made on a P.I. gig back in the fall.

I started down a private road and suddenly hit the brakes as a large house appeared in front of me.

I knew Paulette's dad was loaded—like Bill Gates loaded—but her house blew me away.

It looked like it belonged in Malibu or Palm Springs with its orange tile roof and beige stucco siding. There were palm trees on the property, and palm trees didn't naturally grow or flourish in Virginia's climate. The house had columns and arches and a circular driveway. Horses grazed in the distance. An iron fence in the backyard most likely bordered a swimming pool. Just a guess, but I'd wager some money on it if I were a betting woman.

My beat up work van seemed sorely out of place here, like someone wearing stained, dirty construction clothes in Saks Fifth Avenue. Since I couldn't transform my van into something it wasn't, I put it in park and stepped out.

I glanced down at my old, battered jeans and black T-shirt. Speaking of feeling out of place . . . my outfit wouldn't do much on the impressions front either.

I shoved a curl behind my ear and approached the massive front door. Before I even knocked, it flew open. Paulette stood there, her eyes red-rimmed and bloodshot. Behind her, I saw a glass of wine on the table.

"Thanks for coming," she started. "The police just left."

I squeezed her hand as I stepped inside. "Did they have anything to say?"

We walked together through a massive foyer and into a living room with a ceiling that extended two stories high. A fire blazed and coffee and tea had been set out. I had a feeling Paulette hadn't done that herself.

We sat down in sync on a white leather couch. I really hoped I didn't have any oil or plaster on my clothes that would ruin the lush cushions.

"The police were asking about everyone who's involved with the play," Paulette said. "I had to tell them about the other incidents that happened. They'll be questioning the cast. What if word of this leaks out, Gabby? The whole play will be ruined!"

I thought about poor Scarlet and everything that had been ruined for her. Mainly, her chance at life. But I didn't say that. I knew stress could cause people to think in irrational ways sometimes.

"The play won't be ruined," I said instead. "If anything, more people will show up. Bad publicity is still publicity, unfortunately."

She sniffled again and let out a long, shaky breath. "I have so much riding on this."

She stood and paced over to the window.

I hovered behind Paulette, sensing from her voice and tight body language that she was fragile and needed a friend. "Tell me about Scarlet."

Paulette continued to stare out of the window. "I didn't know her very well, not like some of the other cast members did. I didn't want to get too chummy with them, especially since I was in charge and all. Daddy always says there's a line there. You can't be authoritative and best buddies with people."

"Tell me what you did know about her then."

"She was going to college at ODU. She had dreams of making it big time. She had a really nice voice."

All those things were good, but they didn't even begin to touch the answers I needed.

"What about outside of the play?" I continued. "Was she single?"

Paulette turned toward me, but her eyes appeared glazed. "I think she was dating someone."

"Did she have a roommate?"

"I'm not sure."

"Did she work any other jobs?"

"I have no idea."

I nodded slowly. Apparently, Paulette not only didn't want to be too chummy, but she'd been overall oblivious as well. "I see. Do you know of anyone I could talk to about her?"

"Maybe Arie. Arie helped me handpick her for the role."

"Arie, the playwright, helped handpick the lead?" Arie the Diva had left an impression, to say the least. *Arie Berry the pain in the derriere—y.*

Sarcastic mantras came to me a little too easily sometimes.

Apparently, Arie really wanted to maintain a lot of control still since usually a director picked the cast.

Paulette nodded. "She should be at rehearsal again tomorrow night. I talked to her this morning and smoothed things over. She decided not to talk to her lawyer."

"I'll talk to Arie then."

"I'm not sure she's going to be on board with talking with you. She—"

The front door flew open, and I twirled around. A man charged inside the house. Even from where I was standing, I could see the veins bulging at his temples as he stormed toward us.

Instinctively, I pushed Paulette behind me and braced myself. It wasn't as if I'd ever taken any self-defense courses or anything. But I figured I was more capable than Paulette. Too bad I didn't have my gun with me.

Behind me, Paulette let out a sigh. A sigh? That didn't generally convey fear, more like annoyance. I noticed she stayed behind me, though. Was she . . . cowering?

"Really?" the man exclaimed, getting closer and closer. He held some papers in his hand and waved them like a flag. "You had to send your lawyer to talk to me about this? You couldn't have mentioned it yourself?"

Paulette crossed her arms behind me. "You're not welcome to come and go as you please, Roberto. This isn't your home anymore."

"You're doing everything in your power to make sure that's true, aren't you?" The man looked to be in his early thirties, and he was fit and tan and had a slight accent that I couldn't pinpoint. Brazilian, maybe? He was probably handsome when he wasn't blowing his top, slightly resembling a young Antonio Banderas.

"You knew that when we got married," Paulette said. "There was a pre-nup. None of this should be a surprise."

He stepped closer and thrust the papers toward her, and I could practically see the steam coming from his ears. "This isn't fair, Paulette. Not after everything we went through. I deserve more than this."

Paulette leaned past me, steely determination in her gaze and more fight in her voice than I knew she had. "Everything we went through? That would be one year of marriage. One lousy year at that."

I just wished I wasn't standing between the bickering couple. If there's one thing I wasn't, it was a marriage counselor. I couldn't even manage my own relationships, let alone give anyone else advice.

"You can't leave me high and dry like this." The man—Roberto?—started to reach for Paulette.

I held up a hand. "Maybe you should back off for a minute."

His fiery gaze fell on me, and his eyes widened, almost as if he'd finally noticed I was standing there. "Who are you?"

"I'm a friend of Paulette's. And I don't like your tone. You should treat a lady like a lady."

"This is none of your business," he growled.

I bristled. "It became my business when you accosted Paulette right in front of me."

"Accosted? Accosted? Let me guess—you must be a lawyer! Another one! You're trying to catch me in the act, aren't you? Trying to nail me."

I pushed myself in front of Paulette. "I don't know what you're talking about. I think you need to cool it, though."

His nostrils flared as his gaze burned into Paulette. "This isn't over. Not by a long shot . . . *Honey.*" The word dripped with bitterness and derision. "I'll fight this with everything in me."

With that, he stormed out.

I turned to look at my friend. My heart pounded out of control, so I could only imagine what hers was doing.

Her lips were pulled into a tight line, and she crossed her arms.

"I guess he doesn't realize that if there's anything my dad knows about—besides money—it's how to draw up a contract. There's no wiggle room. Roberto is leaving this marriage with what he brought into it —practically nothing. I thought I was being generous when I let him keep the Mercedes."

Wow. I didn't know Paulette had it in her. She'd always seemed so placid in the past. "Estranged husband, huh?"

She plopped down in a chair by the window. "Yeah, you'd think I'd do a little better job at picking them by now."

I sat across from her, curiosity at an all time high. Just what had happened to my friend in the years since I'd seen her? Life could be a cruel companion at times. "What's that mean?"

"This is my third marriage."

I tried not to flinch or show any judgment. But three failed marriages? Wow. No one could argue that it wasn't a great track record.

"I keep thinking I've found true love, only to realize that they're just using me for my father's money and connections. None of them have really loved me."

"That's got to be hard."

She shrugged, her eyes looking slightly vacant. "I'm accustomed to it. People have used me for my entire life, Gabby. Well, everyone but you."

Talking to her was a good reminder that even being rich, people had problems. Money certainly couldn't buy happiness. I'd seen that enough in my life. But I'd also experienced how not having money could lead to a whole different set of problems.

She stood. "Please excuse me a moment. I feel a headache coming on."

She disappeared down a hallway into one of the wings of her home. The fight I'd just witnessed replayed in my mind all the way up until Paulette returned. She looked a little more composed as she sat across from me on the couch.

"How'd you meet Roberto?" I asked.

"I bought him at—"

My thoughts spun wildly.

"—one of those bachelor auctions for charity. Well, I didn't actually buy him. My assistant did for me. I'm uncomfortable bidding at events like that."

I let out the breath I held. "I see."

"He played soccer for the professional team out of D.C. I thought he was just adorable. But then he had a knee injury, so the soccer thing fell through. He started coaching this minor league soccer team, which barely pays enough for groceries. Plus, he had racked up a ton of credit card debt by trying to live a lifestyle he couldn't afford."

"So, what's he doing now?"

She shrugged again. "I heard he's back to coaching. He's living with one of his old soccer buddies until he can save enough money to move out on his own. Kind of sad for a 32-year-old, wouldn't you say?"

I wondered if she felt at all bad about her role in that. She didn't appear to, and I had mixed feelings on it. Obviously, if the man was just a money grubbing louse, then he was getting what he had coming. On the other hand, it would be hard to go from living a lavish lifestyle to having nothing.

"He was a jerk. He constantly had his hand out, asking for money. He didn't want to work after we got married. He wanted to be a kept man. Daddy didn't approve."

"I can imagine." Mr. Zollin hadn't become successful without a whole lot of smarts. I noticed the time and stood, remembering everything else on my to do list. As much as I'd like to stay longer, I couldn't afford that luxury right now. "Paulette, I've got to run, but I'm going to talk to some people. I'll be subtle."

"That's right. No one can know you're investigating. It's of vital importance, Gabby."

Though that sounded exciting, it actually made things a lot more complicated. In the past, I'd just come right out and asked questions. Being subtle wasn't exactly my gift. I guessed I'd have a chance to brush up on my acting skills in the process.

I walked out to my van, reflecting on exactly how I was going to handle this undercover gig, and paused. Something didn't look right.

That's when I realized that my tires had been slashed.

CHAPTER
SIX

"I CAN'T BELIEVE Roberto would sink this low!" Paulette threw her hands in the air. "He is so dead. He's unbelievable! A jerk if I've ever met one."

We were outside of her house, waiting for the police to arrive and on-and-off staring at the deflated tires of my van. I'd started to call my insurance company, but Paulette stopped me.

"I'll take care of your tires."

"You don't have to do that," I told her.

"Of course I do. This happened on my property because of one of the nitwits I allowed into my life. I know you need your van for your work. I'll have this taken care of."

"You're . . . sure?"

She nodded. "Of course. You can borrow one of my cars in the meantime."

I felt like I should protest, but I really did need some wheels. And I didn't have a lot of cash or a lot of time, so if she wanted to fix my van, who was I to argue? Besides, it was her lousy soon-to-be ex who'd done the deed.

The police arrived and we gave our report. The officer said he would check out Roberto for us but, all in all, he didn't sound very hopeful.

"What's that liquid under your van?" the officer asked.

I squatted on the ground and, sure enough, there was a puddle of something. "I have no idea."

"You might want to have the van checked out and make sure nothing else was done," the officer said.

"It's probably just cleaning fluid," I said.

Changing my tires might take a day. Checking out the van's innards would take much longer.

Roberto must have been a nitwit, as Paulette had called him, if he'd slashed my tires right after he left the house because he was the obvious culprit. Of course, I'd met dumber criminals in my day. I just hated that his rage had to be an inconvenience to me, as if I'd been the one who'd wronged him.

"I've got to get to another job, Paulette," I said when the officer left.

"Of course. Let me get you a car."

I followed her to the garage. Four vehicles—all luxury class—were parked there.

I couldn't even imagine owning one of these cars. I was a used, American car with dents—or lots of personality, as I liked to say—kind of girl.

She stopped in front of a cherry red Bentley convertible.

"Will this work?" she asked.

A smile slowly spread over my face. "This will definitely work. I mean, if I must."

"Your van will be fixed as soon as possible. Hopefully in a couple of days."

I nodded, like I was sacrificing, and then pulled some of my equipment from the back of my old vehicle and filled both the trunk and the back seat of my new loaner. I would look quite fancy pulling up to my crime scene in this.

I got to play practice twenty minutes late. It was all because I'd gotten to my crime scene late. And I'd gotten to the crime scene late because my tires had been slashed. The whole thing had a domino effect on my schedule.

Still, it didn't bode well for the new girl to flounce into rehearsal after everyone else had already started, especially since I was the one who needed to be there the most. Not only that, but I was feeling irritable. Maybe it was because I was so rushed that I hadn't had time to eat. Maybe it was because I'd had to work with the new guy, Braxton, who grated on my nerves. Maybe it was the fact that I was supposed to be investigating and instead I felt like I'd just been wasting a lot of time.

We still couldn't use the stage, so we were in the old chorus room. I flew through the door, feeling a lot like a middle schooler being tardy for class. I had a bad habit of that as a preteen. Maybe some things never changed.

Everyone stared at me when I charged into the room. I tried to compose myself by straightening my back and smoothing out my hair. But I hadn't had time to go home and shower after the job. My haz-mat suit had caught any of the gunk that could have gotten on me, but the scent of blood saturated my clothing and hair. No haz-mat suit could protect you from that.

This was not the way I wanted to start my off-Broadway career. Or my community theater career, for that matter. Or even just make an impression.

"You must be the new girl," someone said.

I looked over and spotted my old drama teacher, Mrs. Baker. She looked nearly just like I'd remembered her, only older. She had petite features and her light brown hair now had a touch of gray.

A grin started to stretch across my face until Mrs.

Baker tapped her pen against a clipboard and pointed center stage. "Please, take your place."

I nodded, my heart sinking. Then I realized that Paulette must have told her I was undercover. That was the only explanation for why she'd act so cold and hard. Mrs. Baker had always been one of my favorite teachers ever. I wasn't sure if she knew the impact she'd had on my life.

I didn't ponder it too long. Instead, I took my place center stage, which was really center of the front of the room.

"We'll be singing, 'Climb Every Steeple,'" Mrs. Baker continued. "I hope you're prepared."

I nodded. Paulette hit a button on the CD player and background music filled the room.

A trickle of anxiety tried to seep into my gut, but I pushed it back. I was undercover. I had nothing to prove to myself concerning my musical ability here. Still, part of me secretly wanted to succeed.

I cleared my throat, listening for my cue. Sweat broke out across my forehead as I tried to remember. I'd been so intent on memorizing the words that I'd forgotten to think about where to come in.

This wasn't good.

"You missed it, Gabby," Mrs. Baker scolded. "You've got to count in your head four measures and then start. We don't have much time to pull this together. I thought Paulette had stressed that to you."

My cheeks flamed. "Of course. I'm sorry. I'll get it."

"Let's try that again," Mrs. Baker instructed.

Paulette started the CD again. I counted in my head, took a deep breath, and then plunged in.

Mrs. Baker stopped me. "You were one beat too slow. I also need you to draw out 'Cli . . . mb ev . . . ery.' You sped through the words."

Wow. What if Mrs. Baker was being cold for real? Had she changed in the years since I knew her? She'd always been so kind in the past, but this woman was like a shark right now.

We went through the rest of the rehearsal. I had more reprimands, a few chuckles, and a whole lot of stress.

This wasn't going to be nearly as fun as I'd hoped.

"Gabby, I need you to stay back so we can work on a few things," Mrs. Baker said. "Okay?"

I nodded as Mrs. Baker wrapped up with the rest of the cast. I glanced at the various members, trying to remember each of them, mostly because every one was a potential suspect in my mind.

There was Arie. I already knew more about her than I cared to know.

Jerome was in his mid-twenties, on the taller side, had a long face, and had studied acting at a local community college. Apparently, he loved Shakespeare and video games, and he worked as an accountant until he could catch his big break. He had an artistic flair and liked to wear scarves tucked around his neck. It gave him a very metro vibe.

Then there were the twins, Karen and Sharen. They were the backstage managers. What could I say about them? They seemed so odd in their own way and reminded me a bit of the twins from The Shining. The sisters were identical and practically joined at the hip. With stringy brown hair, plain looking clothes, and almost no make up, the two were a little eerie. Whenever they laughed, it was in unison and sounded high pitched and awkward—almost fake. Except, the more I heard it, the more I realized they weren't being fake. That's just how they sounded.

There were several other extras and chorus members, but no one else stood out at the moment.

As the meeting wrapped up, I excused myself and hurried to the bathroom, more to collect myself than anything else. I was feeling like I was in over my head, and my nerves felt frayed after such a rough rehearsal.

I splashed my face with cold water. "Pull it together, Gabby," I muttered, staring at my reflection in the mirror and smacking my cheeks.

I felt like an adolescent again. The whole situation was messing with my head and playing on my self-confidence. Being the star of this show was taking me out of my comfort zone and then some.

The door squeaked open, and I jerked my head toward it. It was a girl from the cast. Her name was Bennie, a strange name if I'd ever heard one. Every time I heard it, I started humming the Elton John song, "Benny and the Jets."

The short, athletic-looking woman hurried toward the mirror and smoothed her wavy brown hair into a ponytail. She frowned at her freckles before straightening her poofy purple skirt, one that seemed more appropriate for a three-year-old.

She played the detective in the musical and seemed nice enough. I'd guess her to be in her early twenties.

As she glanced over at me, I braced myself for whatever she might say. *You really stink. You should think about a different career—or even hobby. I know who you are.*

"I just wanted to say I think you're doing a great job," Bennie started.

Some of my guard came down. "Thank you. I appreciate that."

"Ignore the rest of the cast. They're just on edge. Scarlet's death has thrown us all for a loop." She leaned closer. "And honestly, some of us are afraid that Paulette has no idea what she's doing. She seems in over her head."

"Your encouragement is kind, Bennie. I've been feeling some of the tension, so that means a lot."

She shivered. "I hope the ghost will leave us alone until the play's over. I've thought about quitting a few times myself."

"The ghost?" Did the girl really believe that?

Bennie nodded. "Sure. Everyone knows this place is supposed to be haunted. I think the ghost is angry because we're disturbing what's become her home over the past several years. She's had peace up until the renovations started."

I wanted to say something sarcastic, but there was no need to alienate the person who just might be my one friend here. Instead, I nodded. "I hope the ghost will leave us alone as well."

Bennie smiled. "I've gotta run. Talk to you tomorrow!"

I shook my head as she walked away. Ghost? Really?

I pushed inside the choir room, spotted Mrs. Baker talking to Jerome—the guy who played the Specter. As he sneered over at me, I took a seat in one of the old yellow backed chairs in the room. Despite Bennie's encouragement, I felt like an utter failure and like taking on this assignment was a bad, bad idea.

But I liked to stick with things and see them

through until the end. So I was going to do this. Even if it killed me.

As soon as Jerome left, Mrs. Baker's eyes softened. She threw her arms around me in a hug. "Gabby St. Claire! Look at you! It's so good to see you again."

I blinked at the transformation but hugged her back. "It's good to see you, too, Mrs. Baker."

"It's actually Mrs. Harper now, but you can call me Mrs. Baker if you'd like. At first, I kept correcting Paulette, but I finally saw it was doing no good. I'll always be Mrs. Baker to her. So, now everyone here calls me Mrs. Baker, so you might as well, also."

"For old times sake, maybe I'll do just that."

She squeezed my arm. "I couldn't let them know I knew you. Sorry about that during rehearsal. I hated to do it, but I didn't want anyone to get suspicious."

"Totally understand." I'd underestimated her. She was a great actress.

She pulled back, but kept her hands on my arms, just like your favorite aunt might do when she hadn't seen you in a few months. "You look good. Really good."

"Thank you. I'm so excited to be working with you."

She leaned close. "This whole experience has been

somewhat of a nightmare, on more than one level. I mean, Scarlet, obviously. But having both the writer and producer here every evening?"

"I'm sure that makes it difficult."

"Arie is a micromanager who critiques everything I do. She wanted to star in the play, as well, but I insisted there was too much of a conflict of interest and she had to pick someone else. And Paulette is a nervous wreck. Her anxiety starts to wear off on me after a while!"

"I can totally picture all of that."

She waved a hand in the air. "Anyway, enough of that. I'm sorry. You caught me on a bad night. I want to hear all about you sometime."

"I'd love to catch up."

"Come to dinner at my house. You can meet my daughter. Amos would be thrilled to see you again."

I smiled. Amos was a former Navy SEAL. I'd kind of reintroduced the two of them back when I'd been a dog sitter in my younger years. I didn't realize they were married, but now that I knew I totally gave myself credit for it. "I'd love to."

"Great. Tomorrow night before rehearsal? Bring someone?"

Riley was the first person I thought of. I'd love to know what Mrs. Baker thought of him. She'd always been so wise. But Riley wasn't a part of my life right now. However, there was always Garrett. There was nothing not to like about Garrett.

"I'll see if he's available."

She smiled. "Perfect. I can't wait, Gabby. I've never forgotten about you. I'd love to chat more now, but I've got to pick up my daughter from her friend's house. She's thirteen. The same age you were when I first met you."

"I'm feeling old now."

"Then imagine how I feel!"

I chuckled.

Until I stepped into the hallway. That's when I smelled the unmistakable scent of . . . gasoline.

Was someone trying to burn this whole place down?

I wasn't going to stick around to find out.

CHAPTER SEVEN

"MRS. BAKER, call 911. There's gasoline in the hallway," I told her. "But go outside before using your phone, just to be safe."

Her brows furrowed together in worry. "How about you?"

I wanted to leave. Then I remembered Paulette. She was still here somewhere. "I'll be out soon. I just want to make sure the building is clear."

Mrs. Baker hesitated before nodding. "Please be careful."

I didn't have time to explain to her that this wasn't my first rodeo. Despite my experience—or maybe because of it—I knew that one little spark could light up this whole building, me included.

I had to work fast.

I scrambled down the hallway, wishing the lights

hadn't been turned out already. The darkness had an eerie quality that made me want to crawl under a blanket and hide.

A thumping noise in the background made me freeze. The ghost?

I shook my head. No, I didn't believe in ghosts. Bennie had just put the idea in my head, and that was the only reason the explanation had popped into my mind. No ghosts.

But there was definitely a strange sound.

I remembered I had a flashlight application on my phone, and a small measure of relief washed through me. I pulled my phone out of my pocket, found the right button, and finally had some light.

I shone the beam down on the gasoline. Why did it look yellow? What sense did that make?

I didn't have time to ponder it. Instead, I raced down the hallway.

"Paulette!" I called.

I didn't see any sign of her. Where would she have gone? My only guess was her office. Maybe she'd slipped in there to do some paperwork.

I rounded the corner and grabbed the office door. It was locked and all the lights inside were off.

Strange.

Where was she?

I hurried down the hallway, looking for any signs of life.

What if she'd left? What if I was putting myself in danger for someone who wasn't even here?

I'd check a few more places and hopefully by then the police would be here. As I moved deeper into the hallway, the smell of gasoline lessened. It appeared the liquid had just been poured near the chorus room.

The thought didn't comfort me. Someone obviously knew Mrs. Baker and I were in there. But since it still hadn't been lit, maybe they were just trying to scare us.

I swept my light over the floor and something caught my eye. I stepped closer to one of the hallways that had been locked off until Phase 1 of the renovations was complete.

A metal gate with a zigzag pattern stood at the entryway. A padlock normally connected the two sides of the gate, ensuring that no one could get through.

Tonight, there was a crack there and the padlock was unlatched.

Interesting.

Trepidation and curiosity collided inside me. Curiosity won.

I squeezed through the gate. The metal let out a loud squeak in protest. So much for remaining covert.

I looked both ways, saw no one, and continued.

Had Paulette come down this way?

Why would she?

I took leaden steps forward. The sound I'd heard earlier had stopped. Had it come from down here?

This was the hallway where the elective classes had taken place. Art, shop, architecture, newspaper.

I tried the first door. It was locked. Using my light, I peered through the window in the door. Nothing looked out of place inside.

My throat tightened with every step I took.

I turned the knob at the next classroom and, to my surprise, the door opened. I stepped inside the old shop classroom. The scent of sawdust and grease filled my senses.

I stepped across the room, looking for anything out of place. Rows of tables and benches still remained there, just as they'd been all those many years ago.

I paused by a cabinet and, out of curiosity, tugged at the door. It stuck.

I pulled harder.

That's when the entire piece of furniture started falling—right toward me.

I dove out of the way, but the edge of the cabinet caught my foot. A cloud of dust surrounded me, filling my lungs and making me feel like I couldn't breathe.

I heard the door open and footsteps rushing inside. "Ma'am, are you okay?"

I looked up and a bright light shone right in my eyes. I moaned and pulled my leg out. "Yeah, besides a bruised ego."

"I'm Officer Billingsworth with the Virginia Beach P.D. I heard something crash."

I rotated my shoulder as I pulled to my feet. "I tried to open the door, but it was stuck. The whole thing came crashing down."

He kicked something out of the way. "Must be this old building. It looks like that cabinet was just filled with textbooks."

I followed his gaze. Even in the dark, I could tell he was correct. Old books had spilled all over the floor.

"We're evacuating the building," the officer continued. "We need to get you out of here."

I nodded. "I was just looking for Paulette."

"She's outside already."

Great. All of this for nothing.

I brushed some plaster off my shirt and nodded. "Let's go."

Paulette and I stood outside, the night air brisk around us. Numerous police cars filled what used to be the bus ramp. Mrs. Baker had been dismissed, so it was just Paulette, me, and a whole crew of law enforcement officers.

Paulette shook her head, her breaths coming out in frosty puffs. "I just don't understand."

"Someone poured a trail of gas all up and down the hallway surrounding the auditorium and chorus room. However, they didn't ignite it," Detective Charlie Henderson explained.

The police had already been over all of this with Paulette, but she looked dazed and confused. Right now, she wrung her hands together like she might have a nervous breakdown.

I patted her back, trying to calm her down. She claimed she'd been in her office the whole time, trying to track down some receipts to turn in to her accountant. I hadn't seen any lights on in the office, though, and it didn't make sense that she'd be working in the dark.

Currently, Chad and the crew were finishing cleaning inside. I'd called him to help out, mostly because Squeaky Clean had the knowledge and know-how to handle hazardous materials.

I'd helped supervise as we poured kitty litter on the gasoline to soak it up before shoveling it into plastic bags. When that was done, we'd put down some sand to absorb any leftover odors. We'd take all the waste down to a disposal center when we were finished. Thankfully, the damage had only extended down one hallway.

I'd peeled out of my haz-mat suit and left Chad to finish so I could get some information from Charlie.

"Charlie—I mean, Detective Henderson—was it my imagination or was the gasoline yellow?" I asked.

She nodded. "It wasn't your imagination. Someone dyed it."

"How did they do that? Most dyes are water based and everyone knows that water and gas don't mix," Paulette said.

I stared at her a moment in wonder. The question made sense; it just seemed out of character for her to ask that. It required a knowledge base that I had no idea she had.

"There are oil soluble dyes," Charlie said.

"But why? What sense does it make to go through that trouble?" I asked.

Charlie shook her head. "I have no idea. There are some strange people out there."

"What if it was the ghost?" Paulette started. "What if the ghost left a trail of yellow—?"

"It was definitely gas, not an otherworldly substance," Charlie said quickly.

"But maybe someone wanted to make it look ghostly," I suggested.

"It's a possibility," Charlie agreed.

"What I'm wondering is why didn't the person

ignite the gasoline," I continued. "Was it because we stepped out into the hallway before they could or were they just trying to send a subtle threat?"

Charlie shook her head. "I don't know. That's a good question." She turned to Paulette. "Did you have those new security cameras installed yet? The ones I suggested after our last visit?"

Paulette nodded. "I did. Just today, as a matter of fact. Would you like to take a look?"

"Would I ever," Charlie muttered.

"I insist that Gabby go with you," Paulette said. "I'm having her look into this case, as well. I'd like another set of eyes on all the evidence."

"I don't have a problem with that. Show me where the recordings are kept."

We followed Paulette into the school, down the hall, and into the old guidance office. I blinked in surprise at what I saw. Paulette had spared no expense on this equipment. It was state-of-the-art, top-of-the-line stuff.

But I'd also noticed that, when we'd arrived, the door hadn't been locked this time. Had Paulette purposely left it unlocked under the assumption that there was no one else here? Did anyone monitor this area? I had yet to see a security guard on duty.

Charlie took a seat at the desk while I stood behind her, watching the screens.

"I'm not sure how to use all of this," Paulette started, wringing her hands.

"I can probably figure it out, but you'll want someone here who knows how to operate this system if it's to be any good to you," Charlie said.

"Of course." Paulette frowned. "Working within the budget my father gave me has its challenges. He said it's good for me to have limits, though."

"Are these cameras set up all around the school?" Charlie asked.

"Except in the areas we're not using," Paulette said. "Like Corridor D and E."

I stored that information away. Could someone be using those quarantined hallways?

Charlie scrolled backward to nine o'clock, the time right after rehearsal ended.

A shadow appeared in the corner of the screen before everything went black.

"What?" Paulette lurched toward the screen. "How did that happen?"

"I'm not sure," Charlie said. "Let me check some other feeds."

On every camera, the same thing happened. The shadow then blackness.

"I think I know what the guilty party did." Charlie stood. "Follow me."

She led us to the first camera, grabbed a chair, and climbed up to examine it.

"It's just like I thought. Someone spray painted over the lens."

"What?" Paulette looked truly shocked.

"They obviously knew the cameras were here," Charlie continued. "They also knew where to stand in order to avoid detection. It looks like this could be an inside job, Ms. Zollin."

CHAPTER EIGHT

AFTER EVERYONE CLEARED OUT, I sat with Paulette in the auditorium. We were both silent. I wasn't sure about Paulette, but I was taking a moment to absorb everything that had happened.

Finally, Paulette rubbed her hands against her designer jeans and glanced at me. "I didn't mention this earlier, but my stage manager quit."

"Really?"

She nodded. "He said he'd had enough and wanted to get out while he could."

"I'm sorry."

"Ms. Maggie quit too. She said something about wanting to babysit her grandkids, but I know the truth. She wanted out, also."

"I'm really sorry."

"Bennie offered to help out in the meantime."

"She seems nice."

Paulette nodded. "Everything in my life is falling apart, Gabby."

"It's all going to work out. I just know it is."

She looked at me again. "You may not have had money, but you were the successful one, Gabby. You never let anything hold you back. I wish I had some of that gumption."

"You do. Look at this place. It's amazing!"

She smiled faintly. "Do you remember when you found that old time capsule?"

The memory warmed me. It had been "buried" up in the eaves above the auditorium and discovered during a renovation. "That was one of my proudest moments."

"I watched you up on the stage when you did a monolog about it. My dad was sitting beside me and afterward he told me that you were someone to watch for and that he was glad we were friends."

"That was nice."

"I remember thinking that he'd probably rather have you as a daughter."

"I happen to remember that I would have loved to be a part of your family. Besides, that's not true. I know your father loves you."

"That's what one of my therapists says too."

"Therapists?" *One of them?* How many did she have?

She nodded. "He says I've got to let go. That's what I thought I was doing when I took on this project."

"Don't get discouraged. I'm here. I'm going to help you."

"You were always good for that, Gabby." She offered another sad smile and then stood. "I guess I should be getting home. Thanks again for everything."

"Any time."

We walked out to the parking lot. Just as we stepped onto the sidewalk, something in the direction of the bus ramp caught my eye. It was a man walking toward the back of the school!

He froze when he spotted us and then ducked behind the building.

"Stay there, Paulette!"

I took off after him. As I rounded the corner, I spotted him ahead of me. He was dressed in all black, had a stocky build, and wore a dark hat. Other than those things, I couldn't tell anything about him. Except . . . was that a tattoo snaking up his neck? I couldn't tell for sure.

My legs burned as I chased him.

He darted toward the old track. I plunged into the nighttime, away from the overhead lights that made me feel safe. The cold air stung my lungs, but I continued to heave it into my chest. I couldn't afford to slow down.

I raced past the bleachers and stopped cold.

Where had he gone?

My gaze scanned the dark field in front of me. The stands that surrounded me offered too many hiding places to count. The man could have gone anywhere.

I wasn't ready to give up.

I took my first step onto the track. I stayed light on my feet, trying not to give away my presence. I listened for any telltale sign of where he'd gone. There was nothing.

I shivered, suddenly feeling exposed out here on the field. This wasn't a smart idea. I was vulnerable.

This case wasn't worth dying over.

I took a backward step toward the entrance.

As I did, movement in the distance caught my eye.

I looked over in time to see the man on the other side of the field.

It didn't matter, I realized. He was too far away for me to catch. The questions were: Who was he and what was he doing here?

By the time I got back to my apartment, I smelled not only like blood but faintly of gasoline, a little bit of sweat, and probably a touch of Paulette's expensive lilac perfume that saturated the interior of her loaner car.

It was well past midnight and I was beat. It seemed like more often than not I ended up staying awake until all hours of the morning either with my job, my friends, or trouble.

I lived in an Old Victorian that had been cut up into five apartments. It wasn't fancy and the area where it was located seemed about as eclectic as the apartment residents. But it was home, and there was no place else like it.

I dragged myself inside, my physical exhaustion mingling with the waning effects of the adrenaline rush I'd gotten as we uncovered clues about the trouble—and murder—we'd had at my old middle school.

As soon as I stepped into the entryway of the building, the door to my left popped open. My best friend Sierra stuck her head out. Sierra was married to Chad, and the two of them seemed like a match made in heaven. They were attached at the hip and, truth be told, I kind of missed them. Whether anyone wanted to admit it or not, things changed once people got married. Sierra had fewer opportunities to hang out. Less availability. Not as much . . . time for me.

I totally understood, and I was happy for her. But I still missed the old days.

"I heard what happened." She pushed her glasses up on her tiny Asian nose and stared at me.

"You waited up for me? I'm impressed."

"Want to talk? We'll have to go up to your place. Chad's sleeping. He fell into bed after he got home. I guess he had a bad day."

My eyebrows arched up. "What happened?"

I'd noticed he seemed rather aloof at Oceanside, but I thought he'd just been focused on getting the job done. Being married had seemed to bring with it a new side to Chad. When we'd met, he'd been a laidback surfer. Now he seemed more responsible and serious. I guess growing up did that to people.

Everyone seemed to be changing . . . except me. I was changing in my own ways, but not like everyone else. My friends were all getting married, embracing their careers, settling down. Meanwhile, I seemed to be stuck in a holding pattern.

Sierra shrugged. "I guess it mostly had to do with that new guy he hired. Chad's not impressed. Something about Chad still doing the same amount of work for less pay."

I knew it! I knew Braxton was the wrong choice. But I wanted Chad to figure that out himself instead of through me insisting I was right. "I'll talk to Chad later."

Up in my apartment, Sierra and I sat on the couch, and I poured out everything about the investigation. There wasn't enough information to theorize about very many suspects or motives yet, but we agreed that I should keep my eyes on Paulette's ex.

As soon as I finished that purge of information, I launched into another. "Garrett has invited me to go to Africa with him for a month."

Sierra blinked. "What?"

I nodded. "He said I can work as his bodyguard, so it wouldn't be a free ride."

Sierra snorted.

I nodded and pointed. "See! That's what I did, too. That thought is ridiculous, right?"

Her smile slowly faded. "You are very protective. And you're observant. I mean, you being a bodyguard isn't the craziest thought in the world. It's just unexpected. What are you going to do?"

"I don't know. It sounds like a great opportunity to see the world, doesn't it?"

"Garrett really likes you, Gabby. I mean, for goodness sakes—he bought this whole building just so you wouldn't have to move and find a new place."

In the past, I might have hesitated before agreeing. But this time I nodded. "I know. He does."

He had purchased this old house because he'd

known I needed something stable in my life. The place had almost been sold to someone who wanted to turn it into a single-family residence. If that had happened, I would have been out on the street and away from my co-tenants who felt like the only family I had.

"How do you feel?"

At her question, I felt like a huge boulder was placed on my shoulders. "I like Garrett. I really do."

"There's a 'but' in there."

"Sometimes I just wish we'd met at a different time in my life, you know?"

"You mean, before Riley?"

I bit down on my lip. Suddenly chilly, I pulled a fleece blanket decorated with cats over my lap. I wasn't a cat fanatic, but Sierra had given me this as a gift at Christmas. "Yeah, I mean before Riley."

"Have you heard from him lately?"

I shook my head. "No, not really. It's been three weeks, I think." There was no "think" about it. It had been three weeks, two days, and six hours. How long did it take you to get over losing the love of your life?

"It might be time to move on, Gabby. You should give yourself permission to let go."

"But what if Riley decides he's ready to try again? What if—"

"What if that never happens and you turn down a great guy like Garrett?"

The rock on my shoulders suddenly became heavier. "You're right. I would be making a huge mistake."

"Riley may never be the same person, Gabby." She squeezed my arm. "I know you don't want to hear that. I know you want to think that things will go back to the way they were before. But injuries like Riley's—"

"They can change a person forever," I finished. I'd spent hours researching all of this online and hoping that the information I'd read was wrong, even though I knew in my heart it wasn't. "I know."

She wiped beneath her eyes as tears wet them. Sierra? Crying? This was not a sight I usually saw. This subject must be very touchy to her.

"Gabby, none of those other jobs you've applied for with the medical examiner's office have come through yet. If there was ever a time to get out and see the world, it's now. Maybe explore more than the world. Explore what life with Garrett would be like. I like him, Gabby. I know he's not Riley, but he's a good guy."

Garrett's picture fluttered into my mind, and I smiled. "He is. He's handsome, smart, funny—"

"Rich. Don't forget rich. But he's also charitable. And his accent? It's to die for." She let out a sigh.

"I won't tell Chad you said that."

"I appreciate that." She smiled and wiped her

eyes one more time. "How long do you have to think about it?"

"A couple of weeks."

"Garrett's always good about giving you deadlines, isn't he?"

Garrett was definitely a deadline person. Maybe it had something to do with him being the CEO of his own company. He knew that being indecisive only wasted time. "He seems to know I'll waffle around and not make a choice otherwise."

Sierra squeezed my hand. "You'll make the right choice. You always do."

I wished I felt as confident as she did.

"Don't tell Chad, by the way," I implored. "I don't want to stress him out. It doesn't seem right to leave him hanging with the business."

"I don't know if that would stress him out. He's seemed pretty happy lately, truth be told. At least, he's happy when he's at home."

Something about the way she said the words made me pause. "Is there any reason in particular he's so happy?"

A grin spread across Sierra's face. "Because we're having a baby!"

CHAPTER
NINE

MY MOUTH DROPPED OPEN. "What? Are you serious? Congratulations!"

I threw my arms around her. When we pulled out of the hug, she was still grinning. And my friend wasn't a huge smiler. Marriage had softened her up some, and I was sure that having a baby would do that even more. It wasn't that long ago she'd lived and breathed her job as an animal rights activist.

She laughed and pushed her glasses up higher. "Yes, I'm serious."

"I can't believe it. Here I was going on and on about Africa. You should have stopped me!"

"I love hearing about your adventures. There was no reason to stop you."

"Of course there was. You're having a baby! I

want to hear everything. Everything! When are you due?"

"In June."

"June?" I did a quick calculation. "So you're four, five months already?"

She nodded and rubbed her belly. "I'm not showing yet. I wanted to get past the first trimester and then some before I said anything. We just found out this week that it's a boy."

I leaned back hard. "I can't believe this, Sierra. I'm so happy for you guys."

"We're happy, too. This wasn't really planned, but we're ready."

"Are you moving? Will you keep working? Do you have any names picked out yet?"

Sierra laughed at my slew of questions. "We don't know yet. We're still trying to figure some things out. I think this is one more reason Chad has been pushing so hard to really make the most of the business. He's going to have a family to support soon."

"You're going to be a great mom, Sierra." I smiled, imagining her with a baby. It was easy. I just replaced the mental image of her cradling one of her cats with one of her with an infant. If she loved that baby half as much as she loved her animals, motherhood would be a piece of cake for her.

We talked for a few more minutes and then she went back downstairs.

When I was alone in my apartment, I huddled on my couch. One thought remained in my mind. Everyone was growing up except me. I was stuck here in the same place I'd been since I dropped out of college.

Why wasn't I making any effort to change that?

The next day, in between cleaning one crime scene and working on a bathroom remodel at another—that was Chad's idea—I researched various cast members. Paulette had given me a list of first and last names. I hopped on the Internet and searched for anything interesting about them, as well as looked at their social media pages, which generally revealed way too much about people.

At the end of my research, I wasn't any farther along than when I started. I definitely didn't see anything that would indicate I should investigate one cast member over another.

Until I came to Jerome.

Absolutely nothing came up when I searched for him, which was highly unusual for an actor who wanted to make a name for himself. I needed to ask some more questions about him, and I hoped I might get my opportunity to do that at practice this evening.

Out of curiosity, I did a search for "Riley Thomas." I knew it was a long shot that any articles would come up, but this was my once a week ritual.

My eyes widened when a news bit popped up at the top of the screen. My heart fell into my stomach as I read the words.

"Riley Thomas named junior partner at Smith, Gleason, and Aims."

I read the article, just to make sure I wasn't jumping to conclusions. I wasn't. Riley was going back to work. As a lawyer.

He was moving on. Establishing himself again. Taking on commitments, responsibilities.

Even more, he was developing permanency. Up in DC. Nowhere close to me.

I couldn't believe it.

Nor could I believe the fact that he hadn't told me.

Spontaneously, I walked across the hallway to Riley's old apartment. I tried to avoid it as much as I could because there were too many bad memories. Riley was subletting the space to his cousin. She was considerably younger and taking classes at a nearby culinary school. I'd interacted with her a few times and she seemed nice enough.

Before I could second guess myself, I knocked at the door. To my surprise, Olivia answered. Her eyes widened when she saw me. "Gabby! Hi, there."

"Hey, Olivia." I stood there a moment. Why in the world was I going to tell her I was here? This was where planning really came in handy. "I was wondering if you had any flour? I'm going to bake a . . . cake. That's right. A cake. And I'm out of flour, of all things."

Actually, I never bought flour because I never baked. Never.

"It's kind of hard to make a cake with no flour! Of course I have some. Come on in."

I stepped inside, watching her walk into the kitchen. In so many ways, she looked like Riley. They both had dark hair and blue eyes. She had pleasant, even features and seemed grounded.

"So, what kind of cake are you making?" she asked, standing on her tiptoes and reaching into a cabinet.

What kind of cake? I glanced around the apartment, looking for an idea. My gaze fell on a bag of chips. "It's called a potato chip cake."

A potato chip cake? Really, Gabby?

Her head swerved toward me, her nose scrunched in distaste. "I've heard of a lot of things but never that. Have you had it before?"

I shrugged. "Yeah. I thought everyone had. They're all the rage. Sweet and salty."

She raised her eyebrows before reaching back into

the cabinet for a canister of flour. "You'll have to let me know how it turns out."

"Of course."

My gaze fell on the TV stand and I froze. There was a new picture there. A picture of Riley. With a woman.

What?

I inched closer, certain I was seeing things.

No, sure enough, there was Riley with his arm around a blonde wearing hospital scrubs. A lump formed in my throat.

"Here you go!" Olivia handed me the canister.

I pushed away the emotions that wanted to flood out and took the canister. "Thank you," I mumbled.

"No problem. If you have any extra, I'd love a piece! Maybe I'll impress my instructor with it. It could be the next big thing since chocolate covered bacon."

I forced a smile. "I'll let you know." I started to the door and paused. "How's Riley, by the way?"

Her smile slipped. "He's hanging in. Seems to be returning to his old self. That's all we've been praying for."

I nodded. "Me, too."

Garrett picked me up at 4:00 and drove me to my former teacher's house. I tried to put aside thoughts of Riley and betrayal and a million other emotions I was still trying to identify.

Maybe Sierra was right. It was time for me to move on. Riley had. Why shouldn't I?

As soon as I got home, I was going to find a box and pack away all my reminders of him. I still had his sweatshirt. The first rose he'd given me—I'd pressed it between the pages of an old dictionary. I had pictures of us stuffed in my drawers.

My first step would be to get rid of those things. It would be healthy. I had to remove the physical ties to the past before I could remove the emotional ones.

However, it was hard to move forward when pieces of my past continued to resurface. Aside from the whole Riley thing, I suddenly had been thrust back in time at my old middle school, surrounded by people from my tween days, and remembering life as it had been many years ago.

My heart pounded in my ears as Garrett and I pulled into a familiar neighborhood. "This is the same street where Mrs. Baker used to live back when I was in middle school. I dog sat for her once."

I smiled as I remembered those days of trying to earn extra money, of riding my bike all over town, of having my first boyfriend. It seemed like another lifetime ago. Back when Mom was alive. She'd worked so hard to keep the family both afloat and together.

I wondered what my life would be like today if Mom hadn't died. If my brother hadn't disappeared. If my dad hadn't become a drunk.

If my life hadn't taken detours.

My life had taken a lot of unexpected turns. Maybe it was time to take back some control in my life and start calling the shots.

Again, I was traveling back in time. But I had to make peace with my past before I could march into the future . . . right?

"Did you grow up in this area?" Garrett asked.

"I lived only a few blocks away. I haven't been back here since my mom died." I shook my head, pushing away the memories.

"Lots of memories, huh?"

"You could say that. I'll have to show you where I grew up sometime," I told him, my gaze fixated out the window. "It's nothing like your childhood home."

Garrett had grown up in a 10,000 square foot mansion with tennis courts. Well, that was one of his homes. His family came from old money. But even being rich hadn't spared them heartache. In fact, it may have added to their troubles.

"I'm sure it's simply charming."

"I'll let you keep thinking that." I hadn't been

back to my old place in years, nor had I ever shown anyone what it looked like. My home wasn't exactly something to be proud of. While I hadn't lived in a trailer, I had lived in a duplex in a not-so-nice part of town. The grass had always been overgrown, our van had been ghetto with its faded paint and missing hubcaps, and our driveway had boasted oil stains.

I thought I was taking steps to move away from repeating the mistakes of my parents. I'd always wanted to do better for myself. But maybe I was really just heading in the same direction—the direction of going nowhere.

I pointed to a small little bungalow in the distance. "That's it. That's Mrs. Baker's house."

I guess I should have called her Mrs. Harper, but she'd always be Mrs. Baker to me.

We parked and climbed out of the car.

I did a mental "cheers" to myself. *Here's to exploring yet another part of your past, Gabby. And here's to learning how to let go.*

I PAUSED ON THE DRIVEWAY, trying to gather my wits, and Garrett pulled me closer. "I just want to say thank you for inviting me along. I know this Mrs. Baker means a lot to you. I also know that revisiting the days of old isn't always easy."

I smiled up him. "I'm glad you can be here. More than glad—I'm grateful."

He looked at me a moment like he wanted to say more. I saw it in his eyes, in his lingering gaze. But instead he grinned and took my hand. "Let's not keep them waiting."

Something about feeling my hand in Garrett's warmed my heart. At the moment, I didn't feel like I was all alone in the world. But there was so much more at stake here than my loneliness. Would I ever love anyone else as much as I'd loved Riley? I didn't know, but I really needed to start giving that some thought.

Mrs. Baker answered the door, her eyes lighting when she spotted us on the stoop. After a quick round of introductions, we were whisked inside.

I spotted Mrs. Baker's husband Amos standing in the background. His hair was graying, and his face had thinned out some. But he still looked ornery and tough and like the man who'd ultimately made Mrs. Baker a very happy woman.

"Gabby St. Claire." He shook his head and, for a moment, I thought he wasn't happy to see me. Then a grin spread across his face. "First time I met you I thought you were stealing my sister's dog. Look at you now! All grown up."

He actually hugged me before doing that guy hug and handshake thing with Garrett.

Then I met Mrs. Baker's daughter, Larissa. I nearly gawked.

The girl was thirteen with curly hair that had frizzed, almost as if she'd tried to straighten it unsuccessfully. Her gaze appeared determined, curious.

She reminded me of . . . well—me—when I was that age.

For a moment, and just a moment, I wanted to be transported back to my younger days. I wanted to see my mom again. I wanted to eat her applesauce pancakes with candied walnuts. I wanted to hear her call me Tootsie. I wanted to let her know how much I missed her.

I'd had an entirely different set of problems back then, but I'd been too young and naïve to worry about things like food and housing. Instead I'd worried about boys and cliques at school and how I'd ever make up for taking my eyes off my brother long enough for someone to snatch him.

"Let's eat before everything gets cold," Mrs. Baker said. "We have play practice in an hour and a half anyway. I wish we had more time, but I'll take what I can get."

We sat down to roast beef, mashed potatoes, green beans, and rolls—if I ate good food like this every night, I'd gain twenty pounds.

"How's your mom, Gabby?" Mrs. Baker asked, taking a sip of tea.

My throat burned. "She actually passed away while I was in college. Cancer."

"Oh, Gabby. I'm so sorry. She was such a nice woman." She reached across the table and squeezed my hand.

"She was. My dad's still around. He actually has a job now. That's a good first step. About 18 years late, but . . ."

When my brother disappeared, my dad quickly cascaded into a downward spiral that should have made the record books. He'd gone from a champion surfer to couch potato drunk faster than you could say, "Cowabunga, dude!" My mom had worked two jobs to pay the bills while my father had his license and any good sense taken away.

"Better late than never?" Mrs. Baker filled in with raised eyebrows.

"Exactly."

We talked for several minutes, catching up. Then the subject turned to the play. I wanted to get a feel from her about what was going on.

"It's all been very strange, Gabby," Mrs. Baker said, slicing an apple pie. "Someone is obviously sabotaging everything, I just can't for the life of me figure out why. Then there's Scarlet . . ."

"What did you know about her?"

Mrs. Baker let out a long breath as she handed out dessert. "To tell you the truth—not much. I have a feeling no one did. She kept to herself a lot and didn't share many personal details. She was a talented actress. I don't know if she was Broadway material, but she had something there."

"Did you see any arguments between Scarlet and anyone else?"

She sat down and raised her fork. "Now that you mention it, I did see her and Arie whispering rather heatedly about something last week. I didn't think much of it—creative differences, I assumed. I was glad to see that at least they were talking about it."

I stored away that information for later.

"Do you know if she was dating anyone?"

Mrs. Baker shook her head. "Not that I know of. But I do have an idea for you. I think Scarlet took one of the costumes home—the nun habit. She volunteered to have it altered since it was long on her. It would be a great excuse for you to stop by and see where she lives without seeming suspicious. I do believe she mentioned a roommate to me once."

I grinned. "I knew I liked you."

Mrs. Baker laughed. "Oh, Gabby. I'm so proud of you. I always knew you'd turn out well."

Apparently she thought being a crime scene cleaner equated to turning out well. Who was I to argue with her?

"Stop! He's trying to kill me!" I screamed.

The lights in the auditorium went black.

I held my breath, waiting to see what happened next.

To my relief, applause broke out from the cast.

We'd just finished Act Two, and we'd survived.

Despite that, practice today was going worse than yesterday, and that was saying a lot.

To make matters even uglier, Arie had shown up before practice started and she was in a mood.

Primarily, she still wasn't happy about me and felt like she should have had input before Paulette made the decision to bring me on. She addressed the issue in front of everyone right after we'd rehearsed Act One.

I stared at her now, waiting for her reaction, because I was sure she'd have one.

"I just don't think this is going to work," she muttered, casting a withering look my way.

I glanced at Paulette, waiting for her to say something, but she sat there looking like a deer caught in the headlights. I had no choice but to stand up for myself since no one else was.

"I'll be fine in the role, Arie." I really had no idea if I would be fine or not. I wasn't going to tell *her* that, though.

"I don't want *fine*. I want *great*. Outstanding. Stupendous. *Fine* is *failure*." She flung her hands in the air, probably meant to emphasize her stress but instead making her look crazy.

I took a step back. "I think you're overreacting."

That caused her to overreact even more. Her hands flung even higher, her nostrils flared, her eyes widened.

"Overreacting? I've worked for years on this play and I don't want to blow it because some half bit actress was given a starring role without my permission."

"Who are you calling a half bit actress?" I would have totally called myself one, but no way was I letting *her* say it.

She apparently didn't hear me. "There are *no* other plays *out there* like *this*!" she insisted.

"You're right. It's like a mix of *Phantom, Les Mis,* and *The Sound of Music.* Nothing like any other plays at all." I didn't try to keep my sarcasm at bay. Arie was out of control, and I couldn't take it anymore.

"It's *nothing* like those plays," she screeched. "This is a one of a kind *original.*"

The woman really thought this was going to launch her career. She also really thought she was the next great Rodger or Hammerstein, for that matter, or both of them rolled into one too-good-to-be-true package. I had no aspirations of being an actor, and even I wouldn't want this tragedy to go onto my resume.

She stepped closer. "If you ruin this for me, so help me . . ."

Arie had no idea who she was dealing with. I'd dealt with people a lot scarier than her. I threw my shoulders back and raised my chin.

"So help me you'll what?" I challenged.

Her nostrils flared. "I can make your life miserable."

I held up the script and dropped my head to the side. "You already have."

She gasped. "You're an awful person Gabby Whatever-Your-Last-Name-Is!"

She turned on her heel and stormed away.

When I turned around, I realized the rest of the cast had formed a semi-circle around me and appeared to be a rapt audience. And, for the second time today, they applauded for me.

"Someone needed to say it," Bennie muttered.

"Everyone else was afraid of her," one of The Shining twins said.

"You really think this play is horrible?" Paulette asked.

I realized what I'd said in my haste and prayed that Paulette wouldn't be crushed. How was I going to make this better? My words too often got the best of me.

"We're going to make the most of what we have to work with," Mrs. Baker said, always the voice of reason. "We're going to put our best foot forward and make this show a success."

That seemed to cheer Paulette up some. She nodded and attempted to pull herself together. "We don't have any time to waste. We need to get to work. Opening night is only ten days away."

I nodded. I really hoped nothing else happened between now and the opening, though.

CHAPTER
ELEVEN

AFTER REHEARSAL, I hung back to talk to Paulette and Mrs. Baker, waiting for the majority of the cast to leave.

Everyone seemed content to linger, though, so I stepped into the hallway with a group from the chorus line. I looked over to see Bennie coming from the band room, which was where the props were temporarily being worked on until the auditorium was available again. Cast members also kept their personal belongings in there for now.

Bennie stumbled and fell from the room, her bag hitting the floor and some sheets of large paper flying out. She scrambled to stand and gather what she'd dropped.

I hurried toward her to help. As my fingers hit the

paper, I paused. This was no ordinary paper. "This feels so soft."

She took it from me and smiled. "Doesn't it? I was hoping no one would see this. I'm putting together a scrapbook of this play for Paulette."

That would explain the oddly sized paper. "That's awfully nice of you."

She nodded, shoving the sheets back in her bag with a stack of other papers. "It's my thing. It's just what I do." She shrugged.

"If you don't mind me asking, where did you get the name Bennie?"

"Just something my parents started calling me. It's similar to my real name—Bonnie. My mom used to say Dad would talk baby language and say Bonnie Bonnie Bennie Boo. Who knows? Regardless, it stuck." She heaved her bag back onto her shoulder.

"What do you do, Bennie, when you're not acting?" I asked both because I wanted to know and because I had to start socializing with the cast if I was going to get any answers. This wasn't my normal assignment where it was okay to rub people the wrong way. Being undercover, I needed to be in people's good graces. I hadn't done a good job with that so far.

She gripped the bag and shifted. "I mostly do odd jobs for my older brother. He's a mechanic, handyman, and entrepreneur. I've always wanted to be an actress, but my parents always told me I'd never make any money and I'd be poor for the rest of my life. But I lost my parents four years ago and it kind of derailed my already derailed life. I've been floundering around ever since then."

Boy, could I ever relate to that. "I'm sorry to hear that Bennie."

She nodded. "Me, too. We just recently started going through their things. It took us a while, but we were hoping to get closure."

There was that concept again. Closure. Maybe that's what I needed in my life.

She studied me a minute. "You know, you're one of the nicer people here. I'm sorry about Scarlet, but I'm glad you're with us now."

Just then, one of The Shining Twins shrieked. "What's that?"

I glanced over and saw them standing at the main hallway, just beyond the music wing. They pointed to something on the floor.

I hurried toward them, praying it wasn't another trail of gasoline. Instead, I saw wet footprints leading down the hall.

Just as apprehension started to fill me, a cool wind swept through the space.

"This place is haunted!" one of the twins whispered.

I looked back to see her grab another girl's arm. They looked honestly terrified.

"I'm sure this is nothing, guys," I told them.

They weren't moving, so I guessed that meant I was going first. I began following the trail. In order to dispel the emotions that caused so much fear, I tried to focus on logic.

Those footprints weren't all that large, so I didn't think they were from a man. As my foot came down beside one of the footprints, I saw they were only slightly bigger than my own.

The strides between steps easily matched mine, which led me to believe that this person was approximately my height.

As I reached the main corridor, the lights above me flickered. The main lighting had been turned off in favor of energy conserving lighting that was used in the hallway for rehearsals and such. It expelled a fluorescent purple glow that reminded me of the bug zapping lights from my childhood.

The footprints led to the girls' bathroom.

I heard the gaggle of girls behind me gasp.

"What now?" one of The Shining twins asked.

I pushed my shoulders back. "Now we go and check out what happened."

"We'll wait here," the twins muttered together.

I wanted to say, "Call the police if I'm not out in

three minutes." But I kept those thoughts silent and instead said, "I'll check it out."

I couldn't deny that my hands were trembling as I reached the doorway. This was just silly. I didn't believe in ghosts. There had to be a logical explanation for all of this.

I pulled the door open and water cascaded into the hallway. What in the world?

I reached for the light switch, and as it flickered on, I saw that water covered the floor. It was everywhere, probably a couple of inches deep. Steam hung heavy in the air, making it hard to see anything in front of me.

I took a few more steps inside and noticed the water gushing from the toilets. All the sinks were on, streaming hot liquid.

I surveyed the room, looking for a sign of what had happened. The bathroom had not looked like this earlier. This had been done on purpose.

Even stranger: Why did the wet footprints lead to the bathroom and not away from it?

I stepped through the fog to the sinks to turn them off. That's when I saw the message written in blood-red lipstick on the mirror.

I'll get you, my pretty.

Chills raced over my skin and I ran back into the hallway.

As soon as the ladies there saw my expression, they huddled together and gasped. Without words, they knew that something scary had happened in that bathroom.

So much for not alarming anyone.

FIRST THING IN THE MORNING, I stopped by Scarlet's apartment, armed with a box of muffins and the excuse Mrs. Baker had given me about the costume.

Scarlet didn't live terribly far away from me. In the same area, actually—a neighborhood called Ghent. She lived closer than I did to Old Dominion University, in an old brick building that probably had eight units inside. It may have even been a dorm at one time, I guessed, based on some Greek letters that had been artfully arranged within the design of the bricks above the front door.

I knocked on the door and waited patiently to see if anyone would answer. I didn't have high hopes, but sometimes luck was on my side. Today was one of those remarkable days.

The door opened partly, and a woman peered out of the crack with suspicion in her gaze.

"Yes?"

"Hi, I'm Gabby. I'm with the community theater group in Virginia Beach. I just wanted to say that I'm so sorry for your loss."

"Thank you," her voice cracked.

"I know it's not much, but I brought these for you." I handed her the muffins. "I didn't know if you'd feel like cooking, with everything that's happened and all."

She didn't say anything for a moment, but she seemed to be holding herself together okay. I decided to gently bring up the nun habit, praying that my words sounded compassionate.

"I hate to sound insensitive, but I also need to pick up one of the costumes from the play. I heard Scarlet brought it here."

She continued to eye me. "What's your name again?"

"Gabby. We've never met. I actually don't live far away. Right across from The Grounds coffeehouse, if you know where that is."

That seemed to gain her trust some because she nudged the door a little farther open. "I'll see if I can find something. I guess you can wait inside."

I smiled softly. "Thank you."

I stepped inside. The apartment was nothing

fancy: a futon served as a couch, there were various theater posters—*The Lion King, Phantom,* and *Mamma Mia!*—on the walls and a glass top table, wicker and slightly dated, in the dining room. It looked like a typical college student's place.

"I'm Marjorie," she said.

I got my first good look at her. Marjorie had long blonde hair with tight spiral curls cascading down her back. She was dancer thin, but had a smattering of acne across her fair skin.

I wondered if she was always so untrusting or if something had caused her to be this way. More specifically, if something related to Scarlet's death had caused it.

"How are you holding up?" I asked, standing on an island of tile right in front of the door.

She shrugged. "I've been better."

I saw several used tissues on the end table, and I knew she'd been having a hard time. My heart softened.

"How long were you guys roommates?"

She walked over to the breakfast bar and began putting away dishes from the sink. "Since freshman year. We hit it off and moved out of the dorms and into this place instead. I can't believe she's not coming back."

"I'm truly sorry, Marjorie."

She paused, plate in hand. "Who would do this to her?"

"I guess you have no idea?"

She shook her head, putting the plate down and bracing herself against the counter. "No idea."

I decided to take a gamble. I was supposed to remain low key and undercover. But maybe I could push a little harder without raising suspicions. "Marjorie, would you mind telling me a little about Scarlet?"

"What do you want to know?" She drew in a deep breath and resumed drying and putting the dishes away.

I propped my hip against the wall. "Why in the world would someone want to kill her?"

She eyed me from across the room. "I thought you were an actress?"

I forced my shoulders to relax and reminded myself not to sound too anxious. "I am. But I worry that the crime is targeted at the play more than it was Scarlet. Now I'm in her old role, and my gut just feels unsettled. Does that make sense?"

She nodded, tears welling in her eyes. "Yeah, it does. I don't know why she was murdered, to tell you the truth. But I told the police this, and I'll tell you, too. I overheard her arguing with someone four nights ago. I was in my bedroom and the voices drifted up toward my window. I tried to look out and see what was going on, but they must have been standing just around the corner. I couldn't see them."

My pulse spiked. "Was she arguing with a man or woman?"

"A woman."

A casserole dish and plate clattered together, causing my nerves to tighten.

"Could you make out anything they said?"

"No, I couldn't. It just sounded heated." She rose on tiptoes to put the plates onto a high shelf.

Though I wanted her full attention, I understood her need to feel normal, to stay busy in order to create a barrier between herself and reality. "Did you ask her about it?"

"I did. She said I shouldn't worry. She also said everything would be working itself out soon."

"That's strange."

"I thought so, too. Scarlet was passionate about life and a little eccentric at times. She was smart and savvy, and knew what she wanted in life. Nothing held her back."

"What did she want to do for a living?"

"Oh, she wanted to make it all the way to Broadway. She thought this play would be her best chance. At least her starting chance. She was giving it her all and then some."

"Did she have a boyfriend?"

Her lips twisted. "I don't know. She was talking

to this guy. He was Hispanic. Maybe from Mexico? I'm not sure. She only brought him around once."

Roberto? "Did he play soccer, by chance?"

She pursed her lips. "Now that you mention it, I think he did play. I'm not really sure. Their whole relationship seemed kind of hush hush."

"Name?"

She shook her head. "I have no idea. They texted a lot."

At least this was something. I'd take something over nothing.

"Thank you, Marjorie."

She nodded sadly, pausing by the sink. "I guess you want the dress."

"That would be great."

Marjorie walked into a room down the hallway but quickly appeared again with a frown on her face. "I know that costume was in Scarlet's room. I just saw it on her bed yesterday."

I tensed. "What are you saying?"

"It's gone now."

"Isn't it a shame all these donuts are being wasted? Certainly it wouldn't be that bad if we just had one," Clarice said as we prepped the bullet-pocked walls at a local donut shop where, after hours, the owner and two employees had been shot. The place was a mess and had just been released by the police. We were going to get as much done here today as possible, but I had a feeling this would turn into a two day job.

I stared at her. "You want to eat donuts from a crime scene?"

"A donut is a donut. It's not like they got their holes from a gun during a gang fight."

I paused. "Don't touch the donuts, Clarice."

Although, now that she'd put the idea in my head, I was salivating for one of the caramel covered pastries that were in plain view. I could practically taste their sugary goodness, the gooey glaze and the airy pastry.

Stop it, Gabby!

"I bet one of those police officers who worked the scene snagged some. You know how they love their donuts."

"Stereotype," I reminded her.

"Stereotypes are stereotypes for a reason. I don't care what anyone says." She paused from wiping down the walls. "So, how's the case going?"

I continued to sand down a wall that had nine bullet holes. "It's going slowly. Then today, a costume worn by the deceased actress was stolen."

"Stolen?"

I nodded. Marjorie and I had searched the entire apartment. The costume was nowhere to be found.

I'd asked Marjorie if she'd seen any signs that someone else had been in her apartment and she said no. However, the cable guy had stopped by just the day before. She'd been practicing her dance in her bedroom when he was there, so there was a possibility he'd taken it. I'd left a message with her landlord but hadn't heard back yet.

Had the mastermind behind these crimes actually disguised himself as a cable guy in order to steal a costume? What would that prove? I had no idea.

I glanced at Clarice again, my mind snapping back to our conversation. "Not to mention that the play is possibly the worst thing I've ever read."

"The music was pretty bad," Clarice concurred. "Yet strangely familiar at the same time."

"Probably because it's a knockoff of everything else out there." I shook my head. "The playwright and I had it out with each other yesterday. She thinks she's God's gift to Broadway. I'm Arie Berry," I mocked in a high-pitched voice, stopping for long enough to wave my hands in the air. "And *I'm* the *best* thing to ever happen to *show business.*"

"Wait, did you say Arie Berry?" Clarice stopped working for long enough to wiggle her head and morph her voice into a haughty sounding mockery. "That's R-E, not Airy; it doesn't rhyme with Berry."

"Yes . . . ?"

"Arie Berry was on *Cascade Falls.*"

"The soap opera?" Anything pop culture, Clarice knew all about it.

"Yeah, she only had a minor role. It was her shenanigans after the show went off the air that made her practically famous. For a couple of months, at least. She partied hard, showed up whenever cameras were present, and even got into a fight at a baseball game once. She tried to get some other TV deals, but, by that time, she was old news. Her and her boyfriend pretty much became has beens."

I absorbed the new information. "That's interesting."

"I wonder if it's the same person. It has to be."

I shrugged. "I can't imagine there are that many people named Arie Berry. However, if she's desperate for fame, I could see why she'd want the play to succeed so badly."

"Sounds like you've got a lead."

Finally.

WHILE I ATE DINNER, I searched for "Cascade Falls" on my computer. A few minutes later, the show came up and I watched some clips online.

Sure enough, this Arie Berry was the same as *The Specter's* Arie Berry.

The show wasn't highly rated or critically acclaimed, nor was Arie Berry a phenomenal actress. In fact, she seemed typecast because her character in *Cascade Falls* seemed to have the exact same personality that Arie had in real life. She was haughty, arrogant, and important in her own eyes.

Interesting.

But did it mean anything?

I nibbled on a French fry and, out of curiosity, did a search for recent news articles about her.

Apparently, her fame quickly faded when the

show was canceled after one season. Arie and her off camera exploits were more popular than the show, but the public's interest in those only lasted a few months at the most. Then scandal hungry fans moved on to another celebrity who was desperate to do anything for attention.

Arie had tried other failed pursuits—some commercials, an endorsement deal with a deodorant company, starting her own restaurant and bar, and even a web-based reality series—but nothing had stuck or captured people. That must have been when she turned to playwriting, though I found no articles on that pursuit. That was a surprise within itself. What if she was staging the incidents at the theater in order to drum up publicity and then, in effect, her fame?

It was a possibility I needed to seriously consider.

I couldn't wait to share the news with Paulette at practice.

I glanced at the clock on my wall and realized I was running out of time. I still had other things to do today. Domestic-like things.

With a touch of hesitation, I hurried to the kitchen and grabbed a piece of chocolate cake I'd purchased at a nearby bakery. I took a bag of chips, crushed them, and then crumbled them on top. I frowned at the end creation. It looked absolutely disgusting.

I stuck the whole thing on one of my dessert

plates, took a deep breath, and hurried across the hall. A moment later, Olivia answered the door. I forced another smile and held up the cake. "I know you said you wanted to try it."

As her gaze fell on the icing, her nostrils flared in what I assumed was disgust and her lips pulled down in a frown. "Great. Thank you so much."

"You're very welcome."

She took it from me and seemed to notice I stayed in the doorway for a little too long. "Would you like to come in for a minute?"

I tried to compose myself. "I want to see what you think." I pointed to the cake.

She let out a nervous laugh. "Of course, of course. Come in."

I stepped inside, hating myself for using such desperate means to find out more about Riley. But if Riley was pushing ahead with his life, then why in the world was I holding back? I needed to know.

"Let me just grab a fork." Olivia pulled one from her kitchen drawer and stood with it poised above my culinary delight.

I smiled, probably a little too brightly. I had to look sincere. "It's unlike anything you've ever tried before."

"I bet it is."

She drew in a deep breath and dug in. Her face tightened as the food hit her taste buds. "This is very interesting. Where did you say you got the recipe?"

"It's all the rage online."

She nodded slowly, chewing with a tight jaw. "Unlike anything I've had before."

"That's what I thought, too." I paced over to the TV and stared down at the picture of Riley and the blonde. My gut clenched again as I looked at it.

"Have you met Daniela yet?" Olivia nodded toward the photo.

"Daniela?" I questioned. Since Olivia had broached the subject, I picked up the photo and got a better look. I forced myself to keep breathing, to control my thoughts, to ignore the emotions lurking down deep inside.

"She's pretty."

Olivia nodded, her face twisting as she took another bite. Poor thing. I really should put her out of her misery. "She's great. She works at the hospital where Riley's being treated, so that works out really well. She's able to help get him to and from therapy."

I'd offered to do that for him, but he'd refused. The realization pressed on my heart.

"That's good that he has someone to help him."

"Being around people who love and support you is so important." She put the cake down on the counter. "Listen, thanks so much for sharing this, but I've got to get to class. I'll save the rest for later."

I nodded. "I understand. Have a great day, Olivia."

Back in my apartment, tears pushed to my eyes.

I'd thought after five months of this that the realization Riley was dating someone else would come easier, that I would be prepared to accept it. Only I wasn't. Maybe I'd never be.

His nurse! All along I'd had a terrible suspicion he'd end up falling for one of his nurses. I'd just had no clue that I'd actually be right! Was I really this much of a fool?

I picked up one of the last letters he'd written to me. I kept it in my desk drawer. As I read it, a tear hit the paper and blurred Riley's name. Symbolic? A sign from God? I wasn't sure.

So this was it.

Riley really had moved on.

In the meantime, I'd just been sitting around here waiting. Like a fool. Why was it so hard for me to accept reality sometimes?

Using the back of my hand, I wiped away the moisture at my eyes.

I'd wanted to make sure he was happy. That he was really making it on his own okay. That his parents were taking good care of him. Since he'd essentially cut me off, I had no other way of hearing how Riley was holding up. I'd felt so out of touch.

I now knew the truth. What was done was done.

I shoved the letter into my desk drawer.

At least I finally had some answers. Maybe I could finally let go. Maybe I could finally move beyond the events that wanted to chain me to the past. They were like a weight that kept pulling me under water, nearly drowning me.

It was time to cut myself loose and finally breathe again.

I fished out my old pictures of Riley, his sweatshirt—which still smelled like him—and the sweet notes he'd written me. I put them all in a box and stuffed it on a high shelf in my closet.

Forgetting what's behind and pressing toward what's ahead.

That's what I had to do.

I arrived at practice early and tried to find Paulette so I could share what I'd learned. I walked past her office and saw a glass of wine on her desk, but no Paulette. Was that glass a sign that my friend had a drinking problem? Most people didn't bring alcohol with them to work, after all. I'd seen a glass at her house also.

I stepped fully inside her office, curiosity getting the best of me. That's when I spotted a yellow plastic bottle by her stack of mail. Out of curiosity, I picked it up. Pills clattered inside.

I glanced at the label. Some of the typed words had faded, but one ended with "ocotain." What was that used to treat? I would have to look it up. Quickly, I put the bottle back where I found it.

My eyes also skimmed over a red stamp across one of the bills. It clearly said "PAST DUE." Paulette was behind on her bills? Her family had plenty of money. How had that happened?

The gold trimmed clock hanging behind Paulette's desk caught my eye, and I flinched. I was late for practice!

I jetted out of her office and ran into the auditorium and realized everyone had stopped talking and now stared at me. I felt my face warm as my gaze shot around the room. Paulette stood at the front, right beside Mrs. Baker. Jerome paced on stage and several other cast members lingered close.

Then my gaze fell on Arie. She'd positioned herself apart from the others, her eyes shooting daggers at me.

I had a moment of contemplation, wondering if I should confront her or keep silent. I decided to keep quiet and be subtle, which wasn't easy for me. However, I was supposed to be undercover. I couldn't just go around accusing people.

"Glad to see you could join us," Arie mumbled.

Maybe I should rethink that whole being subtle thing.

I reached the stage. "Sorry I'm a few minutes late."

"We were just starting the second act. Why don't you join everyone on stage?" Mrs. Baker said.

I nodded and, as I started toward the steps, the auditorium suddenly went pitch black. A few screams cracked through the air. Something shuffled in the distance.

"What happened?" someone yelled.

"What's going on?"

"This can't be happening again!"

"No one panic!" I recognized Mrs. Baker's voice.

Finally, the lights flashed back on. Everyone let out a nervous laugh as they glanced at each other.

Even Mrs. Baker wiped her brow, a sure indication that she had been nervous too. "Must be some kind of problem with the wiring."

"I had someone look at it, though . . ." Paulette said, knitting her eyebrows together.

"Uh, you guys?" Jerome said.

Everyone turned toward him.

"Where's Arie?"

My gaze darted around the room. He was right.

Arie was nowhere to be seen.

"YOU REALLY THINK A PHANTOM TOOK HER?" Paulette asked, her eyes big and round and child-like.

Mrs. Baker had asked for a private meeting with Paulette, Jerome, and me. Everyone else was on the stage still, probably coming up with their own theories as to what had happened. The four of us stood at the back of the auditorium, speaking in quiet tones so we wouldn't alarm anyone.

"The lights went out and then—boom!—she disappeared. I don't know what else it could be," Jerome insisted.

"How about a vast, complicated, and not-so-smart plot to bring herself back into the limelight," I suggested.

His eyes widened. "What are you talking about?"

"I know about her stint on *Cascade Falls*. Her fifteen minutes of fame faded. Maybe she was desperate to get it back. Maybe she staged all of this just to get attention."

"You think Arie murdered somebody? You're crazy," Jerome said, a New Jersey accent creeping into his voice.

"If Arie disappeared on purpose, she's going to have a lot of explaining to do," I continued. "The police don't like wasting their time or resources on fake crimes."

"I'm telling you—I don't know what happened to Arie, but we need to find her. You've got to believe me," Jerome continued. "Who are you anyway? Why do you sound like some interrogator?"

"I'm someone who's looking out for the best interest of this play. That's who."

"You don't sound like no actress. Not here and not on the stage," Jerome continued.

"You're not doing yourself any favors right now," I warned him.

"Okay, both of you—stop," Mrs. Baker interceded.

Again, I felt like I was in middle school.

I crossed my arms. "There's something he's not telling us."

I had to get the last word in, didn't I?

But if Jerome was telling the truth, then something truly spooky was going on.

"I'm sorry," I conceded. "You're right. We do need to stop arguing. If Arie truly did disappear, we need to look for her."

He nodded stiffly. "Thank you."

Mrs. Baker turned to me. "I think we should call the police."

"Not yet. Not until we know if this is a crime or if Arie wandered off," I said. I didn't trust Arie Berry or her motivations for doing this play.

We wandered back toward the stage, and Paulette addressed the cast. "We're going to split into teams of two and search this building. No one go anywhere alone. Understand?"

Everyone nodded, but I could see the fear in their eyes. No one wanted to leave this room. But, hesitantly, a few groups scampered off. Several people refused to leave the auditorium period, citing safety concerns.

It was time to go search myself.

"Where's your partner?" Mrs. Baker asked.

"I don't have one. You need to stay with Paulette and wait for the police. We can't leave her alone, and you can handle her better than anyone else in the cast."

"But how about you? It may not be safe for you to

go out there alone." Motherly concern was evident in the wrinkles at her forehead.

I glanced back at Paulette. I knew I couldn't fully investigate with someone else by my side. It was a potentially dangerous move on my part, but I needed the freedom to search for evidence without being under someone's watchful gaze. "I'll be fine. Just stay with her. Please."

I decided to hit some of the more obvious places in the building. I checked behind the stage, even up on the catwalk.

Nothing.

With a touch of fear, I opened the door to one of the dressing rooms. It groaned, sending shivers up my spine.

Darkness stared back.

My heart pounded in my ears at an erratic rhythm. The stillness backstage had me on edge. If someone were to lunge at me, I'd never see them coming. Danger could be hiding around any corner, and I'd have no idea.

I shone my light into the room.

No Arie. It was empty.

I quickly checked the other dressing rooms, but they were clear.

Gripping my cell phone like a lifeline, I continued out the back door leading from the stage and into a hallway. With each step, my muscles tightened.

Where was everyone? Was I the only one who'd dispersed? Had everyone else changed their minds and returned to the auditorium, too afraid for their lives? I had to admit—I really couldn't blame them.

Images of Scarlet kept flashing through my mind. I really didn't want to end up like she did. My thoughts fluctuated from condemning Arie for possibly disappearing on purpose to stir up publicity to fearing that Arie might be the next victim. As much as I didn't like the woman, I didn't want her to die.

I moved through the building toward the gated-off wings. After each step I took, I paused to listen for approaching footsteps. I heard nothing.

I shoved down my fear and pushed away images of a serial killer wearing a spooky mask suddenly approaching at the end of the hallway. I'd seen too many scary movies in my lifetime.

As I reached the gates leading to the unused corridors, I checked the locks. They were all still in place and the gates didn't budge.

Where else could I check? That's when I remembered the custodian closet at the other end of the building. It was worth a shot.

I went around the corner, walking toward the half-hallway nestled behind the cafeteria. I walked faster than necessary, mostly because of the bristles popping over my skin.

I reached the hall and froze. The feeling of someone watching me was strong enough that I couldn't breathe.

I twirled around, searching for a sign of someone.

Blackness stared back.

I shone my light but still saw nothing. No one was there. Just me, which was both comforting and disturbing.

The heebie-jeebies came stronger, so I quickly reached the door, grabbed the handle, and twisted it. Slowly, uncertainly, I pulled the door open.

I hesitated to peer inside. Before I could contemplate too long, someone pushed me.

I tumbled into the closet.

"Who are you and what do you want from me?" someone whispered through the darkness.

Fear scrambled across my skin, raising my hair as I pushed myself away from whoever was in here with me. I reached for the doorknob but only felt a blank wall.

"Who are *you* and what are *you* doing in here?" I finally asked as the scent of pine cleaner filled my nostrils. Apparently, this was still being used as the custodian's closet.

"Oh. It's *you*!" Disdain tinged the voice.

My fear dissipated, replaced with annoyance. "Arie? How'd you end up here?"

"You don't think *I* wandered *here* by myself, do you?" The bitterness in her voice grew more brittle with every overly emphasized word.

I bit my tongue. There I'd been, trying to help her, and this was the thanks I received?

"For the record, I was looking for you when I got pushed inside." I leaned back and was pretty sure I'd knocked over a bottle of the granules custodians used to clean up vomit. A horrible smell filled the room. Perfect.

"Some rescuer *you* are then."

If I had to stay in this closet much longer with this woman, I might strangle her myself. "Let's see if we can get out of here."

"You can't open this from the inside. I wouldn't be in here if I could."

I scowled, even if she couldn't see me. "Sometimes locks can be manipulated."

"Like *you'd* know how to do *that*."

I bit my tongue again, refusing to say what I really wanted to say. "You have any better ideas?"

"Pound on the door and scream like crazy?"

"Not bad." I stood and felt around until I found the doorknob. I twisted it, knowing good and well it wasn't going to give. Then I felt around for the lock and shook my head. There was nothing on this side of the door but a blank handle with no lock or keyhole.

I pounded my fist on the wood. "Somebody, help us!"

"No one can hear us. We're too far away from everyone."

"They'll hear us eventually. Besides, this was your idea," I reminded her.

"Yeah, well, I tried it already and it didn't work. We're too far away."

"How about your cell?"

"There's no service in here."

"What?" I pulled out my phone. Sure enough, I didn't have any service either. Then I remembered that there was a boiler room behind us and the air conditioning system was on the other side. Of course there was no reception here. There were too many things to block our signals.

I sighed, resigning myself to waiting this out. Hopefully one of the search teams would head this way. I brushed off some of the smelly granules that had stuck to my hand and tried to focus.

"What happened, Arie?" I asked. "How'd you end up in here?"

"When the lights went out, someone put their hand over my mouth and pulled me here." She let out an annoyed *harrumph*.

"Man or woman?"

"Man, I think."

"You think?"

She sighed this time. "It was complicated. I was scared. He or she seemed pretty strong. Of course, I'm five foot eleven. The height makes it difficult to just grab me."

Well, that didn't help me narrow it down.

"Did he or she say anything?" I needed more information. Certainly she had something else to offer.

"If *they'd* said something I'd know whether *they* were a *he* or a *she*, now wouldn't I?"

Arie was really not likeable.

"Why do you sound like a cop?" Arie muttered. "All these questions make me uncomfortable."

"I assure you, I'm not a cop." I had to tone it down before my cover was blown. "So, you were on *Cascade Falls*?"

It seemed conversational enough to me.

"What about it?" she snapped.

My resolve started to crumble. "You weren't exactly forthcoming."

"I didn't *have* to be forthcoming. Everyone *knows* I was on the show. I don't have to *tell* people. I'm famous."

"I see." The girl had a major ego problem. Perhaps she was delusional as well because I hadn't heard anyone mention the show or treat her like she walked on water.

"You really didn't know I was on the show?"

I'd heard it. There was a crack in her confidence. Instead of going in for the kill, I tempered my voice and tried to soften the blow. "I don't watch much TV. But I do know that all the incidents that have been happening here at the Cultural Arts Center might end up being good publicity for your play."

"What?" she screeched. "What are you suggesting?"

I didn't have to see her to know she had an incredulous expression on her face.

"I'm suggesting that you have fading star power and you want it back. You wrote this play and, to ensure it gets the attention you think it deserves, maybe you staged some of the things happening around the school. Maybe you didn't mean to kill Scarlet. Maybe that was an accident."

"You're crazy!"

I was sure to keep my voice level. "Am I? Because that theory sounds pretty good to me."

"I'll admit—I'd *love* some attention for the show. I *may* have delighted in some of the spooky things happening, only because I knew it would tie in nicely with my musical, which was about a *specter*. But I would *never* stage these things. I especially wouldn't *kill* someone!"

"So, again, you seem like the type who enjoys talking about your accomplishments. I'm not sure I buy into the idea of everyone knowing who you are. You've purposely not mentioned it or talked about it."

"I was waiting to play that card closer to the time of the play's release. Timing is everything, and I didn't want to leak the information to the press too early. This is my chance for a big break, but I wanted to get it the right way."

Wait—so everyone knew who she was yet she was keeping it quiet? I got it that actors were extremely complicated people, a strange mix of arro gance and insecurity. But she wasn't making much sense.

"To clarify—you're saying you're not behind any of the vandalisms?"

"That's exactly what I'm saying." Her voice sounded crispy. "And I resent your implications, Ms. It's-Not-What-You-Know-But-Who."

Maybe she wasn't a killer or a criminal, but she was definitely a jerk.

Silence stretched between us. Awkward, cringe inducing silence. We both sat on the floor of the closet. I pulled my knees to my chest, unable to escape from Arie.

"So, what do you do, *Gabby*?" She said my name

like it was a bad word. "Besides butchering my musical?"

Anger started to grow in me, but I tried to keep a handle on it. Snapping—again—would do me no good. "I have a cleaning, restoration, and renovation business."

"Really? Kind of like one of those gals on HGTV?"

Exactly like that, only different. "You might say."

"Have you ever thought of doing a reality series?"

I laughed a little too hard. "No, someone already talked to me about doing a reality series. I'm not interested." I almost added that the reality series would be based on crime scene cleaning. I was glad I stopped myself before I got there. Admitting that much would raise too many questions and possibly blow my cover.

"I guess you have the look for TV."

I was pretty sure she'd meant that as a compliment. "Thank you?"

"I mean, for a tom boy contractor, at least."

I scowled. *Focus, Gabby. Focus.* This was the perfect time to question her because she couldn't escape. I mentally let out an evil laugh. "How'd you go from soap star to playwright, Arie?"

"I've always had an interest in show business. I figured I needed to strike while the iron was hot."

So she'd picked a start up community theater group? Again, I kept my mouth shut. I was slowly learning that I didn't have to say everything that popped into my mind. It had only taken me nearly thirty years to get that through my thick skull.

"Well, I look forward to seeing it all come together. It sounds like you have . . . quite a bit of experience under your belt. I'm sure it will all benefit this production immensely." It pained me to say the words, but they flowed out anyway.

Silence fell for a minute.

"I guess you're not too bad. Maybe I can stop discluding you from my party invites."

"What party invites?" *And is "discluding" really a word?*

"The ones you haven't been receiving."

"O . . . kay."

"It's true. Almost every night after practice, the cast hangs out. Everyone except you, that is."

"I don't know what to say."

"Say thank you. You're a part of the in crowd now, Gabby. But I can quickly disavow you from the group. Keep that in mind also."

"Just so we're not disclear, I will."

"What?" Confusion clenched her voice.

"Disregard that." I smiled, humoring myself.

"Whatever. You're so weird." Silence stretched a moment. "So, if we get out of here tonight, the cast is going to go hang out. Join us if you want. But don't take this as some kind of professional stamp of approval. I still would have picked a different actress to play Elsa."

"Understood."

Maybe this was the "in" I needed in order to find some answers.

CHAPTER
FIFTEEN

THOUGH SOME KIND of wall had seemed to crumble—slightly—between Arie and me during our confinement together, it had nearly built back up as Arie talked nonstop about herself in the minutes after her party invite.

It wasn't that I didn't want to hear about her Hollywood career, the famous people she'd eaten with, and the gigs she'd almost-but-not-quite gotten, etc.

But I had other things to think about.

Like would the killer come back and finish us off, too? And who exactly had locked us in the closet? Why would someone pretend to be a ghost? Even stranger—Scarlet was dead, but someone continued to sabotage the play. Was Scarlet's death really about ruining the play? Or was something else going on?

Nothing made any sense.

Plus, I would think that a murderer would be on the run after killing someone. Every time he or she did something else here at the school, it only increased the likelihood of being discovered.

Someone jangled the door handle. A moment later, dim light flooded the space. I squinted against it.

"Arie? Gabby?"

The figure moved, his head now blocking the bulb directly behind him. "Jerome?" I asked.

"We've been looking all over for you guys. Are you okay?" He offered his hand, pulling Arie up first and me second.

It felt good to stretch my legs. I wiped granules from my back, my hands, and my arms, and stepped out.

I'd never been so glad to see my old middle school hallway.

"Looks like the phantom has struck again," Jerome muttered as we began walking down the hallway.

"The phantom? You really think a ghost is behind this?" He seriously couldn't believe that. If he did, then there were just too many people around here who were a few rungs short in the ladder leading to logic land.

He shrugged. "Seems a likely excuse to me. The

ghost of Rose doesn't want the show to go on. I don't know about you, but I'm almost ready to run and give her what she wants. I'll never be a famous actor if I'm dead."

"There have been plenty of plays at this school," I began. "Why would she just target this one?" Not that I thought ghosts were real. But in order to connect with certain cast members, I had to get on their level, which meant I had to hammer out this ghost theory.

"Those were middle school plays," Arie said, turning up her nose.

"They were some pretty good plays!" I argued.

Arie raised an eyebrow. "How would you know?"

I remembered that I was undercover. "I mean, I acted in middle school and the work my drama troupe did was pretty impressive. I bet it was the same here."

"Hm." She eyed me. "I think Rose is afraid we'll make history and outdo her."

Outdo her? No one here had even heard the story about her! I kept my mouth shut.

I really needed to check with Clarice to see if she'd done any research yet. Was there any truth at all to this crazy story?

"Where is everyone?" I decided to change the subject.

"They're all quarantined in the choir room. We didn't want anyone else to disappear," Jerome said.

Paulette looked like a nervous wreck when we arrived. She walked over to me and pulled me into a hug. I wanted desperately to remind her that we weren't supposed to know each other, but I kept my mouth shut in order not to draw any more attention to the situation.

I noticed a smudge of dirt on Paulette's cheek and some dust in her hair. Just where had Paulette been and what had she been doing?

Mrs. Baker clapped to get our attention. "I know the past few weeks have been crazy—to say the least —but we only have a week to pull this together. We've got a lot of work to do, gang. I'll need to make sure you're all committed."

I glanced around. Arie, Jerome, The Shining Twins, and Bennie all nodded. Paulette stared off into space. Was the guilty party in this room? I hated to think it could be true, but that's what I was leaning toward more and more.

"We need to get back into the auditorium and run through this from start to finish," Mrs. Baker continued. "We don't have much time and we still have a lot of kinks to work out."

"Tickets are on sale and we've nearly sold out. But I can't afford to refund the money to people and go in the hole," Paulette said.

Sold out? A couple of articles had run about Scarlet's death. Had the bad publicity bolstered sales? Would that give Paulette motivation for murder? The thought startled me. How could I suspect my old friend? Being objective was so hard sometimes. Of course I didn't want to doubt the innocence of someone I considered a friend.

"The future of this theater is riding on the success of this play," Paulette continued. "I'm going to up the security here at the school and do everything in my power to prevent any more of these vandalisms from occurring and acting as obstacles to our success."

Everyone nodded again. A new somberness had come over the cast. I'd have bet more than one person was considering getting out while they could.

Mrs. Baker's eyes met mine, and I saw the concern there. She was as worried about all of this as anyone else.

We filed silently back into the auditorium and took our places, everyone's movements wooden, stiff, almost hesitant.

Bennie placed her hand on my arm. "You okay? You look a little shaken."

I nodded. "I'm fine."

"Not everyone stayed in groups, you know," she whispered.

"What do you mean?"

"I mean that I saw several people wandering

around by themselves or slipping out to the bath-room. It makes me wonder if one of them locked you in that closet."

"Like who?" I whispered back. I glanced around to make sure no one was paying attention.

"Like Jerome, for example. Arie mentioned that he was alone when he found you. Isn't that suspicious?"

It was true. But what reason would Jerome have to be behind these acts? Then I remembered that I hadn't found out anything about him when I did my Internet search. Maybe he wasn't who he claimed to be. That would explain why he had no web presence. Actors usually wanted as much attention as they could get.

"Elsa, you're up."

I cleared my throat and swirled on stage while the chorus began singing, "What Do You Do with a Slightly Flighty Nun." This was the opening where everyone at the convent gave me their blessing to go off to the theater and, in the meantime, out of their hair—or maybe I should say their "wimples."

After I was whisked out of my home at the abbey, the lights went down. Stagehands wearing all black moved flats and set pieces for the next scene, a theater within the actual theater.

I mentally ran through my lines as I stood on the black stage, waiting for the lights to come back up.

You're the Spector. Please don't hurt me. What do you want? Why can't you leave us all alone?

My mental voice deepened as I silently repeated Jerome's lines also. *You're all I've dreamed about, Elsa. You came to me. I knew you would. I've been waiting.*

The lights came up. In the blackness, I hadn't even realized that my gaze was fixated on the orchestra pit below. With no live music, the space was used for storage now and filled with old chairs and music stands.

Something else in the pit caught my eye.

As the music started for "Climb Every Steeple," I did a double take.

There was a body in the pit. A dead body.

I let out a blood-curdling scream.

CHAPTER
SIXTEEN

"I'M TELLING YOU, if that body had been down there for more than a few hours, we would have smelled it. It was placed there some time between when the lights went out and when play practice started," I whispered to Detective Charlie Henderson.

"I assure you, we're investigating, Gabby," Charlie said.

Everyone else had been sequestered back in the choir room, but I remained with both Paulette and Mrs. Baker.

No one was allowed to leave until after they were questioned. Which essentially made everyone a possible suspect or witness.

Bennie's words kept coming back to me, though.

Not everyone stayed in groups, you know.

Jerome.

As I glanced over at the body of the man from the pit, I realized I'd never seen him before. He could possibly be the man I'd seen in the parking lot that day, but I couldn't even be sure of that. He definitely wasn't a cast member, and Paulette confirmed he didn't work here at the building.

"May I?" I asked Charlie as the gurney came closer.

She stared at me uncertainly.

"I did work for the medical examiner before budget cuts," I reminded her.

As if to confirm my theory, Danny—the medical legal death investigator—paused to say a few words. We'd worked together on a couple of cases, which I hoped only helped my credibility.

"Go ahead," Charlie muttered. "But make it quick."

Danny pulled the sheet back. I soaked in the man's face. It was round and thick like his neck, giving him a stocky, heavyset appearance. He had a scar on his cheek and a sleazy looking mustache boasting long strands of sparse hair.

I quickly examined the rest of him.

There were no signs of foul play. No blood. No visible bruises. No swelling or knots or anything.

"We should have the results in a few days," Danny told me. He must have read my thoughts.

"How long has he been dead?"

"In my estimation, just based on factors determined here at the scene like body temperature, livor mortis, and rigor mortis, this man has been dead about five hours."

I nodded, and Danny continued to wheel him away. I walked back over to Charlie, who was talking to some of the crime scene techs. My mind turned over the facts again and again.

"Did you find Scarlet's cell phone?" I whispered.

"Yeah. Why?"

"I suppose you checked her messages for anything suspicious."

"Of course I did. It had been wiped clean, though."

"Were you able to recover anything?"

She crossed her arms. "No, we weren't."

"Didn't you find that strange?"

"Of course. Either she was very careful or she didn't like texting people."

I stored that information away. Was it a clue? Or a coincidence? "Most people her age love texting."

"There are exceptions, though." Charlie shifted. "There's something I need to ask you about, Gabby."

"Anything." I figured she'd ask about cast members or suspicions—my gut instinct about the case.

"Why was your business card found on the

man?"

I blinked. "Excuse me?"

Charlie continued to stare. "We found your card in the man's pocket. Did you question him?"

"I've never seen that man before."

"Then how did he get your card?"

I shook my head, dumbfounded. "I have no idea. I promise you, I have no clue who he is."

"We're going to need to question you, Gabby. You know that, right?"

Dread pooled in my stomach. This was just part of the routine, I told myself. However, I didn't feel any better. "Am I a suspect?"

"Just a person of interest."

"That means suspect," I told her.

"Not always. I'm asking you to do this on your own free will."

I bit back a sigh. "When do you want me to come in?"

She glanced at her watch. "Thirty minutes? Give me more time to wrap up things here."

"Are you bringing everyone else in also?"

She shook her head. "Not unless we have reason to."

I closed my eyes. This wasn't good. It wasn't good at all.

I crossed my arms over my chest as I sat in the interrogation room. I'd dreamed about being in this very place many times—but in all my fantasies, I'd been on the other side of the law. The *right* side of the law.

Right now, I felt exposed. There was no table between Charlie and me. I desperately wanted to put something between us, but crossing my arms over my chest was the best I could do at the moment.

"Are you sure you've never seen this man?" Charlie repeated, pushing his photo toward me.

"I'm positive, Charl—I mean, Detective Henderson. Besides, I was locked in a closet when this happened. I couldn't have done it."

"Apparently, you were only in the closet the last thirty minutes. There were thirty minutes prior to that when no one saw you."

"That's because I was looking for Arie!" I insisted.

I had to keep my voice down. I wasn't doing myself any favors by getting wound up, and I knew that. Applying it was much harder.

"Then how did your business card get in his pocket?"

"It's like I've told you already: I have no idea. I guess someone put it there? Maybe we have mutual acquaintances. I'm not sure."

"Is there anyone involved with the play who you've noticed acting suspiciously?" Charlie asked.

I let out my breath. At least the spotlight was off me for a minute. Should I mention Paulette? She'd had dirt on her cheek. But that didn't make her guilty.

Arie? Again, I had suspicions but no proof. If I mentioned either of their names and happened to be wrong, then I wouldn't be doing myself any favors.

"I heard several people went out by themselves searching for Arie," I said instead. "I suppose any of them could have had the opportunity. I still have no idea what anyone's motive would be, not to mention the means. There was no sign of foul play on the man."

"His body didn't end up in the orchestra pit by accident."

"I agree. I think someone put him there to make a statement."

"About what?"

"Quite possibly about me! He was planted there to make a point. I think it's obvious he didn't die in the pit."

Charlie squinted. "Why would you say that?"

"He wasn't there during the first act, for starters. It looked like he'd been positioned on the floor. If he just happened to be vandalizing the school and fell, the scene would have been much uglier."

Another detective entered the room and slid a file

toward Charlie. I held my breath as she opened it and read something there.

I hated this. I hated being on the opposite side of the law—even if I wasn't really on the opposite side. The justice system was supposed to work in favor of the good guys, not condemn the innocent.

Jesus, who was innocent, was condemned for your sins and paid the ultimate price.

The thought slammed into my mind and I drew in a deep breath. The trials I faced on this earth were just temporary, no matter how consuming they could feel. All the hardest moments in life could lead to some of the deepest character growth.

I'd learned that time and time again over the past couple of years. I couldn't let myself forget it now.

"Does the name Oliver Cartwright mean anything to you?" Charlie asked.

I thought about it a moment and then shook my head. "Nope. Not a thing. Who is he?"

Charlie glanced up, her gaze no-nonsense. "He's the man from the pit, and he's got a list of petty offenses, apparently. No real job. That doesn't explain why he was in the school."

Silence fell, and I rubbed my temples as the seriousness of the whole situation hit me even more. I could be in big trouble. I hoped I was overreacting, but better safe than sorry. "Do I need to call a lawyer?"

Charlie shook her head. "No. A business card isn't enough to book a person for a crime. But you should stay in town, Gabby, just in case we have more questions."

I leaned closer. "You don't really think I'm guilty, do you?"

Certainly she knew me better than this. We'd had dinner together. I'd given her and Parker my blessing, even when Parker was dating me and had feelings for her. I'd fussed at Parker for being irresponsible and not marrying her. Basically, I'd been on her side.

For a brief moment, I regretted that. I regretted misplaced loyalties. I regretted kindness that wasn't returned.

"My feelings have nothing to do with this, Gabby. My job is to follow the evidence. I thought you knew that."

At that moment, I realized that Charlie wasn't my friend. She was my ex-boyfriend's scorned baby momma. Any ties we'd had were gone. In fact, Parker's betrayal of her might even make her dislike me more.

"Of course I know that you have to be objective. But—" I stopped myself. Arguing would be futile. "Never mind. I'm not going anywhere. I'm not guilty either."

Now I just had to prove it.

CHAPTER
SEVENTEEN

WHEN I LEFT the police station, I only wanted to go home and be alone. But I still had a job to do. I had a killer to find. The investigation was even more important now because the last thing I wanted was to be framed for the crime.

With a bit of anxiety pressing on me, I walked toward the Slug House, an unappetizing name if I'd ever heard one. This was apparently where the cast went after practice to unwind. It had taken me a few days to get an invitation from Arie, who was evidently the ringleader of this motley crew, but at least I was here now.

I paused before walking inside. The night air was bitingly cold around me, but I needed to check something out with the assurance that no one was looking over my shoulder. I pulled out my phone and noticed

I'd missed a call from Garrett and a couple of calls from Chad. I ignored them and did a quick search for Oliver Cartwright instead.

There wasn't much information on him, but I did find one of his mug shots. Having his picture up on my phone and readily available could come in handy. I took a screen shot and then slid my phone back into my pocket.

I pulled open one of the heavy double doors leading to the restaurant, which was located in a strip mall down the street from the school. This wasn't my kind of place—it was really more bar than restaurant. As always, I'd stay away from the alcohol, but I would try to uncover some answers while inside.

Besides, maybe someone would suffer from loose lips while they were here. Alcohol could do that to people. While I didn't encourage the drinking, I would be using it to my advantage, if I had to.

I spotted the group at a table in the corner and sauntered over to them. Bennie was the first one to see me. A wide smile spread across her face.

"Gabby! So glad you could make it. Scoot over, guys. Make room for her."

Everyone scooted around. Thank goodness I had at least one person on my side. Good old Bennie.

"So, they questioned you first, huh?" Jerome started. "That's what Paulette said. That's why you were able to leave when you did."

My heart rate slowed. Paulette had given me a cover story? I supposed I needed to thank her. "That's right. Since I discovered the body, I guess it made sense to talk to me first."

Arie glanced at her watch. "So, where have you been between then and now?"

"That's really none of your business," Bennie said, giving Arie her best sassy girl duck lips.

"Thanks, Bennie," I told her. "But if people really want to know, I had some business to attend to."

Miraculously, no one asked any questions.

"So, we're taking votes on who thinks the show won't go on anymore. What's your vote?" Jerome asked before chugging some beer.

I shrugged. "I think we should press ahead."

"After two murders?" Bennie asked, her mouth parting with surprise.

"We don't have enough information yet. There were no signs of foul play on the man we found tonight."

"How do you know that?" Arie asked, her eyebrows arching together.

"Because I saw him. Not only from the stage; I was in the room when they hauled him off to the medical examiner's." I paused as I noted the incredulous looks around me. "Look, I agree that it was all very strange. But we shouldn't jump to conclusions. Besides, you heard Paulette tonight. She's depending on this play to launch the entire Cultural Arts Center. If this bombs, the whole place could close and then there would be fewer opportunities for any of you—I mean, us—to get our acting chops."

A few people shrugged.

"I guess you're right," Bennie said. "I just don't want to see anyone else get hurt."

"Paulette is upping security. Maybe that will thwart some of this nonsense," I added.

"Why do you sound like you know so much about this?" Arie asked, suspicion staining her eyes.

I shrugged. "Maybe I watch too much TV."

"Or maybe you're involved with this somehow." A new emotion gleamed in her eyes. Was she gloating?

"That is just as likely as you being somehow involved. I wasn't even a part of this show when this stuff started happening." I stared at Arie. "You were."

She scowled.

"All of this pointing fingers will get us nowhere," Bennie said. "Besides, this is reminding me too much of my family life growing up. I'm blowing this joint if this keeps up."

"You're right," I concurred. "You know what? I think I'm going to run to the restroom. If the waiter comes around, I'd like a water."

"You sure you don't want something stronger?" Jerome asked.

"Positive."

Once I was out of sight of the table, I bypassed the bathroom and leaned against the bar. The bartender came over and I pulled out my phone. "You ever seen this guy?"

It was a long shot, but if the man who'd died had been casing out the school, maybe he'd also been lurking around unknowing cast members as they hung out here also. I'd never know if I didn't ask.

He studied the picture. Based on the way his head bobbed to the side, I thought for sure he'd say "no," but he nodded instead. "Yeah, he's been in before."

"Remember anything about him?"

"Not much." He wiped a glass dry. "Why?"

"He's dead."

"You the police?"

"P.I.," I whispered.

He stared at me another moment, continuing to dry the same glass. "Yeah, he was in a couple of days ago. I remember him because he paid for everyone's drinks. Kind of generous—not that anyone was complaining. But you remember things like that."

"Was he with anyone?"

"I think he was with a girl and a guy. Neither seemed happy with him. In fact, I'm pretty sure they led him out of the bar right after he paid a major tab."

"Remember anything about them?"

He stared off in the distance for a moment before shaking his head. "I can't say I do. Not really, at least. The girl had curly red hair—kind of like yours."

I swallowed hard. Red hair? Like mine?

That wasn't good. Someone *was* setting me up, weren't they? "How about the guy?"

"He wore a ball cap. They had a strange smell to them. It was a mix of gasoline and something else."

Gasoline? Maybe he'd been here the night when someone had left a trail of it in the hallway. My pulse spiked.

"Can you describe the other smell?"

He sighed and set the glass down. "You know, not really. Maybe like newspaper, though. It's the closest I can get to the actual scent."

Someone called for a drink farther down the bar. I slipped my phone in my pocket again, armed with new information. I wasn't sure what to do with it exactly, but I hoped the pieces would start snapping together soon.

"Gabby?"

I looked over and saw Bennie standing there. I straightened, realizing how strange I probably looked. "Hey."

"Everything okay? You were taking so long I

thought I should check on you." She glanced back and forth from me to the bartender.

"I was just checking the weather. Someone told me we might have a snowstorm on the way."

She snorted. "Don't tell Paulette that. It will just be one more thing to stress her out. Snow means nobody's coming out for our play, you know what I mean?"

I nodded and started walking back toward the table. "Yeah, the bartender seemed to remember that forecasters are thinking it will miss us and head north instead."

Bennie hooked her arm through mine. "Let's go back and sit down."

I mentally took a few steps back in time. Bennie also smelled faintly of . . . gasoline.

Today was Saturday, and I actually didn't have any firm plan for the morning hours. We had an afternoon rehearsal, and I was having dinner at Garrett's place tonight. In the meantime, I was really hoping I didn't get called into any jobs today. Chad and Sierra were doing some kind of fundraiser for her animal rights organization, so I'd be taking any calls that came in for the business.

I needed some downtime. I'd been either working

or rehearsing for the play all week, and I was tired. Plus, I needed to let my thoughts settle.

I'd hung out with the cast last night, hoping to discover something about someone. But I hadn't discovered anything about anyone. I'd mostly heard people complain. Watched them get drunk. Listened to them laugh at things that weren't funny.

I'd stayed for about an hour before I couldn't take it anymore. I'd feigned exhaustion and slipped away, no closer to answers now than I'd been before. Bennie left when I did.

She'd hopped on her motorcycle and ridden off into the night.

It was then I'd realized that she smelled like gasoline because of her bike. Had the man who'd died also ridden a motorcycle? Was that the smell that had saturated him?

I had so many questions.

All I had in my cupboards was some coffee, so I made myself a pot and then sat down at my desk. The first thing I wanted to do was call Marjorie's landlord again.

He answered on the first ring, and I explained who I was.

"Right, right. You called earlier. Sorry. I've had other things to do besides return phone calls."

"I only need a moment of your time. I just need to

know if you called the cable company for one of your residents."

"No, I didn't call the cable company for anyone this week. I have no idea what you're talking about. Was one of the residents complaining that they weren't getting their TV stations again? Those young people. Don't they have anything better to do than watch TV?"

He went off on a tangent and, at the first opportunity, I bowed out of the conversation. I had the answer I needed. Someone wanted to get his hands on that costume. Why? Was there something special about it?

Next, I looked up the prescription I'd found on Paulette's desk. I wanted to know what she was taking medication for.

I typed in the last seven letters and only one RX came up. A drug called Exocotain. I read the description and discovered it was for anxiety and depression. I scrolled down to read the fine print. It was also capable of causing hallucinations and paranoia.

I sat back and chewed on that information, sipping on my coffee as I did so. What if Paulette's medicine was causing her to act in strange ways? What if she was behind some of the acts at the school?

I shook my head. Not Paulette. I didn't want to believe she could be behind this. I wanted to think my old friend had her life together and that her motivations in hiring me were pure.

Then who?

I mentally ran through my clues, evidence, and suspects.

The two biggest clues were Scarlet's dead body and the man who'd been found in the orchestra pit.

There was the vandalism, the girl with red hair, the smell of gasoline, the unlatched padlock on the gated hallway, the wet footprints leading to the bathroom, and the man I'd chased through the parking lot.

Arie could have the most to gain from the publicity generated by everything happening at the theater. Except there hadn't been a lot of publicity yet, not when I really thought about it. I'd yet to see one news article mentioning her. Plus, Arie had been locked in that closet with me.

Bennie had smelled like gasoline, but that was only because she drove a motorcycle.

Someone was arguing with Scarlet outside of her apartment a week before she died. I had no idea who.

Then there was Rose, the supposed ghost. I wondered if Clarice had done any research yet. Maybe now was the time to find out.

I WALKED across the street to The Grounds, my favorite coffeehouse. I mumbled good morning to my friend Sharon, who owned the place, and ordered a latte and a cranberry muffin.

"Clarice here?" I asked. Clarice was Sharon's niece.

"She's upstairs. I'll call her down."

I sat down at a corner table. I'd no sooner taken a bite of my pastry than Clarice appeared.

"I've been hoping to catch up with you!" She slid into the seat across from me, some papers in her hands. "Rose is real."

"What?"

She nodded adamantly. "It's true. Rose was a teacher at Oceanside. She was only there for three months before she died. Everyone was very quiet about her death because they didn't want to frighten the students."

"Tell me more."

"Her first play was going to be *The Wizard of Oz*."

I swallowed hard, remembering Scarlet's shoes and socks sticking out from behind the curtain. I remembered thinking that it reminded me of the Wicked Witch after the house had been dropped on her. Coincidence? I didn't know.

Then there was the message on the mirror. *I'll get you, my pretty.* Could the trail of yellow gasoline represent the yellow brick road? What would be next . . . flying monkeys?

"Rose was there working on some props," Clarice continued. "When the police arrived at the scene, they discovered one of the props had fallen over, close to the orchestra pit, which was the very place her body was found. There was nothing to prove foul play."

Uh oh. She'd been found in the orchestra pit, the same location where the man had been found last night? Coincidence? Or was someone making a statement?

"Was it unusual for her to work late?"

"Funny you asked." Clarice grinned. "I hope you don't mind that I did this. But I actually found Rose's mom and called her."

I raised my eyebrows. "I'm impressed."

"Yeah, I know. Right? So, she said that Rose was very concerned about doing a good job with this play. She wanted to start off at the school on the right foot, and she had a tendency to be a perfectionist. She spent many evenings working late, so it didn't come as a surprise to her mom that she was at the school alone at that hour."

"So her mom had no suspicions that there may have been something sinister at play?"

Clarice shook her head. "Nope. Not at all. She did tell me one thing that I thought was interesting, though."

"What's that?"

"Rose's brother, Peter Hines, now works for Zollin Industries."

It was a crazy whim. I knew it was. Despite that, I pulled up to one of the sports complexes in Virginia Beach. I knew very well this could turn out to be a rabbit trail, but it was a chance I needed to take.

I walked in and a woman behind the front counter said the Virginia Beach Sand Sharks were practicing—just what I was hoping. The receptionist was young with a rope of blonde hair braided down her back. Perhaps her youthfulness could work in my favor.

"I really need to talk to the coach," I told her, leaning casually against the desk, hoping to convey a friendly vibe.

"I'm afraid that's not possible." She shook her head and stared at me, cheerfully stern.

"It's important," I told her.

"It's not possible." She continued to stare.

This was going to be harder than I thought. "We're old friends."

She squinted, doubt lacing her eyes. "Really?"

I nodded. "Really."

She shrugged. "You still can't see him."

I let out a long, drawn out sigh. I needed a Plan B. In the distance, I spotted a young man walking down the hallway with an armful of balls. Two teetered precariously on edge. At the same time, someone entered the building behind me.

This was my chance.

As the receptionist turned to greet a man in a business suit, a wayward ball bounced from the loaded arms of the young man in the distance. I grabbed it and subtly kicked it toward the semi-important looking man who'd just walked in. He dodged it but ran into a potted plant in the process.

"Johnny! You've got to be careful!" the woman

scolded before turning back to the guest to apologize. "Mr. Jennings, are you okay?"

At that moment, I ducked below the desk and slipped around the corner. I had no idea where I was going, but I kept moving, especially when I heard the receptionist ask where I'd disappeared to. Finally, the wall changed from solid concrete to plastic windows. On the other side, I saw the soccer field.

I slipped through the next door and hurried onto the field. I quickly spotted Roberto with a whistle in his mouth, yelling at one of the players. He wore soccer shorts and cleats, as well as a yellow jersey.

Yes, he definitely looks like a young Antonio Banderas.

"Roberto!" I said, approaching him.

He didn't even look my way.

"Excuse me! Roberto!" I waved my arms, drawing nearer.

He glanced at me and professionalism washed over him for a moment. Something in his gaze changed as I got closer. He was trying to place me, I realized. I wouldn't let him know who I was.

Yet.

"Can I help you?" he asked, an annoyed edge to his voice.

"I just need a few minutes of your time."

He pulled his eyes away from the game for a moment. "Do I know you?"

I shrugged. "Not really. I met you the other day."

"At Club 9?"

I shook my head. "At Paulette's."

The smile disappeared from his face. "That's right. You're her lawyer friend." He said "lawyer" with the same disdain others used when saying "taxes" or "colonoscopy."

I was surprised anyone would even entertain the idea I was a lawyer since I was dressed in jeans and flip-flops and had my hair pulled back in a ponytail. "I'm not a lawyer."

His gaze hardened. "What are you doing here? Spying on me? Reporting back to Paulette? Because I'm not doing anything I shouldn't be. Even if I were, Paulette and I are separated now. I'm allowed to."

"You really don't like Paulette, do you?"

"She kicked me out of the house and onto the street with nothing but the clothes on my back. And my car," he added. "But that was only because the title was in my name. I made sure her father wasn't with us when we were shopping for some new wheels. But still, I would have done anything for her."

"Then why did you cheat on her?"

"I never cheated on her!" His voice rose, his Brazilian accent with it.

"She thinks you used her for her money." I was inclined to agree after his remark about the car. He'd plotted that devious move.

"She thinks wrong. She was never around for me to show her how much I appreciate her."

"Where was she?"

"Working out, for starters."

"Paulette works out?" I tried to form a mental picture but couldn't.

He nodded. "Every morning. She's stronger than you think. When she's not with her personal trainer, she's usually at home drinking."

I shifted. "Does she do that a lot?"

"She's trying to pretend she's not a disappointment to her father."

I didn't know whether to argue or agree. Instead, I changed the subject. "Look, I'm not here to talk about you and Paulette. I'm not a lawyer, and I wasn't hired to follow you. I just have questions."

He bristled. "About?"

"Does the name Scarlet ring a bell?"

He shook his head. "Can't say it does."

"Were you dating her?"

"I'm not dating anyone. Even if I were, I'm allowed now. Paulette ended things." He looked back on the field. "Keep doing the drills. Keep your eye on the ball, Wickerson!"

"So you're denying your involvement with Scarlet?" I clarified.

"Unequivocally. Now I need to get back to work. Excuse me." He raised the whistle to his lips.

"Wait! One more question!" I still didn't believe him, but I had more questions in the meantime.

"Look, lady." Roberto stared daggers at me. "Are you trying to get me fired? Because this is all I've got. If I lose this job, I'm done."

"It's about Oceanside Middle School."

He rolled his eyes. "Oh, that. It was Paulette's pet project. She was obsessed with it. She was the one who convinced her father to buy the place. She's desperate to prove herself, especially after the dinner cruise fiasco."

"Are you desperate to do just the opposite?" I locked my gaze with his.

His nostrils flared. "What's that mean?"

"I mean, are you desperate to see her fail? She hurt you. Humiliated you. Left you on the street with almost nothing. Maybe you want to see bad things happen to her."

He stepped back. "If you think I'm the one vandalizing the property, you're crazy. I'm barely holding on as it is. I don't want to be deported."

"Even if it means ruining Paulette?"

"Look, I don't like the woman for what she's done to me, but I'm not stupid. I'm not going to kill someone to get revenge."

Something about his unwavering gaze made me believe him. "Know anyone who might want to shut the whole place down before it ever really gets off the ground?"

He looked at me, long and hard. "Yeah, I do."

I waited. When he didn't say anything, I tilted my head. "Who?"

"Paulette."

CHAPTER
NINETEEN

CERTAINLY I HADN'T HEARD him correctly. "What was that?"

"That's right. Paulette. She's the one I'd investigate." He forcefully pointed toward the ground as if to drive home his point.

"Again, this goes back to ruining her. You're just blowing off steam."

He straightened as a player went past. As soon as the other man was out of sight, he leaned toward me. "I'm not blowing off steam. I'm telling you—Paulette is losing it. I think she's going crazy."

"I've seen people sink low, but really?"

Even as I said the words, guilt began to rush through me. I'd wondered about her innocence myself, so I really had no room to talk.

"I'm not joking. Pay attention. There's something not right with her. She was behaving bizarrely in the weeks before she kicked me out, and I'm not just saying that to be mean. I'm really worried about her. We both started drinking too much. I got help; she didn't. That was part of the reason we had so many problems."

What? I wasn't sure what to do with that new tidbit. I knew she'd been drinking, but this confirmed that she was drinking too much.

Still, Roberto had too many reasons to lie. I couldn't believe him too easily.

"I think she should give up on that whole Cultural Arts Center and stop trying to impress her dad so much."

I shook my head, trying not to soften as I listened to his rolling Brazilian accent. "I think you've got this all turned around. You're the one who's acting crazy. You slashed my van tires."

His eyebrows shot up. "I talked to the police about that. I didn't do nothing. I'm telling you—it was Paulette."

"I was talking to Paulette the whole time."

"The whole time?"

I ran through our conversation again. Paulette did leave the room for about ten minutes to get some Tylenol for her headache. But that wouldn't have been enough time to go outside and slash my tires herself. Would it?

The evidence seemed to be building—against the person who'd hired me.

One thing I knew: I didn't like where any of this was going. Not one bit.

I left the sports complex in time to make it to afternoon practice.

I had to get my thoughts under control, though, because there were too many people I could visualize as being guilty. That fact was making my emotions yo-yo everywhere—between trust and distrust, suspicion and wanting to see the best in people. In between those thoughts were snippets from the articles Clarice had found on Rose, images of the man I'd found dead last night, and remembrances of how cold it had felt in that interrogation room.

We went through practice and, shockingly enough, nothing happened. I kept waiting, anticipating. But there was nothing.

Maybe it had something to do with the fact that we were in the choir room again today. The police hadn't opened up the auditorium again, not until they were sure there were no more clues.

Paulette looked tenser than a klutz walking a tight rope.

Certainly she realized that there was a good chance this play wouldn't come together. Everyone involved with the production had to know that. We were less than a week away from opening night and unable to use the stage. Everyone's nerves were frazzled, especially considering there was a killer out there who seemed a little hung up on this play.

At the end, after everyone cleared out, I turned to Mrs. Baker and lowered my voice. "I don't know if I'm ready for this."

Even I wasn't sure if I was referring to the play or my life.

She squeezed my arm. "You're doing fine."

I decided I'd been referring to the play. It seemed like safer, less vulnerable territory. "I forgot more lines today. And I got the verses on one of the songs mixed up. I'm pretty sure I'm more frustrated with myself than anyone."

"It's just nerves. Remember shakes on eight?"

I smiled. It was one of the warm ups she used to have us do in drama club. "I sure do."

"Just do exercises like that. I promise you, this will all come together." She straightened up the chairs, just like she used to do as a teacher. I guess some habits never died.

"You're not nervous at all?"

She paused. "About you?"

"About the play."

She glanced around. Paulette was in the hallway now talking to Jerome and Arie. "I really wanted to help out Paulette by doing this. We were up against a lot with this script. But add to that everything that's been going on? I'm not really sure if this is the way she wants to introduce the Cultural Arts Center to the area."

I nodded in agreement. "Speaking of which, have you heard anything else about the man we found yesterday?"

She shook her head. "No, but the police wouldn't tell me anything. I stayed last night until everyone had been questioned, though. I feared some of the cast members would be shaken up."

"And your motherly side emerged."

She smiled. "I suppose it did. But when I was leaving, I heard a clanking sound in the building."

A chill raced through my blood. "You believe in ghosts also?"

She laughed. "No, not quite. But I couldn't figure out what the noise was. I keep having this feeling that someone is watching us, you know? It's quite eerie. I'm not sure if the play has put ideas in my head or what. Something just doesn't feel right, and

I'm afraid these incidents are going to continue until the person behind them is arrested."

"I've thought about that myself."

"Be careful, Gabby." She cast me a motherly glance.

I nodded. "I will."

I slipped out the door and ran to catch up with Paulette, who was walking toward her office. She offered a small smile as I fell into step beside her. "Hey Gabby."

"Have you heard anything new?"

She shook her head. "Not yet. I guess the autopsy will take a couple of days. Until then, we wait."

"I have a question, Paulette. Do you have the keys to Corridor D and E?"

"Of course I do. Why?"

"I'd like to go down there."

"Why?"

"Just a hunch. It could be nothing. I'd like to see inside some of the classrooms."

"Let me grab the keys then." She went into her office and emerged a minute later. She jangled metal against metal as we walked down the hallway.

She paused at Corridor D. This was the hallway I'd gone down that night after I'd found it unlocked. After she released the padlock, she shoved the metal gate back.

It made a screeching sound.

Was this what Mrs. Baker had heard? She'd said she heard a clanking noise. That's definitely how I'd describe this sound. I'd have to ask her.

We slipped inside. As soon I stepped foot in the hallway, I noticed it smelled like a garage. Was this a clue? I also remembered that the shop classroom was farther down this way. Maybe the scent of woodwork and tools hadn't left this area in all these years. I didn't want to jump to conclusions.

Paulette opened the first room. I stepped inside. At once, I remembered being in here for my FACS class—Family and Consumer Science. It was funny how places could so quickly take you back in time.

I wasn't 13 anymore, I realized. Back then, I'd thought I had forever. I'd seen too much since then, lived too much with death to hold on to that notion. With age, the years only seemed to fly by even more quickly.

I only had one chance at this life and, if I wasn't careful, my time was going to slip away. Maybe God had connected me with Paulette and this old school just to remind me of that.

"Gabby?"

I snapped out of my thoughts and turned toward Paulette. "Sorry about that. I went back in time."

She smiled. "I know. It's easy to do. I have so many great memories of hanging out with the gang here at Oceanside. It's one reason I really wanted to preserve this building."

How could I ever consider that someone who sounded that sincere could be behind the incidents here at the school?

"I wonder whatever happened with the old gang," I said.

"I heard Pete was working for some tech company out in California. It sounded right up his alley."

I smiled. Pete was my first real boyfriend. I hadn't talked to him in years. "How about Brandon? Ever hear anything about him?"

Brandon was only the most talented actor and dancer I'd ever met. I'd had a major crush on him during middle school.

"He's doing his first show on Broadway."

"What?"

Paulette nodded. "I tried to get him to come here and do this play, but he'd already signed a contract. He doesn't have the lead role, but he will one day."

"I always knew he'd make it. You're right."

"Do you ever talk to Becca?" Paulette asked, closing the door as we moved down the hallway to the next classroom.

I shook my head. "I'm ashamed to say it, but no. I haven't talked to her since my freshman year in college. She went to the University of Florida to study marine biology. She loved it so much down there that she stayed. Her parents were even moving there, last I heard. They both retired and wanted to be closer to her."

We wandered to the next classroom. The moment felt so normal. How could I have ever suspected Paulette? She was my old friend. Besides, why would she hire me if she was guilty? Unless she thought I was totally incompetent.

I pushed that thought out of my mind.

We checked the next three classrooms. I kept halfway expecting someone to jump out, but there was nothing except stale air and lots of memories. The cabinet that had nearly toppled on me remained on the ground in the old shop classroom.

What if that wasn't an accident, just set up to look like one?

What if all the things that had happened were the work of someone devious and purposeful, someone who was setting everything up to look like accidents?

Who would be smart enough to do that, though?

I paused outside of the newspaper classroom. Paulette unlocked the door, and I stepped inside.

My gaze perused my surroundings and came to stop on a massive machine. "What's that?"

"That's the offset press they used for the old school newspaper."

"What? They had a press?" I didn't remember that

She nodded. "That was after we attended. My father bought it. He thought it could offer some good practical experience for the students."

Newspaper. The man at the bar had said he'd smelled gasoline and newsprint on the man who'd died. Did it have anything to do with this machine?

Even if it did, why would someone break in here to print their own daily? What kind of criminal enterprise would that be? Unless it was some subversive, underground paper done by whackos.

"Why's this still here? I'm surprised they didn't sell it off." I leaned down to examine it more closely. I ran my finger down the side of it, expecting to find my skin covered with dust. It was clean.

"I don't know for sure why it's still here. I never thought to ask."

"It looks incredibly big and awkward," I mused aloud. "It would probably have to be taken apart just to get it out the door. Plus, so many things are digital now. I'm not sure how much use there is for it in today's society."

"True." Paulette nodded.

This school had stayed in the past and it had been abandoned for years. Was that what happened when you refused to change? You became stagnant and not useful? Was that what was happening with me?

I glanced around the room again. To the left there was an old dark room, leftover from the days when people actually developed their own photos. As I tiptoed toward the room, I bent over and scooped something up.

"What's that?"

I examined the crinkly orange paper. "It's a candy wrapper."

"That's strange. It's probably so old it belongs in a museum."

I pulled out my cell phone and shone the light on the paper. Then I shook my head. "The expiration date is next month."

Paulette leaned over my shoulder. "Are you sure?"

I nodded. "Positive."

I stored that information away and peered in the dark room. Everything appeared to be in place, even the old wire line where photos were hung out to dry.

I closed the door and crept over to the closet. It was almost completely empty except for some papers on the bottom. I shined my light there before bending over to pick up something.

I held up a photo. "Remember this?"

She leaned closer and squinted. "Can't say I do."

"It's *Oklahoma*, Paulette. The production we did in middle school."

"Why would that picture be out? That was years ago."

"That's an excellent question."

I picked up one more paper from the bottom of the closet. It was another photo. This one was of Mrs. Baker and me at rehearsal from back in the day. Only, the photo was torn in half.

Seeing it made my blood go cold. There was no ghost here at Oceanside, but someone was definitely haunting the place.

Paulette glanced at her watch. "Look, Gabby. I need to run. I have a late meeting. Is there anything else you need?"

I shoved my new evidence into my purse, feeling in my blood that I was getting closer to finding some answers. "No, I think I'm good for now."

"So, how was practice?" Garrett asked.

I dropped my purse by the door to his downtown apartment and walked with him toward the couch. "Uneventful."

"And that's good. Right?"

I nodded and sank into the soft cushions. I was tired and my mind was racing.

There were just too many questions clamoring for my attention.

Garrett had a toasty fire crackling in his ultra-modern fireplace. The structure was situated in the middle of the living room, not against a wall. Acoustic rock music crooned in the background, an old Lisa Loeb song about only hearing what you want to. The lights were low and soft, and I could see the twinkling lights of downtown Norfolk from his twelfth floor home thanks to a wall of windows.

"You look tired." Garrett sat beside me. "Here. Face the other way. Let me rub your shoulders."

Normally, I might have said no. But a back massage did sound kind of nice.

I turned and he kneaded my tight muscles. As he worked the knots there, I remembered the photos of Riley. I remembered his job announcement.

Riley wasn't coming back. Riley and I weren't happening anymore. Not right now. Not in the future. The sooner I accepted that, the easier my life would be.

"So, tell me what's going on," Garrett said as he rubbed my overwrought muscles. He leaned closer, close enough that I could feel his breath easing through my hair. "You smell good, by the way."

"Thanks. And what's going on is that I was hired as a private investigator, and I'm failing on the job. That's what."

"Oh, come now. You always pull through. Sometimes it just takes a bit longer, does it not?"

I loved the way his "does it not" sounded with his British accent.

"I haven't let an investigation beat me yet," I concurred.

"And most assuredly, you won't now. So, tell me what else is bothering you so much."

My ex-fiancé has moved on with his life. Of course I didn't say that. It was only one of my problems anyway. Problems came in groups, that's what my whole life had taught me. Not groups, more like flocks. Flocks of angry birds that nose-dived at you with a vengeance.

I ran through the investigation with him, including being interrogated, and ending with my conversation with Roberto.

"Sounds like an interesting case. I find it especially interesting that the brother of this Rose lady who died has been hired by Zollin Industries. Do you know what area of the company he's working in?"

I felt myself loosening up some. "Not yet. I need to talk to Paulette about it. Tonight would have been the perfect opportunity, but I guess I missed that. Had too many other things on my mind, I suppose."

"What do you think about what Roberto said about her?"

"He's just trying to make her look bad."

"She does have a bit of a reputation in the area."

I turned to Garrett. "What do you mean?"

Garrett dropped his hands. "I mean, sometimes she looks a bit vacant and other times she looks all fired up. She seems a little off sometimes. I hate to say it, but it's true."

"I didn't know you knew her even. She never gave any indication of that, nor did you." I felt a little insulted by this twist.

"Of course I know them. A lot of the business owners in this area know each other from the various luncheons and fundraisers we attend. Paulette and I aren't friends, not even acquaintances really. But I know who she is. Trent Castlerock spoke about her quite a bit when the acquisition of the school was taking place. He thought for sure that she'd fail and the whole project would shut down. The Cultural Arts Center made it farther than he ever assumed."

"You mean, Donabell's husband?"

Garrett grimaced. "Perhaps I shouldn't have brought him up."

"No, it's fine. Anyone who'd marry Donabell can't be that great a judge of character, though." I heard my harsh words and flinched. "That wasn't nice."

Garrett put his hand on my back. "No, it wasn't."

I rubbed my temples. "I'm a work in progress."

"You're too hard on yourself."

We sat there for a moment and I realized just how good Garrett was to me. He was patient and encouraging and he was always there for me to lean on. He made my heart flutter and had so many qualities that I admired. He'd even started coming to church with me.

Maybe I needed to stop looking back and just focus on what was ahead. I needed to keep applying for new jobs. I needed to keep my options open. Most of all, I needed to cut myself some slack.

I stood and walked to the sliding doors leading to his balcony. "You mind?"

"Not at all."

I stepped outside. Instantly, the fresh, frigid air revived my senses. I crossed my arms and looked over downtown as I tried to sort my thoughts.

"What are you thinking, Love?" Garrett asked.

He stepped behind me, and I could feel the heat emanating from him. It made me want to cuddle in his arms and stay warm and cozy.

I looked up at him, my heart pounding in my ears. "I'm thinking you're a really good guy, Garrett."

He leaned closer. "Is that right?"

My throat felt achy as I absorbed his very pleasant features. Was I ready for this? Really ready? "It is."

His fingers brushed my jawline. "I'm really glad to know you think that."

Electricity crackled between us as we moved closer to one another.

Maybe I'd never know if there was something between us unless I gave it a shot. Maybe I just needed to stop holding back.

I leaned toward Garrett.

Before our lips connected, the door to Garrett's apartment flew open. A loud bang shook the room as smoke filled the air.

Just what was going on?

CHAPTER
TWENTY

"POLICE! DOWN ON THE FLOOR! NOW!" a voice demanded through the smoke.

What in the world? I clutched Garrett's hand as we stepped inside, ready to clear this up.

"I said down on the floor!" A man appeared from the haziness with some kind of high-powered rifle in his hands. He had full body gear on and a SWAT vest.

I was coughing so badly I could hardly think. I didn't have time to argue—and I had better sense. I lay on the floor, face down and hands out. Garrett did the same.

I turned my head, and at least six police officers in SWAT uniform came into view.

"Sir, are you okay?" one of the officers asked

Garrett. He helped him to his feet and pulled him back.

"Of course I'm okay. What's going on?" he demanded.

I started to stand, also. The officers had obviously realized this was a terrible misunderstanding. That's why they were talking kindly to Garrett now.

"Stay down!" the officer yelled my way. "Cuff her!"

"Cuff me? What is going on?" I was seriously confused.

"Don't hurt her!" Garrett lunged toward me, but an officer held him back. "What's the nature of this?"

Another officer slapped some cuffs on my wrists and pulled me to my feet with enough force that my arms felt like they might snap. He pushed me against the wall.

"Search the house!" the oversized, testosterone-filled, man-in-charge ordered.

Another officer kicked the remains of a flashbang grenade out of the way. Finally the air started to clear, revealing a whole army of police officers dressed like they were going to war. The terror coursing through me intensified. In fact, as more details came together in my mind, I felt more distressed than ever.

I caught a glimpse of Garrett's door, hanging loosely on one hinge. Had the police used a battering ram to get inside?

Something was seriously messed up now. If there was an emergency in the building, like a fire or bomb threat, we'd already have been ushered out in an evacuation.

Instead I felt like we were *the* danger. Or, in all reality, that *I* was the danger.

"I insist you take those handcuffs off her!" Garrett started toward me again.

Rambo's bossy twin brother stopped him again. "We'll decide that."

"I demand to know what's going on—why you've charged into my residence like this!" The veins at Garrett's temples bulged and his eyes were wide with outrage.

"We received a report of a hostage situation here at the house," Rambo informed us.

"From who?" Garrett asked. Emotion charged through his voice.

"From you," the officer said, a tinge of exasperation in his voice. "Gabby St. Claire went over the edge and was holding you at gunpoint. You feared for your life and requested immediate assistance."

"I never made any such call. Now, can you please let her go? You have a lot of explaining to do."

"Everyone, stand down!" Rambo Jr. ordered. He raised the shield covering his face and lowered his gun. "Sir, the call came from your IP address."

"From my IP address? That's impossible. Ms. St.

Claire and I have been conversing for the past hour. We haven't been apart once. Besides, why would I make a call from my computer?"

I nodded in agreement, desperate for them to know that Garrett was telling the truth. "No one's been on his computer. At least . . ." Another thought occurred. "No one that we know about."

"The apartment is clear, sir," another officer said.

"Ma'am, I'd like you to go with Officer Klausen. I need a moment alone with Mr. Mercer," Rambo said.

Garrett reached for me. "She's not going anywhere, not until I have some idea what's going on here. This is my home, and you've all just invaded my space—and what was starting as a lovely evening with a lovely woman."

If there was one thing I could say about Garrett, it was that he knew how to be in charge. He didn't run a successful company by being indecisive. I appreciated his protective gesture now.

Rambo sighed, long and hard. We'd obviously disrupted his plans for the night—said plans being doing a war zone-like raid on someone's home. What was second on his agenda? Doing Tarzan calls and beating his chest? Scaling downtown buildings simply for the practical experience of it?

"Someone logged into the 911 service that's meant for hearing impaired residents in this area and wrote that a woman named Gabby St. Claire had entered this residence and was holding you hostage. Immediate assistant was requested."

"I assure you that I did not."

"We knocked to announce our presence, but there was no answer," Rambo continued.

"We were on the balcony and the music was playing," Garrett continued. "We didn't hear you."

"We take these calls seriously," Rambo said.

My mind was in another world, though. "Someone must have gained access to his IP address and hacked into it," I mumbled. "But why?"

"If it's a joke, it's a dangerous joke for someone to play," the officer continued. "I'll gather up my guys and let you return to what you were doing. We'd like permission to have one of our forensic techs look at your computer. It's doubtful we'll be able to trace the person behind this, but it's worth a shot."

"I want some answers," Garrett said, wrapping his arm around my waist. "I want to know who did this."

"There's a new crime wave called swatting sweeping the country," Rambo continued. "It's where people, oftentimes gamers, place fake calls warranting SWAT team raids. It's causing many dilemmas in the law enforcement community."

Was this in some way tied in with the crimes going on with the musical? Someone had known my name. They'd known where I was. They'd known there was a possibility that I'd get hurt or even be arrested.

Who could be behind this?

Roberto? I'd certainly ruffled his feathers earlier.

Arie? This didn't seem like her style.

Another more disturbing thought occurred. What if it was Paulette? Did I think she could orchestrate this all on her own? No. But she definitely had the funds to pay someone to do it for her.

There was a big, bright target on my back. I just had to figure out why.

CHAPTER
TWENTY-ONE

GARRETT WENT to church with me the next morning. I'd always known he believed in God, and I knew he had a lot of goodness inside him. I wasn't totally sure he really got "it," though—"it" being the gospel message. The brokenness of man. The desperate need for a Savior that required laying down your life and living with an eternal perspective. We'd had some good conversations, and I thought I'd seen some progress. I prayed that all of this was real for him and not just something he was doing to impress me.

After services, we grabbed lunch at a nearby Italian restaurant. We never had finished our conversation that had started right before the SWAT team invaded his apartment. The officers had finally cleared us, but the whole incident had been disturbing on more than one level. By the time the SWAT team had left, Garrett and I were both exhausted. We'd skipped dinner and called it a night.

"What are you up to now?" Garrett asked as we climbed back into his car after eating.

"I might sit back and read some more stupid criminal stories. They always cheer me up."

He sent me a sharp look. "You really don't read those, do you?"

Should I admit that I really had taken up the reading habit in my spare time? "Actually, I do, but I'm not going to do that now, truth be told. I think I'm going to go talk to Rose's brother. It's Sunday, so there's a better chance that he'll be home and not working."

"So you're giving credence to this whole ghost thing?"

I shook my head. "No, I'm not. Not really. But I want to find out more. Plus, I want to know what his affiliation is with Zollin Industries—if there really is a connection."

"Sounds interesting. Mind if I tag along?"

"You really want to?"

"Sure. I wouldn't mind seeing you in action again. I thought you were very charming on that last case."

Though he said it with a smile, I knew the last case was hard for him, mostly because it involved the decade-old death of his family. "Then I'd love the company."

Twenty minutes later we pulled up to an apartment complex in Portsmouth. The area was one of the rougher neighborhoods in town, so I was glad Garrett was with me. I'd made enemies of one of the gangs that frequented this area, and a girl could never be too careful.

I'd found the address for Peter Hines on the Internet. What did people ever do without it? I wasn't 100 percent sure this was the right Peter Hines, but I was willing to give it a shot.

Garrett placed his hand on my back as we walked toward the rusty metal stairs. Peter's apartment was on the third floor.

I thought Garrett might look like a fish out of water in this area, but to my surprise he looked at ease. Which was only one more thing to admire about him. He was rich, but he cared about the plights of those with little to nothing.

I knocked at apartment 341 and waited for a minute. I had started to walk away and chalk this up to a wasted afternoon when the door cracked open.

"Can I help you?" Gray eyes surrounded by wrinkled skin stared through the slit.

"I'm looking for Peter," I said.

"Who are you?"

"I'm Gabby St. Claire and this is my friend

Garrett Mercer. We just wanted to ask you a few questions about your sister, Rose."

The door opened a little more, revealing a frail looking man. "Rose? Why are you asking about her? Nobody ever asks about her anymore."

"I've been doing some work over at the old Oceanside Middle School and her name has come up quite a bit, actually."

He stared at me more until finally the door opened wide. "Come in. Excuse the mess."

"Thank you," I told him.

We stepped into his apartment, which was surprisingly not messy at all. He pointed to a couch and instructed us to have a seat.

Garrett and I lowered ourselves onto the old plaid sofa while Peter sat in a blue wingback chair across from us. He looked stiff and uncomfortable. "Why are you asking about Rose?"

"She was your older sister. Is that correct?" I started.

"That's right. Six years older. Would have been 59 this year. Hard to believe. She was a wonderful teacher. Very passionate about theater. She really wanted to impress everyone during her first year at the school. I guess she left an impression." He shook his head sadly.

"Did you have any doubts that her death was an accident?" I asked, keeping my voice gentle.

"There are always questions, especially when someone dies so young and so unexpectedly. There was an investigation, but no sign that anyone else was there at the school that night. It was just like Rose to work all hours of the night to make sure things were perfect."

"Some people say that Rose is still hanging around the school." I waited carefully to see his reaction.

"That's nonsense. Rose is gone. People just like making up stories. Besides, Rose loved those kids. She's not the type who'd try to scare students."

Relief softened my shoulders. I hadn't been sure what I would have said if he'd thought Rose's spirit was still hanging around the place.

I shifted, deciding to move on. "I heard you work for Zollin Industries now."

He nodded. "I do. Have for the past two months."

"What made you want to work for them?"

He shrugged. "Paulette Zollin asked me herself. One day out of the blue. Offered me a decent salary. How could I say no?"

My thoughts came grinding to a halt. "Out of the blue, you said? You mean, you hadn't even applied for a position?"

He nodded. "That's right. She called me and said she needed to hire someone and that my name had come to mind."

Garret and I exchanged a look. Something sounded suspicious.

"What exactly do you do for Zollin Industries?" I asked.

"I work maintenance at the new Cultural Arts Center."

After we left Peter's, Garrett and I sat in the car for a moment, heat blaring.

"What did you think of that?" I asked Garrett.

He shook his head. "Something doesn't sound quite right, does it?"

"Not at all. Why would Paulette cold call Peter, of all people? What even put the thought in her head?"

"What are you thinking?" He put the car in drive and took off.

I pinched the skin between my eyes. "I don't know. I realize this sounds crazy, but I wonder if there's some truth in the idea that Paulette is either insane or behind some of this. She did mention something about a therapist . . ."

"Just because someone sees a therapist doesn't mean they're crazy."

"I know that. But something is not adding up, and I'm trying to figure out what." My cell phone rang. "Speak of the devil . . ."

"Hey, Gabby. I just wanted to let you know that your van is ready," Paulette said. "You want to swing by and switch it out?"

"Sure thing." Thankfully, I wasn't too far away. Garrett agreed to drive past her house.

"One more thing I wanted to mention," Paulette continued. "I got a strange email this morning. You'll never believe from who."

"No idea."

"Donabell Bullock's husband."

My curiosity spiked. There his name was coming up again. "Really? What did he want?"

"There was a bidding war on the property between him and Zollin Industries. Obviously, we won. I hadn't heard from him since then. Until today. He sent me an email that said, 'You ready to sell yet?' Isn't that strange?"

"That is strange." It almost sounded like he knew what had been going on at the school building.

The bigger question was: Could he be behind the vandalisms? Maybe there was an attempt to shut down the Cultural Arts Center so he could finally buy the property. It was something to consider.

"I wanted to mention it to you," Paulette said. "You know, in case it helped with your investigation."

I thanked her before hanging up and turning to Garrett. "You want me to drop you off?"

He raised an eyebrow. "Are you kidding? I'm yours for the rest of the day. Besides, this whole case has gotten me curious now."

Fifteen minutes later, we'd dropped off Garrett's car, picked up the loaner from Paulette, and pulled up at her place. Paulette met us outside. Her eyes were red rimmed.

I really wished Roberto hadn't planted the thought in my mind that she was crazy because now, whether I wanted to or not, I kept thinking about the possibility. Evidence seemed to be mounting to confirm it was more than a theory.

"Hey, Gabby." Paulette smiled weakly and pulled her sweater tighter across her shoulders.

"Paulette, this is Garrett."

She held out a hand, something flickering in her gaze. "I've heard of you."

"Pleasure to meet you," Garrett told her.

She crossed her arms over her chest as a chilly wind swept across the lawn. "I'm sorry again about what happened to your van. The good news is that they don't know what the fluid was underneath your van. It was probably just condensation."

I wasn't sure that was good news, but I nodded anyway. "Right."

"The police have no idea who did it."

Could Paulette have done it? I'd assumed Roberto was guilty. But if not Roberto then Paulette would make the most sense. She had slipped away for a few minutes—for long enough to do the deed.

"I appreciate you having the van fixed for me," I told her.

"It was the least I could do, especially since you were just an innocent bystander in all of this. Divorce is ugly." She frowned. "I don't recommend it."

Whenever I got married, I wanted it to be for life, no matter how hard the journey might be. My mom had stuck with my dad, even though he was a lazy louse for most of my childhood. I had to admit—I didn't want that either. But one could never be certain exactly what life would hand you, good or bad.

"I also had the van detailed for you, by the way," she continued. "I guess your AC was going bad, so I had that replaced, as well."

"You didn't have to do all of that."

She shrugged. "I wanted to."

"Thank you." Gratefulness filled me.

Before I could gush anymore, my attention turned to a figure stepping out the front door. My eyes widened in surprise. Roberto? What was he doing here?

Paulette actually blushed for a moment. She pulled a hair behind her ear but offered no explanation.

Roberto came and stood beside her, eyeing both

Garrett and me suspiciously. Garrett introduced himself and then a moment of tension stretched between all of us.

"Fancy seeing you here, Ms. St. Claire," Roberto finally said, narrowing his eyes at me.

"I was just thinking the same thing," I mumbled in return.

I waited again for Paulette to say something or for her to ask him to leave. She did neither.

Finally, I cleared my throat, deciding that I should get down to business. "Paulette, quick question for you. Why in the world did you hire Peter Hines?"

"The maintenance man?" she questioned.

I nodded.

"I heard what happened to his sister and felt terrible. I wanted to do something to help him. Of course. He only works there a few days a week, during the daytime when no one else is here. Why?"

I needed more. "How did you hear about his sister? About Peter?"

"Arie told me."

Arie just happened to mention it? That seemed suspicious within itself. "Then what happened?"

She pursed her lips and fine lines formed around them. "Then I did some research, I figured out what Arie said about Rose Hines was true, and I called Peter. It just made sense. Do you think I shouldn't have hired him?"

The worry in her eyes made me second-guess my questioning. "No, no. That was very kind of you. I was just checking. Thank you." I supposed her explanation made sense—if she was telling the truth. "Let me just grab my stuff out of the trunk."

I was going to miss this car, I realized as I circled around it. For just a few days, I'd imagined my life if I could afford a vehicle like this. Sure, it was just a car. But I'd felt like a million bucks—quite the opposite of how I felt when I drove my white work van.

I popped the trunk open and started to reach for my supplies.

What I saw there stopped me cold.

It was a costume—a nun habit like the one Scarlet had taken home from the show—as well as cans of black spray paint.

"GABBY?" Paulette whispered.

I took a step back, shaking my head vehemently. "I did not put those things in the trunk."

"What's going on?" Garrett asked. A wrinkle formed between his eyebrows.

I pointed to the costume and the paint cans. "That habit is one of the missing costumes that was last seen with Scarlet. The spray paint? It could have been used to paint the security cameras at the Cultural Arts Center."

"And now they're in your trunk," Paulette muttered.

"Stolen items?" Roberto said. Accusation flared in his eyes.

"Not Gabby," Paulette whispered.

In all our years of being friends, Paulette had

never once doubted me, even when I deserved to be doubted. That's what made the look in her eyes right now even harder to swallow.

Yet, at the same time, I had no room to talk. I'd been doubting her, as well. It was never fun when the tables were turned. And even I had to admit that I looked guilty.

"Paulette, you've got to believe me," I told her. "I have no idea how those things ended up there."

"We're calling the police, Ms. St. Claire," Roberto said, a satisfied gleam in his eyes. "Guilty or not, this could be evidence in murder. Paulette told me everything. You're not going to take advantage of her."

"Take advantage?" My mouth dropped open. I decided he wasn't worth speaking to anymore. "Paulette—" I took a step closer, desperate to explain. Yet I had nothing to explain. I was just as clueless as anyone else here.

Before I could finish my sentence, Roberto pulled out his phone. "I'm calling the police."

"Fine. I'm not guilty, nor am I hiding anything."

"Gabby?" Paulette questioned again.

"You've got to trust me, Paulette. I'm being set up."

She crossed her arms over her chest, glancing back and forth from me to Roberto. Snippets of Roberto's conversation floated across the air to me. I heard enough, including "murder," "stolen," and "evidence," to know this wasn't good.

Garrett put an arm around my shoulders and leaned in close. "You think someone planted those things there?"

"I know they did. Someone is desperate to make me look guilty." As possibilities of who it was ran through my mind, I realized the most obvious person was either Paulette or Roberto. Both had access to this car—I'd bet Robert even had a key still—and could have easily slipped the evidence into the trunk.

Roberto—maybe he was involved.

But Paulette? Why would she bring me into this, only to make me look guilty?

Charlie showed up at Paulette's place fifteen minutes later, and we went through the whole story with her.

Too many people talked at once, however, making the explanation confusing. Charlie's head volleyed back and forth as Roberto and I both told our sides of the story, with Paulette and Garrett inserting opinions frequently. The detective furiously scribbled in her notebook.

"You're telling me you have no idea how those things ended up in the trunk?" Charlie asked me.

"Absolutely." I glanced at Garrett, Roberto and Paulette. "Can I have a word? Alone?"

"Of course."

We stepped away from the crowd—namely, Roberto. He didn't need to know all my business. "That's exactly what I'm saying, Charlie. I have no idea how the dress or the paint got there. The only other person who would have a key to it is Paulette."

"So, you're accusing the person who let you borrow her car and who fixed your van?"

I frowned. "It does sound awful when you say it that way. I guess I'm not really accusing anyone. I'm just pointing out the facts."

"The most obvious fact is that this points back to you. I know you talked to Scarlet's roommate. You knew about the costume."

"How'd you know that?"

"We questioned her in our investigation into Scarlet's death. She mentioned that you'd stopped by and that the costume was missing."

I shook my head. "I didn't take the costume."

"I'm not saying you did. But you do realize how this looks?"

"Of course I realize how this looks! No one realizes that more than I do."

"This isn't enough for us to bring you in. Yet. But you need to be careful. To repeat myself, just because

I know you doesn't mean I can cut you slack. I'll follow the evidence wherever it leads."

"I'd expect no less." I knew what this meant. I was now moving up on the suspect list.

"One more thing," Charlie said. "I'd tell your little friend that Parker isn't relationship material."

I froze. "What are you talking about?"

"Parker went out with a friend of yours apparently."

"No he did not."

Charlie tilted her head. "Does the name Clarice ring a bell?"

My mouth dropped open. "No. They. Didn't."

Charlie nodded. "They did."

After Charlie left, my mind still raced through a multitude of thoughts. None of them were good. Garrett said nothing but squeezed my hand.

To make things worse, I still had to get my car keys back from Paulette, which meant that we had to interact again.

"I'm sorry about that, Gabby," Paulette began. "You know I didn't want to call the police. Roberto just jumped in."

"What's he doing over here, anyway?"

Her cheeks flushed. "He was trying to talk things through."

I glanced over at him. He was on his phone,

talking in Spanish or Portuguese. "And did he succeed?"

She shook her head. "No, he didn't. He just got here a few minutes before you did."

I shook my head, feeling a steady ache coming on. "Do you still want me to work this case?"

"Oh, yes, Gabby. Just because Roberto called the police doesn't mean I don't trust you. You still want to investigate, right?"

I thought about it a moment before nodding. "Yeah, I don't like stopping things before I complete them."

"Then I'll see you at practice tomorrow evening?"

"I'll be there."

She tossed me my van keys. "Great. I hope there are no hard feelings."

As soon as she disappeared inside, I turned to Garrett.

"You're probably not going to want to hang out with me for the rest of the day after all."

"Why's that?"

"Because I'm going to go talk to Donabell's husband." I crossed my arms. "This investigation is getting too personal."

SURPRISINGLY, Garrett stuck with me. I figured he'd bail at the first opportunity, and I'd certainly given him an escape route. If things went downhill from here, he'd only have himself to blame.

That's what I told myself, at least.

As I pulled up to Donabell's house, I wished I'd taken the time to trade my van for one of Garrett's sleeker cars. But it was too late for that.

I also wished I'd had the chance to freshen up a bit—maybe reapply my makeup or check my clothes for wayward pieces of my lunch. But it was too late for that also.

At the door, I paused. "I'm supposed to be undercover."

Garrett raised his hands. "Okay . . . ?"

"So, would you mind playing along? I'm not

investigating per se. I'm simply a member of the cast, after all. Undercover and all."

"Play along, I will."

Before I could ring the bell, compose myself, or even check my breath for the garlic bread I'd eaten earlier, a man answered the door. He was tall, and big boned, and had a thick stomach.

His gaze fell on Garrett and a larger-than-life grin spread across his face. "Garrett Mercer! How are you, man?"

Trent, who wore jeans, cowboy boots, and a Dallas sweatshirt, also had a slow drawl and a loud voice—the epitome of a man from Texas. He gave Garrett a man hug, slapping his back with enough force that I cringed for Garrett.

"I'm doing great. Just happened to be in the neighborhood, and I thought I'd stop by and take a look at those golf clubs you were telling me about."

I could have kissed Garrett. Seriously. He was a lifesaver because I had no idea what my excuse was going to be for dropping by.

"Absolutely. It's like I told you—any time." Trent's gaze traveled to me. "And who is this?"

I grinned. "I'm Gabby."

"Nice to meet you, Gabby. Why don't you both come inside?" He stepped back. "Get out of that weather."

Trent lived in a contemporary brick house on a

decent sized lot. Two kids ran around in the background, chasing each other. The smell of something
spicy—Mexican, maybe?—drifted out toward me,
along with the children's squeals.

"Donabell! We have guests."

A woman came around the corner.

"Gabby, this is my wife—"

"Gabby St. Claire?" The woman stopped in her
tracks. Her lips parted in surprise.

"Donabell."

"You two know each other?" her husband asked.

"We went to middle school together," Donabell
said, wiping her hands on a dishtowel.

"Well, isn't it a small world? Sit down. Donabell
will get us some drinks, won'cha, hun?" he asked,
sounding at once jolly, firm, and in charge.

Donabell scowled. "Of course."

In what was every unpopular girl's dream,
Donabell had aged.

Don't get me wrong—she still looked good. But
she looked much more ordinary than I'd imagined
she would. She had a distinct apple figure—a small
apple, but still an apple. Her hair looked thin and like
all the bleaching she'd done had made it brittle. And
perhaps most unfortunately, she already had some
wrinkles, probably due to the hours she'd spent in
the sun working on her tan when we were younger.

Garrett sat on the couch, chatting away with

Trent, who'd probably never met a stranger. I started to join them but decided to help Donabell instead. I found her in the kitchen.

Dishes were piled in the sink, meat simmered on the stove, and the dishwasher moaned on the other side of the room, steam seeping from its edges. Juice had been spilled on the floor and water puddles could be seen on several surfaces.

I cleared my throat, realizing she hadn't heard me come in. "Can I help?"

"Kids, no water guns in the house. Haven't I told you that before? You're going to ruin the paint!" Donabell shouted.

So that would explain the puddles.

Donabell turned to me and sighed. "I'm fine. Thank you. Why don't you sit down?"

I'd imagined this moment many times, especially as a middle schooler on the occasions when Donabell had belittled me. Put me down. Publically insulted me. And never once had my imaginings included me feeling sorry for her. Never. Ever.

But that's what I felt now. I just couldn't shake the feeling that Donabell was overwhelmed, tired, and maybe even neglected or ignored. So much for the Donabell who wanted to be famous, center of attention, and in the limelight.

I'd obviously caught her off guard because she was wearing old jeans and a sweatshirt. Her hair was pulled back in a ponytail. She'd always been put together back in middle school.

I didn't get the satisfaction I'd expected.

"I insist. Let me grab these two glasses." Before she could argue, I took my and Garrett's glasses of tea.

"Thank you," she muttered as we joined Trent and Garrett in the living room.

Small talk went around the room for a while. Finally, at a break, I decided I could delicately bring up an undelicate situation. "So, you'll never believe this, Donabell. I'm actually acting in a play at our old middle school."

She raised a thin eyebrow. "Are you? Just like old times, huh?"

"Paulette Zollin is managing everything there. I do, at times, feel like I should be back in seventh grade."

"The old middle school, you said?" Trent chuckled. "That's funny. I was trying to buy that property."

I tilted my head and stole a glance at Garrett. "Were you?"

Trent laughed. "Yes, I was. I really thought I was going to win the bidding war, but I didn't. Then everything started happening there, and I was glad I didn't win. Or, I should say, I wondered if Paulette had changed her mind."

"What do you mean?"

"I saw the article in today's paper. Arie Berry was interviewed. She talked about all the strange things happening at play practice. I guess I shouldn't say strange when two people were found there dead."

"That was in the paper?" I'd missed it and was surprised that no one, especially Paulette, had mentioned it.

"Yes, ma'am, it was. As soon as I read it, I emailed Paulette, asking if she'd changed her mind. It was all in good fun. She probably didn't take it that way, though. She was determined to buy the old school."

"I wonder why. I mean, it just doesn't really seem like her thing," I said, fishing for more information.

"Paulette was lucky to find her way to class without getting lost," Donabell muttered. "I'm not exaggerating."

I wanted to argue and stand up for my friend. I really did. But what Donabell had said was true. Paulette had been like a lost little puppy dog who desperately needed someone to guide her. Her money and looks did nothing to enhance her personality or smarts.

"Paulette apparently is like her mom," Donabell continued. "You know Mr. Zollin married a model who was twenty years his junior. All looks, no brains. That's the rumor, at least."

"Well, she's determined to make a go of this." I refused to talk poorly about her.

Donabell shrugged. "Well, best of luck to her, then." Just then, one of her kids ran past with a water gun. "Chris! I told you not to play with those in the house." She scurried off after him.

I chewed on what I'd learned by being here. I didn't think Trent was behind those vandalisms. Either that or he should really consider a career change and go into theater because he was a great actor.

At least I'd ruled him out.

Now I needed to figure out who else I could eliminate.

An hour later, Garrett had seen Trent's "amazing" golf clubs and it was time for us to go. I'd attempted to make conversation with Donabell, but almost every time it was interrupted by one of her children. Her boys were a handful, for sure.

Donabell walked me to the van while Garrett and Trent chatted about an upcoming community fundraiser.

"Are you happy now?" she muttered when we were out of earshot of the men.

"Happy about what?" I asked, genuinely confused.

"Happy that the girl who caused you so much

grief in middle school is a miserable mess, all while you're dating a rich, famous CEO and starring in community theater productions?" She crossed her arms and huffed.

"Why would that make me happy? Besides, you have two beautiful children, a nice house—"

"A chauvinistic husband. My life is my kids. I spend all my time driving them around from practice to practice. Trent thinks that's my job."

My heart panged. "I'm sorry."

"Don't feel sorry for me," she snapped.

"I'm sorry that you're not happy."

"Don't be nice."

I raised my hands, realizing that nothing I said would be right. "I'll pray that you find peace and wisdom in your life, Donabell. If you ever need to talk, call me. I'm pretty good at listening."

She stared at me and opened her mouth to say something when Garrett reappeared. He called a jolly goodbye before we climbed into my van and took off down the road.

"Did you get the answers you wanted?" Garrett asked.

"As a matter of fact, I did. And by the way, you were great at improvising back there. Like, amazingly great."

He grinned. "Anything I can do to help."

"Donabell didn't look happy, both about seeing me and about how her life has turned out."

"You don't think?"

I shook my head and tried to remember how to get where I was going. "No, not at all. It seems like she's lost herself in the process of becoming a wife and mother."

"Being a wife and mother is a noble calling."

"They are. But Donabell had big dreams. She may have changed in the years since we last spoke, but I'm pretty sure none of those dreams included being a housewife. Maybe a pampered housewife, one with a nanny and a cleaner. But I just sensed this underlying discontent in her."

It was also strange to see someone my age seem so much older.

Though in my heart I felt like I was still 23, I had to face the fact that my clock was ticking. I was nearly thirty and my life was flying by. I didn't have much to show for it except for a business that I co-owned. I didn't own an apartment, a nice car, or even nice clothes. I didn't have a family of my own. I felt like, in some way, I was lagging behind.

As we started down an overpass, I hit the brakes to slow down.

Nothing happened.

I pressed harder.

Still nothing.

My eyes widened in realization as we charged toward the red light ahead.

"Gabby?" Garrett asked.

"My brakes are out," I rushed. Adrenaline surged through me, heightening both my senses and my fear. "Hang on!"

As the intersection neared, I saw the cars crossing the highway. An oversized truck. A minivan. Several sedans. If I didn't slow down, I was going to hit at least one of them.

I braced myself for the worst.

Lord, help us!

CHAPTER
TWENTY-FOUR

"GABBY!" Garrett yelled.

In a split second decision, I pulled the wheel hard to the left. The van spun and spun. A blur of asphalt and cars and blue sky muddled around me.

They said that before death your life flashed before your eyes. Right now, everything played at fast-forward in my mind. My brother disappearing. My mom dying. Starting my crime scene business. Losing Riley.

All the way up to where I was today. Stuck in a cyclical cycle of my own doing. Acting at times like my own worst enemy.

Was this it?

Somewhere in the chaos, I screamed. My hands gripped the steering wheel with white knuckles.

I was going to die and what kind of legacy would I leave behind? I'd solved a few crimes. A few of my friends would miss me. But life would go on. In a few days, it would be like I never existed.

I waited for a crash. For impact. For the van to roll.

Instead, we came to a halt.

My head was still spinning, my breathing labored, and sweat dripped across my brow as I sat there in total shock for a minute.

"Are you okay?" Garret asked.

I glanced over at him. Blood trickled down his forehead, causing another moment of panic in me. That could have ended horribly.

I grabbed his hand and squeezed, desperately needing human contact at the moment. "I'm okay. You?"

He nodded. "I'll survive. Come on. Let's get out of here before another car rams us."

When I stepped on the road, my knees felt too weak to hold me up. Thankfully, a whole army of bystanders surrounded us. Someone grabbed my elbow before I sank to the ground.

I couldn't stop thinking about what had happened.

My brake lines had been cut. I felt certain of it.

And Paulette had been the one with the most access to do just that.

A police officer gave us a ride back to Garrett's place. After hearing the officers at the scene talk and thinking through things in my own mind, I'd come to the conclusion that my brakes had been cut, just not all the way. That way, whoever had done the deed wouldn't look as guilty since the accident hadn't happened immediately.

Back at Garrett's, he'd insisted that, this time, I borrow one of his cars. My van had been hauled away to be examined by forensic techs. Thankfully, Garrett had walked away with only a cut on his forehead and some butterfly bandages. I'd walked away shaken.

But everything in my life seemed to be telling me to stop being chained down by my past. As my life had flashed before my eyes, that thought had only been re-emphasized.

Even in church today, the pastor had said something about "the old is gone and the new has come."

I really needed to get the hint.

Garrett and I walked through the parking garage outside of his apartment building. It was dark outside now, and the light in the garage was dim. The cold air crackled around us.

"You want to come up to my place a minute?" he

asked at the elevator. "I'll try to make sure no SWAT teams interrupt us."

I appreciated his attempt at humor, but I couldn't even smile. "I really should get home and return some phone calls that came in today. I've got to get my work lined up for the week."

"You sure?" His gaze seemed to draw me toward him.

Before I could second guess myself, I leaned forward and planted a kiss on his lips. His hands went to my waist, encircling it, silently asking permission for more.

I expected the whole scenario to feel foreign. I waited to feel like I'd betrayed Riley. But instead of negative emotions, I felt hopeful. For the first time in a long time.

"What was that for?" Garrett asked, keeping his hands firmly planted on my waist.

"It was to say thank you. For everything."

"Feel free to say thank you anytime. I'll do whatever I can to make sure you're grateful."

My hands slipped around his neck. "You've been really good to me, Garrett. I appreciate it. Any normal person would have run from me today."

He leaned closer. "It's a good thing I'm not normal then."

Our lips connected again, for longer this time.

"I'd invite you up again, but now I'm thinking that would be a bad idea."

I smiled, my lips still tingling. "Yes, a bad idea. But we'll catch up later. Lunch maybe?"

"And the play is this weekend. You can't forget that."

"Believe me, whether I want to or not, I can't block that from my memory."

His thumb brushed against my cheek. "You're going to be safe, right?"

"I will."

He dropped his hands from my waist and intertwined my fingers with his. "Let me show you to your chariot then."

My brain was still swirling with more than its fair share of dueling thoughts as I headed to my first job the next morning.

I met with the homeowner first and went over instructions for what we were doing today. She signed a contract that I'd printed out last night, and I began making a list of what needed to be done and the order we should complete it all. This would at least be a two-day job, and I'd probably need to call in Chad and maybe even Braxton.

Clarice arrived on time to help. I was pulling up some carpet that was officially considered a biohazard. The homeowner had left the house abandoned for the past six months and, in the meantime, it had become a hangout for druggies. There were needles and stains and even a couple of bullet holes. The whole place should have probably been condemned. Here I was instead.

I didn't waste any time engaging in small talk with Clarice. I couldn't forget what Charlie had mentioned at Paulette's house.

"I heard you went on a date," I started, keeping a watchful eye out for needles.

She pulled her safety goggles on. "I started to tell you the other day but we got interrupted."

"Don't forget to wear thick gloves," I told her. "We have to be really careful with the scene." The job sometimes required living on the edge.

"Got it."

"So, how'd the date go?"

Her face lit up. "It was great. I think he could be the one."

I blinked. I'd been trying to play it cool, but this was going to be much harder than I thought. "Wow. That serious, huh? You've got to be careful. You know that, right?"

"You sound like my Aunt Sharon," she muttered, her smile slipping. She stepped over the carpet.

"What can I do?"

"Start patching those walls. Everything you need is in that bucket." I didn't want her any closer to these needles than she had to be.

She picked up a patch kit and stared at it a moment. I could tell she wasn't in a work mindset.

"So, who's the lucky guy? Someone you met at the coffeehouse maybe?"

I watched as she stiffened ever so slightly. "No, you were actually with me when I met him."

"That guy who hit on you at the crime scene last week?"

She shook her head. "No."

"I know! That cute police officer who helped us move the furniture right after the scene was cleared at the shooting out in Chesapeake?"

Clarice frowned. "It was actually . . . Parker."

I thought I'd have to fake my surprise and indignation, but it came back to me easily when I heard the words roll from her lips. "Parker? Have you lost your mind?" I dropped the carpet I'd just rolled, watching as it spread open again.

She shrugged, scooping up some putty. Suddenly, she was very interested in working. "No, I haven't lost my mind. Why would you ask that?"

"You know he just had a baby. With another woman."

She shrugged again. "The baby is six months old now."

"But Parker was still with Charlie up until a month ago."

"Things were bad between them, though." Offense stained her voice, but she paused for long enough to glance my way.

I couldn't see her eyes because of her goggles, but I felt the death rays shooting from them.

"He's older than you," I reminded her.

"That's a plus. Guys my age are total duds." She turned back to patching holes in the wall.

I stopped what I was doing, walked over to Clarice, and laid a hand on her arm. "I'm not trying to tell you what to do, but—"

She shrugged my hand off. "Then don't. Don't tell me what to do."

I pulled back. Clarice had never spoken to me like that before. "I just don't want to see you get hurt."

"Worry about yourself, Gabby. Certainly you have enough going on in your own life that you don't have to butt into mine." Derision dripped from her words.

"That's not fair, Clarice. I know Parker. I know what he's like."

"He's perfectly charming. The first time we met, he gave me advice on getting a degree in criminal justice. We realized there was something there."

Frustration built inside me. Why couldn't I get through to her? "Clarice, he's no good."

"Says the woman who's still obsessed with a man who has no intentions of moving back to this area."

My lips gaped open. "I've moved on, thank you."

"You certainly don't act like it." She put the putty down. "You know what, I think I'm calling in sick today. I'm just not feeling this."

"Clarice . . ."

"Parker warned me that you'd be judgmental."

I could only imagine how that conversation had gone. "I just want what's best for you."

"That's for me to determine."

And with that, she left.

I rested my forehead against the wall, trying to figure out how I could have made that go better. Trying to think of what I should have said as opposed to what I did say.

I had no idea. Literally. No idea.

***

"Tonight, you need to practice being on the wire," Paulette said as I stood center stage during rehearsal.

I tugged at the harness I'd struggled to both get on and adjust. With a final pull at one of the belts around my hip, I stole a glance at Mrs. Baker, hoping she'd object to this unnecessary torture. She shrugged.

"Don't worry. We had everything checked out today," Paulette continued. "It's safe. Sharen and Karen filled in for you."

Sharen and Karen together probably didn't weigh as much as an empty sack of flour.

The other cast members took steps back, their body language indicating that they were glad it was me and not them. I couldn't blame them.

I cleared my throat. "How long ago did you check the wire?" All it would take was one minute of the stage being out of sight for someone to sabotage something.

"Just about an hour ago," Mrs. Baker said. "How's the harness feel?"

I tugged at it, dread filling my stomach. "It feels good."

"You remember the instructions we gave you?" Mrs. Baker continued.

I nodded and mentally ran through the safety precautions. Don't jerk around. No horse play. Nothing unexpected. "I got it."

"Let's give it a whirl then." Mrs. Baker patted my shoulder.

This was just . . . awesome.

This was the final scene, where the Specter tried to

take Elsa McGovernness with him to live in the secret confines of the theater because, of course, he'd fallen in love with her. Even though he was really a person and not a phantom, for some reason we still had to ascend into the ceiling—to make it more dramatic, I guessed.

I was all harnessed up, but my throat burned and my neck muscles were knit tighter than my grandmother's old afghan blankets. I was willing to take a lot of risks and do a lot of things to solve a mystery. But this one in particular had me seeing my life ending painfully.

"Hold Jerome's hand," Mrs. Baker instructed.

Arie smiled up at me from her safe little seat in the audience. "Break a leg."

I scowled.

"What? That means good luck."

"Hm hm," I muttered.

Bennie leaned closer. "Don't worry," she whispered. "There was only one glitch when we tested it on Sharen and Karen. Everything's fine now."

The blood drained from my face.

Before I could argue anymore, I was hoisted into the air. The sudden motion caused a rush of air to leave my lungs. I gripped Jerome's hand. At least if my wire had been cut, maybe his hadn't and I could hold on to him for dear life.

Or I could pull us both to our deaths.

"Don't forget, as they hoist you, you've got to sing," Mrs. Baker reminded.

My mind went blank. What were the words?

I remembered finding Scarlet below the catwalk. Was that how I'd look when I died? Would someone even add some striped, colorful socks?

Did Scarlet feel any fear before she died? Did she have a pit in her stomach like I did now?

I glanced at the stage below. It looked so far away.

Who was operating the rig on this anyway? Did they know what they were doing? One wrong move and the whole line could give. I could end up worse than Scarlet. I could end up splattered on the stage floor, like some kind of thespian road kill.

Rose and I could haunt this place together.

I shook my head. Everyone stared at me, waiting for me to begin. I could hardly breathe.

"Gabby?" Mrs. Baker asked. "Is everything okay?"

"It's okay." My voice squeaked out, pitched higher than a cartoon mouse's.

"It's going to be just fine," Jerome whispered. "I've done this a million times before. I only got hurt once."

"That doesn't make me feel better."

"Gabby?" Mrs. Baker asked again.

Just then, the line gave a little, sending me free

falling. I screamed the girliest scream that had ever left my lips.

The line caught and I jerked to a halt mid-air.

"Sorry about that! It was a little glitch," one of the stagehands called from somewhere out of sight. "Everything's good now."

"Do you want to get down?" Mrs. Baker asked. A worry wrinkle snaked between her eyebrows.

Everyone stared at me.

I wanted to scream, *Of course I want to get down. Are you crazy? I don't want to die this way!*

As panic threatened to overtake me, I glanced over at Mrs. Baker's daughter Larissa. She sat there on the front row, watching me with her eyes wide.

I remembered sitting in that very place, watching the lead of *Oklahoma* in awe. I pulled myself together, for the sake of the 13 year old me who'd wanted to star in a play more than anything.

"No, I've got this," I finally said.

Dear Lord, please help me survive this.

Shaky at first, eventually my lines flowed out.

I kept waiting for the wire to fray. Remarkably, it didn't. It held me, even as we began to sway back and forth.

The ending was going to be magical—if no one died in the process.

As I sang out the last line, the cast broke out into applause. My cheeks flushed.

"That was wonderful you two. You could really feel the fear and anxiety Elsa felt as she was faced with the possibility of leaving everything familiar behind," Mrs. Baker said.

That's because my fear and anxiety are real, no acting involved.

I cleared my throat as the wire lowered me back to the stage. I'd never been so glad to feel something solid under my feet. But I also had a rush of adrenaline as I realized that I'd just conquered a big fear of mine. At the moment, I felt like I could do anything.

"Let's take a break and then we need to run through all of this again. Meet me back on stage in five," Mrs. Baker said.

As the rest of the cast dispersed, Mrs. Baker came on stage. "You're doing a really fantastic job, Gabby. Especially for someone who had to fill in at the last minute. I always knew you were a natural."

"Thanks, Mrs. Baker."

"And I've been meaning to tell you that the guy of yours that you brought by—Garrett, right?"

I nodded.

"He seems like a keeper. He looked at you like you could do no wrong."

"We're not actually together. Or, we're taking it slow, I guess I should say." I shrugged. "I was engaged to someone else up until a few months ago.

But now he's moved on with his life. I guess I need to move on as well."

"You know what Nathanial Hawthorne said, don't you?"

"I'm afraid I don't."

"He said, 'The past lies upon the present like a giant's dead body.'"

"There's wisdom in that quote." In other words, I couldn't let the past conquer me and hold me back. That's exactly what I'd been doing. I'd have to chew more on those words later.

As the cast gathered, I noticed Paulette slipping backstage. Interesting. Where was she going?

I snuck backstage but saw no one. Where had she gone?

I moved quietly through the dark space, my gaze scanning my surroundings.

Strange. It was like Paulette had never been back here.

I moved toward the dressing rooms. Slowly, I pushed the first door open. It was dark inside. Whose room was this again? I was pretty sure four other cast members shared this space. I flicked the light on.

Everything appeared normal.

I went to the next room, reminding myself to move quickly. I didn't want people to get suspicious that I was gone. This was Jerome's dressing room, if I remembered correctly.

I turned the lights on and examined the space.

There was no Paulette.

But there in the corner were some tools—nuts, bolts, wrenches, a hammer.

I stepped closer, wanting a better look.

That's when I heard a voice behind me. "What are you doing here?"

I swirled around. Arie stared at me with accusation in her eyes.

TWENTY-FIVE

"I THOUGHT I saw someone come in here," I muttered. "I was just making sure everything was okay, that no one was up to any mischief."

"How do we know that you're not up to any mischief?" Arie stepped closer. "I'm beginning to think it's more than a coincidence that you were picked to fill in for Scarlet's role. You just happened to be at the right place at the right time, huh?"

I swallowed hard. "That's right. Lucky me."

"There's something you're not telling us."

I shrugged. "Everyone has dreams and wants a better life. I thought maybe I could find mine with the theater. You can't blame me for that." As the words poured from my mouth, I pondered the truth in them.

I guess everyone did want something a little more

for their future. That's why we all worked hard and pushed ourselves to do better. I could do better than the position I was in right now in my life.

"I researched you, you know." Something gleamed in her eyes.

"Did you?" I tried to keep the tremble from my voice.

"I know about your past."

So much for being undercover. "It's not what you think—"

"You and Paulette were friends. That's how you got this role."

My heart slowed for a minute. "You're right. We do go way back. I'm sorry we weren't upfront with you."

"Is everything okay back here?" Paulette appeared with a clipboard in her hands.

"I'm fine," I started. "I was just making sure everything was okay here when Arie barged in and started making accusations."

"I'm just concerned because of everything that's been going on lately. I'm sure you can understand." Arie glared at me.

The noise from the stage area suddenly disappeared. Everyone was probably trying to eavesdrop. Nosy little actors.

Great. I had an audience at a time when I didn't need one.

"Enough of the bickering. We've got to run through this again and none of us want to be here all night," Paulette said.

Begrudgingly, I left the backstage area and joined the rest of the cast on stage. Everyone looked at the three of us as if we'd been sent to the principal's office.

"Everyone in place," Mrs. Baker instructed.

I took my place center stage. I noticed Amos had come to pick up Larissa. He waved my way. Unfortunately, the girl had been here to witness the not so flattering moment. My hopes of being a good role model for a member of the younger generation quickly faded.

Acts One and Two went smoothly. I was able to put everything out of my mind and focus on my performance. At the beginning of Act Three, I had to climb some scaffolding that represented a roof scape (hence the song, "Climb Every Steeple, Scale Every Roof") with a row of houses below.

I'd just started the number when I glanced down and saw one of the huge screws at the end of the roof was a good inch from being completely twisted into the wood. Something clicked in my head.

Those nuts and bolts in Jerome's dressing room: Could they have been used to hold this part of the set together?

Before I could think about it, the bottom of the stage collapsed—me with it.

I rubbed my hind side. I'd walked away from the accident with a few bruises and a pounding headache. That was the good news.

The bad news was that the set was a crumpled mess behind me. It could be fixed—maybe. The scaffolding had definitely been sabotaged, and Mrs. Baker had called the police.

Charlie stood on the stage right now, addressing the rest of the cast as if she were an award-winning actress. She paced the glossy wood, a hand on her hip by her gun. Her gaze was intense. The only thing that ruined her tough girl image was the spit up on her shoulder.

"Someone is trying to harm both this production and the people involved," she said. "I want to know who. I want to know why."

No one said anything for a moment.

Charlie looked back at the cast. "Does anyone know who might have messed with the set?"

"We used it for our first run through and it was just fine," Bennie said.

"Did anyone see someone messing with it between practices?" Charlie asked.

I braced myself for what I knew was inevitable.

"Gabby was backstage doing something when I walked back there," Arie barked.

Everyone's eyes fell on me.

I raised my hands in defense. "I thought I saw someone go back there. I was just checking things out. Besides, why would I rig part of the set to hurt myself?"

"What were you doing back there, Arie?" Bennie asked, crossing her arms and sending an accusing look to the has-been starlet.

Her cheeks reddened. "I was doing the same. I was making sure everything was okay since someone is determined to ruin my play."

"Someone's determined to ruin something," Charlie muttered. "Where was the scaffolding prior to Act Three?"

"It was backstage," Mrs. Baker told her. "We didn't bring it in until Act Three."

"Maybe it was the ghost," Bennie said. "Besides, a house almost landed on Gabby. Does no one else see the irony in this?"

"Are you saying I'm like the Wicked Witch who dies in *The Wizard of Oz*?" I asked. But it was true. A house had almost landed on me. Coincidence? I couldn't be sure.

"Ghost or no ghost, whoever is behind these acts needs to be brought to justice. Someone here knows something. We're going to get to the bottom of this. I promise you that," the detective said, sounding all Charlie's Angels tough. Good for her.

"What should I do? Should I cancel this performance?" Paulette asked, tears glimmering in her eyes.

I remembered seeing her go backstage. Could she be responsible for this? I wasn't ready to express my theory to anyone yet, especially not Charlie. There was too much at stake.

Charlie shook her head. "I don't know what to say except act at your own risk. If I were in this play, I'd be running away screaming right now."

I glanced around, standing on the periphery of the crowd so I could see people better.

Most people looked paler, frightened at her announcement. But Jerome and Arie exchanged a glance. What was that about? Was there more to their story than they were letting on? I was starting to believe that was true.

Meanwhile, there was Paulette. She looked genuinely distressed. Could she be guilty *and* truly frightened? Or was she a better actress than anyone had guessed?

The Shining Twins stared.

Bennie looked confused and determined.

Could the guilty party be right here?

It made the most sense that someone on the inside

was behind these acts. Had Scarlet discovered them and been killed because of it?

That was exactly what I needed to figure out.

When play practice was over, I checked my phone. I had three missed calls from Chad, which seemed unusual. I wandered to the back of the auditorium for privacy and called him back.

"We've got problems," Chad started.

"What's going on?"

"Clarice just quit and so did Braxton."

"What?" My voice came out louder than intended.

"Yeah, Clarice said you'd had creative differences." His voice sounded hard.

"Creative differences?" I repeated.

"She said that was putting it nicely."

"She's dating Parker and I warned her against it. She got offended. I tried to be gentle and compassionate. I promise that I did." I sighed, wishing sometimes that I could rewind my life. "What about Braxton?"

"He said he can't work for a woman."

"What? He actually said that?" My voice level climbed again.

"Yeah, he actually said that. So that leaves you

and me, Gabby. We've got a full workload this week. I wouldn't have committed to so much if I'd known we'd be short staffed."

"What are we going to do? Should we call our clients and ask for extensions?"

"You know how that goes. Then we'll suddenly start getting all these bad online reviews and that drives business away."

"This is the week before opening night. I'm going to have trouble putting in overtime hours."

"Yeah, I know." He sighed, long and hard. "We're essentially re-launching our business. I don't want it to fail now."

"I don't either, Chad."

"So you're committed to what we're doing?"

"Of course I am." Even as the words left my mouth, I wondered if they were really true. In my mind, I was fully committed. But in my heart I knew I was thinking about the future—and about change—even more than usual lately.

He remained silent for a moment and, with each second that passed, the tension between us grew. "I feel like you're looking for any opportunity possible to ditch work for other prospects."

As I felt my defenses rising, I decided to take a mental step back. "Look Chad, maybe we shouldn't be talking about this now. It's obvious you've had a bad day, and I don't think you're thinking clearly."

"I don't know, Gabby. Things have just felt so complicated lately."

Maybe Chad had been feeling resentful about my absences from work. In truth, I couldn't blame him. Despite that, part of me still felt wary.

"We'll just talk later, Gabby. You're right. I've had a bad day. The way it is now, I'm going to be working eighteen hour days."

"Look, I'll recruit my brother and my dad to help if I have to. We'll get it all done." Certainly he realized I was concerned and serious if I'd go so far as to suggest that.

"I hear you. Later, Gabby."

I hung up. I hadn't thought it was possible to feel any worse. But I sure did.

"I'M GOING to do a stake out here tonight," I told Paulette. "You okay with that?"

"What will that prove?"

I shrugged. "Maybe nothing. Maybe everything. I don't really know. If something is happening here after hours, I want to know what."

Paulette nodded. "If that's what you need to do."

Now more than ever, I had to solve this case so I could begin to mend fences with Chad. Maybe I could only handle one job at a time and this whole being a private eye on the side wouldn't work. This play had been more work than I anticipated and it had eaten into my time. Chad had worked several night jobs because I had play practice. Normally, we would have split the time between us.

Maybe I'd been egocentric and self-absorbed this

whole time. It wasn't beyond me to act that way, although I'd thought I'd conquered those weaknesses.

"You going with us to the Slug House?" Jerome asked.

I shook my head. "Not tonight. I have some other things I need to do."

"Have it your way."

I lingered, pretending to study my script. When the last cast member was out the door, I gave up on the façade and stretched.

"You sure you're going to be okay?" Paulette asked.

I nodded. "I should be fine. Maybe I'll finally get some answers."

"Just be careful."

When she left and I was truly alone, a sense of foreboding gripped me. I might as well have been left alone in a creepy old haunted house. That's what the school felt like at the moment.

"Rose, I don't believe in ghosts. I don't believe you're haunting this place. But something's going on," I whispered, staring at the stage.

I walked over to the orchestra pit. I pictured the man lying there dead.

Then I pictured Rose.

Three people had died here. Three people.

All, by initial impressions at least, had seemed accidental. But they weren't.

I wasn't sure what being here tonight would prove. But at least I could check things out without fear of being caught.

I decided to start in the dressing rooms. I hit Jerome's first.

The police had taken the tools I'd found on his floor and were checking them to see if they were matches. I had no doubt they were. Really, anyone could have left them in his dressing room, though. The rooms weren't locked, so it would be easy for someone to frame him.

I wandered around but saw nothing out of the ordinary.

Out of curiosity, I went down into the orchestra pit next. I moved aside some of the chairs and music stands there. I stood in the spot where I'd found the man and looked up at the stage.

Why had his body been left here? What were his connections with the crimes?

I had more questions than answers.

I had more suspicions than I had confirmations.

For every theory, I had a doubt as to its accuracy.

That left me feeling like I was going around in circles.

I climbed out of the pit.

That's when I heard a door close in the distance.

Someone else was here, I realized.

The questions were who and why.

I realized I was standing out in the open where anyone could spot me. I ducked low and hurried toward the wall. I hit the light switch and the auditorium went dark.

The dark both concealed me and terrified me.

I lingered by the wall, waiting for another telltale sign.

My heartbeat was the only thing I could hear. It drummed at a hard steady rhythm.

Who else was here? Just what were their reasons? To wreak more havoc? Or were they plotting something more deadly like another murder?

I heard another door squeal open. I glanced at the entrance at the back of the auditorium and saw one of the doors there was cracked open. The hallway outside had a purple emergency light that illuminated a dark figure as it slipped inside.

My senses tingled as the shadow lingered by the door.

If the intruder turned on the lights, I'd be spotted. I couldn't let that happen.

As if on cue, the lights above me flickered.

Quickly, I hit the switch above me and flipped them off.

The process repeated itself several times until finally the intruder gave up. Did he or she think it was an electrical short? Maybe they didn't know I was here.

Someone came down the aisle. The person didn't sound especially heavy, but I supposed they could just be walking softly. What were they up to?

I was about to find out.

I couldn't exactly be unarmed, though. I felt beside me and grabbed an old microphone stand. The base was heavy and weighted. Maybe that would work in my favor.

I gripped it, just in case I needed a weapon.

The figure, best I could tell, started toward the stage but paused. Did this person suspect I was here? That I was watching?

I pressed myself harder into the wall. I would have ducked, but I feared the motion would only confirm my presence. Instead, I froze. I still gripped the microphone stand, just in case.

I sensed the footsteps starting again, coming closer.

Alarm raced through me.

Was I about to come face to face with a killer?

My pulse quickened.

I had to take a risk and see who this person was.

Before I could second guess myself, I flipped the light switch. As the overheads flooded on, I gripped my microphone stand, ready for a fight.

"Wait!" someone screeched.

I blinked at the figure standing there. "Bennie?"

"Gabby?"

We stared each other down.

"What are you doing here?" I started, lowering my makeshift weapon.

"I forgot my wallet. I didn't think I would get in, but the outside door was unlocked."

Again? Why was that door continually unlocked? There was something wrong about that. Majorly wrong.

"Don't you have a key?" I asked.

"No, Paulette didn't give me one. With everything that's been happening around here lately, I wasn't sure I wanted the responsibility, to be honest." She eyed me. "Your turn. Why are you here?"

I swallowed hard, wanting to pour out the truth—that I was investigating. But Paulette really wanted me to keep this quiet. "Paulette gave me permission to stay after hours. She's worried about the play and thought it would be a good idea for someone to be around. She hasn't found a suitable security guard yet."

It was the truth . . . only not completely.

Bennie's eyes narrowed before widening. "So, you're, like, on a stake out?"

I shrugged, trying to appear like I had no idea what I was doing. "I guess."

"Can I help?" She said it like a little kid asking if they could go to Disney World.

I searched my brain for an excuse as to why she couldn't possibly help me. I came up with nothing. "Sure. The more the merrier."

My words lacked conviction but she didn't seem to notice.

"This is going to be so fun. A stakeout. I feel so . . . detective-y." She giggled. "But before I forget, let me grab my wallet. You'll leave the lights on this time, right?"

I nodded. "Now that I know it's you."

Her eyes widened again. "That's right. I could have totally been a bad guy. What happens if the bad guy does come tonight, Gabby?"

"We call the police. That's it. We don't rush in and try to be heroes. We don't try to tackle him or her ourselves. We're merely observers."

She nodded crisply. "Observers. Got it. I'm going to get my wallet."

I watched her disappear. Great. This wasn't what I had planned. I liked the girl well enough, but I wasn't sure if she'd be in the way or not. The last thing I wanted was to stay awake into the wee hours of the morning, all for nothing. Or, even worse, to have Bennie ruin it.

It didn't matter anymore. I'd told her she could stay, so now I was stuck with her.

She appeared a moment later, waving a bright blue wallet in the air. A huge grin stretched across her face. "Found it. Now, how do we start?"

"I'm no expert on this, but we mostly just chill. We stay quiet and low key and listen for anything suspicious."

"You think we'll find something?"

I shrugged. "Who knows? It appears that whatever is happening is in some way connected with this school or this play. I'd like to walk the halls, see if we hear anything."

"You really think we will?"

I shrugged again. "I have no idea. I understand if you don't want to stick around. This could be boring."

"Not at all. I wouldn't miss this for the world."

I offered a smile, though it took everything in me to muster it. "Let's go then."

We walked down the eerily silent hallways. It just wasn't the same here without the students darting to and from class. Without teachers fussing. Without custodians cleaning up barf and trying to trip students with their "Wet Floor" signs—which I'd always thought were more dangerous than the wet floors themselves.

We wandered down the main hallway, past the offices, past the various corridors. Except for the buzz of the lights, the school was eerily quiet, reminding me somewhat of a graveyard at midnight. Mentally, I pictured an impending storm in the distance, as well. What was a creepy graveyard without lightning and thunder?

Something fluttered behind me before swooping by my ear. Bennie and I both screamed and ducked.

As we rose, we saw a . . . bird. The little guy flew away, toward a window where he landed on the sill and stared at us.

I let out a weak laugh. "Just a feathered friend. Wonder how he got in here."

"He's probably more scared than we are."

Just then, something groaned in the distance.

"What was that?" Bennie asked.

"I have no idea. Let's check it out."

We walked toward the opposite end of the building, and I paused by the gym. "That's strange."

"What?" Bennie asked.

I walked toward the outside door. Using only one finger, I pushed on it. A gust of wind pulled it the rest of the way open. "This door isn't latched."

"That's not reassuring."

"I'll tell Paulette to look into it. Maybe the latch is

broken." Even as I said the words, I wondered if there was more to it.

"Since that mystery is solved, I'm going to run to the bathroom, Gabby. I'll be right back."

I watched as she disappeared through the doorway, and I wondered if this whole evening would be a bust.

As soon as the thought entered my mind, movement at the end of the hallway caught my eye.

Someone *was* in here!

"Stop where you are!" I shouted.

The intruder—who wore all black—froze. Then, in an instant, he darted into the gym.

I took off after him.

TWENTY-SEVEN

I SHOVED through the double doors leading into the room that gave nightmares to unathletic students everywhere and paused.

Where had he gone?

I saw no movement. But I couldn't stand here all night and let the man get away. I inched along the wall, past the pull up bars and the banners proclaiming state championship titles. Bleachers lined the opposite wall and on either side of me were basketball hoops.

My eyes were wide, watching for anything suspicious. At the center of the wall, I paused again. There were only so many places someone could hide in here. There was an office that the coaches used, a weight room, a small room where the wrestlers practiced, and . . . the locker rooms.

A shadow moved in that direction.

I sprinted toward it.

As soon as I burst through the doorway, I froze. I sucked in a quick breath as the darkness surrounded me.

There were too many nooks and hideouts here. Rows of ugly blue lockers. Splintered wooden benches. A bathroom. Shower stalls. Any one of those places could be a trap. Someone could be waiting for me and I'd be walking right into his or her lair.

I'd always hated this place. Hated changing in front of other girls who'd turned their noses up at me. Hated wasting my time playing dodge ball and tinikling, a Filipino dance using bamboo sticks.

I hated being in here now just as much.

I inched forward, remaining on guard, anticipating the heart-pounding fear of someone jumping out in front of me.

What are you going to do when you catch him, Gabby? Tackle him?

I silenced my inner voice. But the truth was that I had no idea. At least maybe I'd catch a glimpse of him. That would be something.

I reached the end of the first row and peered around the bank of lockers.

Darkness stared back. I had no idea what I was plunging myself into. No idea what kind of danger awaited around the corner.

Was catching the person behind this really worth it? This could be the only way I found any answers. Maybe I was being foolhardy. But I didn't want to turn back now.

I edged toward the end of the row, reaching the second aisle where students used to change clothes. I was going to have to cross the great divide, losing the security of having something at my back.

I held my breath, counted to three, and then rushed into the abyss.

Just as I did, I saw the man. He darted from around the corner directly in front of me. I reached for him, my fingers connecting with his hat. I jerked it off and spotted a bald head. But not before he rammed himself into the lockers. The entire row crashed toward me.

I threw myself out of the way. As I did, the man darted into the darkness.

The lockers bounced off my head and shoulders and pinned my leg. My face knotted with discomfort, then pain. I was going to have a few bruises, but I'd take bruises over broken bones

My heart raced. The man was gone. There was no way to catch him now.

At least I'd caught a glimpse of him. I now knew there was a bald man involved in this somehow. That man was probably the same one I'd chased through the parking lot.

I pulled my foot out from under the wall that smelled like a shrine to dirty socks, grateful that a bench had prevented the lockers from trapping me completely. As I drug myself to my feet, I rubbed my shoulder and the back of my head. That could have been really ugly.

I did a mental check of myself, and I was pretty sure I was okay.

I hobbled out of the gym and down the hallway, wondering if my ego or leg hurt more. I kept my eyes open for anything else suspicious. I figured that guy was long gone now. He'd seen his opportunity to get away and done just that.

I had to make sure Bennie was okay. What if something happened to her? If the man had snatched her? What if I found her, just like I'd found Scarlet?

I reached the bathroom and stuck my head inside. "Bennie?"

Silence answered.

Strange.

I stepped inside, looked under each stall. There was no one in here. Where had she gone?

I went back into the hallway and called her name again.

Still no answer.

Just where was she? An even worse thought occurred—what if that man had grabbed her?

I quickened my steps, looking in every classroom, every office, anywhere I could think of.

She was nowhere.

The only place I hadn't checked was the gated corridors.

I hurried toward them. Sure enough, one of the padlocks was undone.

I slipped between the metal and the wall. The hallway appeared clear. But what lurked behind the closed doors, in the places unseen?

I ran into the first classroom.

No one was there.

I pushed into the next one. The shop classroom.

A figure there caught my eye. "Bennie?"

I rushed toward the woman in the corner. She stood, hunched as if in pain. "Gabby?"

"Bennie! What's going on? What happened?"

She shook her head, a dazed looked in her eyes. "I don't know. One minute I was looking for you, the next minute something hit my head. I woke up here."

"Are you okay?"

She nodded, still looking uncertain. "I think so."

As she pulled her hand away from her head, I saw the blood covering her fingers. Alarm spread through me. "We should get you to the hospital."

"I'll be fine. Really. It's just a little cut. No big deal."

I held on to her arm. "Regardless, this stakeout is over. Come on, let's get you home."

When we stepped into the parking lot, I spotted a car parked on the street in front of the school. It was a Mercedes.

Roberto had a Mercedes, I remembered. It was all he was keeping in the divorce.

I couldn't help but wonder if the car was his.

The next morning, Chad and I worked silently on a dining room. A hot water heater on the other side of an adjoining wall had burst and caused extensive water damage. No, this wasn't a crime scene but this job encompassed the new "restoration" portion of our business.

The two of us had barely said a word to each other since we started the job.

Last night, after I'd gotten Bennie home, I'd gone to the police station and dropped off the hat that I'd snatched from the intruder. Maybe there'd be some DNA on it. I'd take anything I could get, at this point.

Whenever I wasn't being haunted by what happened at the school, Chad's words had haunted me. The last thing I wanted was to let down people who were depending on me. I had responsibilities. That meant that if I went to Africa with Garrett, I'd essentially have to sign my portion of the business over to Chad. It just wouldn't be fair to him if I took a sabbatical. He had big visions for the company, and maybe I was still used to being a one-woman show.

After we'd torn out the floorboards and some drywall, we set up an air scrub to pull the moisture from the room. We also set up a portable heater to help dry the space out. Thankfully, none of the soffits had been damaged; otherwise, it would have been a huge job. We'd enclosed the room, just in case there was any dangerous mold. We tried to contain the damages to one area.

Our work here was done for a few days until the wood could dry out.

We slid through the plastic covering at the doorway, gave the homeowners an update, and then stepped outside. Chad started walking to his car without saying anything.

"Shouldn't we talk?" I called to him. The wind hit my face, bringing with it a smattering of icy rain.

He paused, his back toward me. I could see his muscles tighten and release. He wasn't happy with me.

"I almost think you want us to fail because you're too stubborn to give the business up," he muttered, still not facing me.

I blanched, feeling like I'd been slapped. "What are you talking about?"

"You ran off the two employees we had—"

"Honestly, Chad. That was hardly my fault. And could you please look at me so I don't have to talk to your backside?"

He turned, his jaw clenched. "Even still, you just don't seem committed. Getting a new business off the ground takes blood and sweat and effort. I don't see it in you."

"I was doing just fine on my own before we joined forces!" The words slipped out.

"Maybe people are right. Maybe friends shouldn't work together." His gaze was smoldering.

I blinked rapidly, hoping I'd misunderstood him. "What are you saying?"

"I'm saying that we should both take some time to cool down and really think about whether our goals match up, Gabby."

His words caused unease to wage in my heart. "What about our commitments for this week?"

"We still do them. But we reevaluate. Gabby, I have a wife, and soon I'm going to have a baby. I can't afford not to take this seriously anymore. I can't keep on living like I'm this single surfer without a care in the world."

I nodded, the weight on my shoulders pressing harder. "I understand."

"Please don't mention any of this to Sierra. I don't

want to stress her out, especially with her pregnancy and all."

"I won't."

He stared at me a moment before bobbing his head up and down slowly. "I'll see you at the next crime scene?"

"I'll be there."

But as soon as I climbed into the car, all I wanted to do was disappear and cry.

CHAPTER
TWENTY-EIGHT

THE SECOND CRIME scene was as painfully awkward as the first. Chad had never acted like this toward me before, and it made me feel terrible.

I had this crazy vision of one day having everything together. I guess life didn't work like that. At least *my* life didn't work like that. But, in truth, there was a restlessness stirring inside me.

Lord, what are you trying to tell me? Is all of this unease a sign? And why do I keep returning to the same areas of struggle? Is there any hope of me overcoming these strongholds? Is there any such thing as a life without struggle?

After Chad and I finished at the second scene, I realized I didn't have enough time to go back home. Instead, I headed toward the Cultural Arts Center. I needed to study my lines. Opening night was only three days away, and I still had a lot of work to do.

When I pulled up at the school, there were no other cars in the lot. On a whim, I decided to see if any doors were unlocked. To my surprise, the first one I tried opened.

"Hello?" I called.

There was no answer.

Just to be on the safe side, I checked the office. No Paulette.

Peter, the maintenance man, wasn't here either, nor was volunteer assistant Bennie.

I perched myself in a chair in the auditorium, trying not to stare at the stage too long. I had too many visions of both dead bodies and choking while performing—choking as an actress, not actually choking. Though that was horrifying in its own right. None of those thoughts were appealing. Instead, I read my lines, trying to ingrain them in my memory.

"Gabby?"

I looked back and nearly jumped out of my skin.

The Shining Twins stood there staring at me.

I pulled myself together, fanning my hot cheeks with the script. "You two scared me to death. You're both as quiet as . . ." *serial killers from a 1980 horror flick.* I didn't say that, though. I stuck with the well known instead. "Quiet as mice."

"We arrived early to work on the set," one of them said.

"How'd you get in? I thought the door was locked."

"No, the door by the old gymnasium is always unlocked. Other times, the maintenance man lets us in."

I stored away that information. "Oh, Peter?"

The one who always wore red nodded. "Yes, he's nice."

They glanced at each other and when they looked back, both had wrinkles on their forehead.

"We have something to tell you," Blue said.

"Yes, Karen?" I asked.

"I'm Sharen," she said.

"Sorry. Go ahead, Sharen."

"We feel like we should tell someone," Karen said. "But we don't know who, but you seem more down to earth than some of the others here."

I lowered my script. "You can tell me. What's going on?"

They glanced at each other. Finally, Sharen spoke. "We overheard Arie bragging to someone on her cellphone before practice on Saturday. She didn't know we were here."

"What did she say?"

"She told someone that she'd convinced Paulette to pay her off. Something about a contract."

I shifted, letting their words sink in. "Did you hear anything else?"

They both shook their heads.

"That was all we could make out," Karen said.

"Thanks for sharing," I told them, mulling over what they'd said.

I remembered that Arie had threatened to take her play elsewhere. Had Paulette paid her to ensure she wouldn't do that? I knew Paulette was desperate to keep this production going and prove to her father she could be someone. Would she take it that far?

I tried to put the idea out of my mind and study the script for the remaining forty-five minutes until practice started.

But I also stored away the information about the gym door. Was that how someone was getting in and out?

Twenty minutes later, Paulette walked into the auditorium and cast a faint smile my way. "Hey, Gabby."

"Paulette, I need to talk to you," I whispered.

"What's going on?" She set her purse to the floor and swiped a hair behind her ear.

"Did you pay off Arie?" I watched her face closely.

Part of her lip pulled down in a frown. "What . . . what do you mean?"

"I mean, did you give her hush money?"

Paulette looked away. "I simply decided to give her a bonus royalty for letting us use her work."

"Why would you do that?" I tried to keep my voice quiet but it rose in volume anyway.

"She was going to pull out! I had to do something." Panic built in Paulette's voice as well.

"She was under contract. She couldn't pull out!"

"She said she had ways out of it."

"Paulette, it's like you said when we were talking about Roberto at your house. If your dad knows anything, it's contracts. I'm sure whatever Arie signed was iron clad."

She sighed. "I just couldn't risk it. I figured if a little more cash would make her feel better, then it was worth it."

At the moment, I wanted to shake my friend. "How much did you pay her?"

"Ten thousand."

My mouth dropped open. "Are you crazy?"

She raised her tiny chin. "I did what I had to do."

"What about your bills? Aren't you overdue on some of them?"

She stared at me a moment, an unknown emotion flashing in her eyes. "How do you know that?"

"I went into your office looking for you. You left a 'Past Due' notice on your desk."

"My manager here quit. I've been trying to juggle a lot. I didn't know what else to do." She sat down hard and buried her face in her hands. "I'm going to blow this, aren't I?"

I sat down beside her, trying to put all my suspicions about Paulette out of my mind. I patted her back. "You're not going to blow this."

"Everything is falling apart, Gabby."

My phone buzzed. I wanted to ignore it, but I knew by the double vibration that I'd just gotten a text. Since Paulette's face was still buried and she couldn't see anything, I slowly pulled my phone from my back pocket. I glanced at the screen. The text was from Clarice.

"I'm still not speaking to you. But I can't resist solving a mystery either. Follow this link and watch the video. I knew I recognized that tune from somewhere."

I looked at Paulette. "I think we need to go to your office."

<hr>

"I don't understand," Paulette muttered.

She's said that ten times already. Her eyes were fixated on the computer screen.

I put my hand on her shoulder. "It's clear, isn't it? Arie stole this script from someone else." The wretchedly awful script. Why hadn't she at least picked a good one to rip off?

"How could she do this? Can things get any worse?"

I'd learned not to ask that question because things could always get worse. Silence fell between us, so I continued watching the video link that Clarice had sent me. It was for this web-based reality show that was looking for the next great American musical.

A woman named Harlot Jenkins had written a play called *The Specter* but had been voted out before getting to finals. The music and storyline weren't exactly like Arie's play, but they were close enough.

Harlot may not have been the brightest bulb in the socket because she'd actually posted the play online in hopes of selling it. As a result, anyone could read it or claim it as their own.

So, Arie had been that person. She'd seen the musical and, like a predator, she'd seized the opportunity. Maybe she'd even scoured local theaters, looking specifically for one with a history. Oceanside Middle and Rose Hines were perfect. That still wouldn't explain the murders, though.

"We've got to talk to Arie."

"No!" Paulette popped out of her seat. "Not now. Wait until after the play. Please."

"If Harlot Jenkins finds out we're doing her play, we're going to be in serious trouble." And by *we're*, I meant *Paulette*. I didn't say that, though.

"I can't believe she would do this to me." Paulette buried her face in her hands. "How could she?"

"I can't help but wonder if this all ties in with everything that's happened here with the musical, Paulette. I'm still trying to sort out the details, but there could be something there. I just need more time."

Paulette grabbed my arm, her gaze pleading. "We've got to get to practice, but promise me you won't say anything yet. Give me a day, at least, to figure out what to do."

I stared at my friend a moment before nodding. "Okay. One day. Then no promises after that."

Even as I said the words, I regretted them.

TWENTY-NINE

AS SOON AS the lights came up on Act Two, the auditorium went black.

Again.

Everyone screamed around me, a familiar sense of panic filling the air, but I didn't feel fear. No, I felt annoyed.

Why did this keep happening?

"Everyone, calm down!" I yelled from center stage. Though no one could see me, I put my hands on my hips and firmly planted my feet. It was a power stance, one I'd learned from Wonder Woman, for that matter.

Suddenly, it got quiet. I couldn't believe my order had worked.

"Everyone stay where you are. I'm going to get to the bottom of this, once and for all." I *sounded* brave, at least. I made my way off the stage, careful not to step off the edge. The last thing we needed was another casualty. The last thing I wanted was to be that casualty.

"Watch out for Rose," someone said.

I couldn't make out the voice, but I ignored it. It wasn't worth the energy.

"Where's the electrical panel?" I asked.

Just then, the lights flickered and finally turned on. A cool breeze swept over the stage at the same time.

Bennie screamed and grabbed Jerome's arm. "What was that?"

"The heat came on," I explained. "There's always a burst of cold air before it gets warm. Typical for old buildings like this."

Silence fell and I could feel everyone's gaze on me.

"The panel is in the office," Paulette said.

I nodded and made my way there. The longer this case went on, the more irritated I felt. Why did someone keep pushing this? What was his or her purpose?

I found the panel in the office and studied the breakers. After a few minutes, I shook my head. I had no idea what to make of all this.

I decided to swallow my pride. I called Braxton,

who had a background as an electrician's apprentice. He wasn't an expert, but he knew enough.

"What's going on, Gabby?" He sounded matter-of-fact without a hint of warmth in his voice.

That pretty much summed up our relationship.

"I have a question for you. The lights keep going out at the school where I'm working. Any idea why?"

"Bad wiring?"

"Why does it only happen every so often?"

"What are the common elements?

I ran through it in my mind. "I suppose it could be because of the spotlights."

"They suck up a ton of power. In an old building, that could very well be a factor. There you have it. There's your answer." He sounded like he just wanted to get off the phone.

"So, the power goes out because too much power is being used on one circuit," I clarified.

"Right, like when you vacuum and run the dishwasher at the same time."

"But to fix that, wouldn't you have to flip the breaker?"

"Makes sense to me, Brainiac." His voice dripped with derision.

"You really—" I stopped myself before my aggravation got the best of me.

"I really what?" He prodded.

"Nothing," I muttered. "Thanks for your help."

"I like the sound of that. Don't hear it enough."

"You've got to be kidding me. I spend half of my time correcting the things that you've done wrong, because you haven't bothered to ask how the job should be done in the first place! And I'm supposed to thank you constantly? You're out of your mind."

"You just have to accept that there are other ways of doing this."

"You were my employee!" I felt like steam was coming from my ears. "You know what? I need to go."

I hung up before he could say anything else. I took a few minutes to compose myself, sucking in deep breaths. I truly despised working with Braxton. I'd worked with worse before, but I'd also worked with much, much better.

I turned my thoughts back to the electricity.

So who had turned the power back on? Did that mean there was someone else in the building? If so, where were they now?

With baited breath, I stepped into the hallway. I paused and listened. Nothing.

Instinctively, I was drawn toward the hallway with the unlatched padlock. I'd only taken one step there when movement caught my eye. There was someone there!

I stepped into the shadows and braced myself.

The figure continued to walk toward me. I ran through mental scenarios of what I could do to defend myself and finally decided to remain hidden.

As the man came nearer, I got a better look at him and stepped out. "Roberto?"

He scowled at me. "You. What are you doing here?"

"I'm in the play," I reminded him.

He raised his chin. "That's right. How could I forget?"

I placed a hand on my hip, already riled up from talking to Braxton. "Is there a soccer game nearby tonight? I can't imagine why else you would be here."

"That's none of your business."

"Gabby?" a softer voice said behind me.

I turned and spotted Bennie walking down the hallway toward me.

"We're waiting for you and wanted to make sure you're okay," she said. "Paulette sent me to find you."

I nodded. "I was just on my way."

With one last glance at Roberto, I followed Bennie to practice. This case just got more interesting all the time.

CHAPTER
THIRTY

AFTER REHEARSAL, I walked into The Slug House with the rest of the gang, minus Arie, who'd been absent from practice because of some prior engagement. We sat at the corner table, gabbing as usual.

This was so not my scene, but I needed to be here in case anyone revealed a clue of some sort.

Everyone seemed content to talk about TV shows and football instead.

Arie showed up ten minutes into the gathering, offering no clue as to where she'd been. "How was practice?" She looked at me when she asked the question.

"It was fine," I answered.

"I hope you don't let me down." Her glare turned icy.

So many snide comments were on the tip of my tongue, but I kept them silent. Every time I held back my sarcasm, I counted it as a victory.

"Hey there, Love," a familiar voice said behind me.

I looked up and saw Garrett. He kissed my cheek and then slid in beside me. He'd called earlier and asked if he could come by. His timing was impeccable.

Everyone stared at Garrett, but people had a tendency to do that. It wasn't just his looks, it was the way he carried himself. He had a natural charisma that couldn't be learned.

I noticed Arie's gaze volleying between me and Garrett and her lips parting in what appeared to be surprise.

"Everyone, this is Garrett. Garrett, this is everyone."

"Pleasure to meet you, everyone," he quipped with a charming grin. He surveyed the establishment, which was anything but first class. "This is quite the place."

"It's so honky tonk, isn't it?" Arie said, all iciness gone from her voice. "But it's close, so that's why we choose it."

He glanced around. "It's got personality, at least."

"That's what I always say, too." Arie smiled.

I wanted to roll my eyes. I really did.

Garrett nodded toward my new "friends." "I've heard so much about all of you. I can't wait to see the play. In fact, I bought everyone at my company a ticket."

I felt the blood drain from my face. "You really did that?"

"Of course I did! We like to support our local community, not only communities around the world."

"You support communities around the world?" Bennie asked, her eyebrows jammed together in confusion.

"His company builds wells for impoverished areas globally," I responded.

"Global Coffee Initiative," Garrett finished like any good entrepreneur might. "Maybe you've heard of it?"

"I *love* GCI coffee. It's the *best*!" Arie gushed, suddenly coming alive. "It's your company? Like, *your company* your company?"

I glanced over at Jerome and saw him scowl. Did he like Arie? Why else would he act like this as Arie turned all her attention to Garrett? He almost looked jealous.

While Garrett charmed everyone, I noticed the bartender from the other night. When our eyes connected, recognition washed over him and he waved me over.

"Excuse me one minute," I whispered to Garrett.

I sauntered over to the bar. Just as before, the bartender was wiping a glass dry with a clean white towel.

"You were asking about that man the other night," he started, lowering his voice.

"That's right. The one I showed you a picture of."

"I thought you might want to know that someone else came in looking for the same person."

Things suddenly got interesting here. "Really? What did this person say?"

He gave me a look that reminded me of someone trying to scalp fake tickets to a major league baseball team. "What's it to you?"

He was asking for money?!? I couldn't believe it. Looking around me again, maybe I could. This place hadn't bothered to upgrade the tables or chairs in at least twenty years. That made me doubt the owners could afford to pay the employees that well either.

Sighing, I reached into my purse and pulled out a twenty.

He shrugged. "I don't remember that much after all."

"Are you serious?" I sighed again and pulled out another twenty. It was a near miracle I even had this much cash on hand. "Good enough?"

He pulled his chin up in a homeboy nod. "Now you're speaking my language. He said that the man owed him some money. I told him that I stayed out of other people's business and that I hadn't seen him in more than a week."

"And he said?"

The bartender shrugged. "Nothing. He grunted and left."

"Did he leave a phone number? A name?"

"Nope."

My lungs deflated. "What did this man look like?"

"He was on the smaller side with his hair cut so short he was almost bald."

"Military short?" I asked. We had so many military personnel in the area and that could describe any number of them.

"No, shorter. I think he was bald but his hair was just growing back. It had a red tint to it."

"Thin? Stocky?"

"Thin," the man answered. "He wore all black. I'll tell you what—the man may have been small, but I sure wouldn't want to get on his bad side. He screamed trouble, you know what I mean?"

I nodded. "Yeah, I do. Thanks for sharing."

I wished I could say the information was helpful, but the truth was that I still had no idea who he was.

Garrett insisted on driving me home. He said he'd send his assistant to pick up my car in the morning and have it back at my place before I even woke up. Normally, I would have told him no, but having some extra time to chat with Garrett had its appeal, for more than one reason.

"Did you find out anything interesting while I was gone from the table?" I asked, relishing the heat pouring from the vents at my feet. The car was nice and toasty, a pleasant contradiction to the frigid weather outside.

"I'm not sure. How do you define interesting?" His hands were draped casually across the steering wheel as we started down the road.

"Noteworthy."

"I'll give you my take on everyone there. How about that? I consider myself an excellent judge of character."

"Do you?"

"Well, I think you're great. That should say a lot." He cast me a glance out of the corner of his eye.

I almost blushed. "I won't hold that against you. Give me a rundown. What are your thoughts?"

"The Twins are creepy," he started.

"I know, right?"

"Jerome has shifty eyes," he said.

"I thought that same thing!"

"Speaking of which, he was texting someone as

we spoke. I just happened to look over his shoulder at one point."

"Did you see who it was?"

"I saw that the email address contained 'Entertainment Now.'"

"The news magazine?"

He nodded. "That's what it said."

I chewed on his words for a moment. "Well, that's interesting."

"Noteworthy, isn't it? It seems like lots of people would like to get some publicity for this musical."

"But of all of them, I didn't think he'd have any motivation to bring attention to the show. He didn't write it. He doesn't own the theater."

"But he's your costar. Besides, something about him just doesn't ring true. For instance, the scarf he's wearing. He kept tugging at it, like he wasn't comfortable with it around his neck. It made me wonder if he's trying to create a persona that doesn't feel natural."

"The need for attention seems like a bad reason to murder someone."

"What does a need for attention boil down to, though?"

I thought about it a moment. "Greed?"

"Exactly. The desire for more can cause people to do irrational things."

I supposed that Garrett, of all people, would know that. His money had made him a target before.

I shook my head. The answers seemed like they were so close, but I still needed more details before anything would fit together.

I turned my thoughts to another subject.

"What did you think about Arie?" I felt a touch of possessiveness toward Garrett as I asked the question, which was crazy.

"She was quite gregarious."

"Gregarious? That's one way to describe her. She was all about you." In fact, when I'd returned back to the booth, she'd been beside Garrett, her eyes wide as she leaned toward him.

Thankfully, Garrett had stood and let me slide into the booth, which then meant I was sitting smack dab between Arie and Garrett. It also meant that when Arie tried to have a conversation with Garrett, she had to talk loudly over my head.

I'd only lasted ten minutes after that and then I was ready to go. I'd had enough of that place, of those people, and the meaningless conversations.

"Are you jealous?" Garrett asked with a sparkle in his eyes.

"Jealous? Me? No. Besides, she's not your type . . . is she?"

He reached over and squeezed my hand. "No, you're my type."

This time, I definitely blushed. Garrett was a good guy. I could be very happy with him.

I knew at that moment what my answer would be to his proposition concerning Africa.

When we reached my apartment, I'd tell Garrett. I wanted to be able to look in his eyes, though, with nothing to distract us.

The problem came when we pulled up to my apartment. Police cars surrounded it.

I exchanged a worried glance with Garrett. "I wonder what's going on."

As soon as the car was in park, I rushed out the door and into my building. To my horror, I saw officers parading in and out of my apartment.

I sprinted up the steps, desperate to find out what was going on. I pushed my way toward Charlie. "What happened?"

She held up a paper. "We've got a search warrant for your residence."

"A SEARCH WARRANT? FOR WHAT?" I screeched.

"You're a suspect in the vandalisms at Oceanside Middle School," Charlie informed me.

"That's ludicrous. Why would I vandalize the school?" I jabbed my finger into my chest so hard I might have left a bruise.

"That's a good question." She raised an eyebrow, looking perfectly calm and in control.

Garrett joined me at the top of the stairs, concern etched into the wrinkles around his eyes. "What's going on?"

"They're searching my apartment. They can look all they want because I don't have anything to hide."

"We'll be the judges of that." Charlie motioned for the officers to continue.

I looked around and saw that everything in my house had been ruffled and tousled.

I closed my eyes, lifting up a prayer. I hadn't misunderstood. This was really happening.

"Detective," one of the officers muttered. Charlie joined him by my desk.

Nausea pooled in my stomach. Garrett put his arm around me and kissed the top of my head. "It's going to be okay."

"Nothing feels okay right now. I'm being set up, Garrett."

Charlie held something in the air as she approached me. "Articles on Rose? The woman who died at Oceanside? Could that be because you set up this elaborate scheme?"

"Again, why would I do that? Besides, the vandalisms started before I even knew this play was going on."

"The evidence is saying otherwise. You're under arrest."

My mouth dropped open. Certainly I hadn't heard her correctly. This couldn't be happening.

"Excuse me? You can't possibly have enough evidence to arrest me." My voice came out shriller than I anticipated.

"We can and we do. You have the right to remain silent, anything you say can and will be used against you . . ."

I glanced at Garrett and saw his eyes widen.

"You can't be serious." His hands went to his hips as he stepped closer.

"We're more than serious," Charlie said. "I'm really sorry, Gabby. But I warned you that I'd go wherever the evidence led."

My heart rate quickened. "How in the world did it lead to me?"

"We had two witnesses who spotted a woman with red, curly hair snooping around at the time of the vandalisms. A woman matching your description was also seen at a bar with the man who died. There was the dress and the paint cans in your trunk. We also found gasoline cans outside behind your trash."

"I would be smarter than that! If I did this, I'd know to hide the evidence. You know it's true!"

Charlie narrowed her eyes. "The fact that you've disappeared often right before the acts occurred doesn't help your case either."

"All of that is circumstantial!"

"It's corroborating," Charlie said. "Put it all together and it leads to you. I'm sorry, Gabby."

"Then I was set up. I didn't do this!" I insisted.

"We can't arrest you for the murders, Gabby, but we can take you in for the vandalisms."

"You're out of your mind!" A rock formed in my stomach and I thought I might be sick.

"We can make this hard and use handcuffs or you can cooperate," Charlie said.

I glanced at the officers behind me. They had the cuffs in their hands just waiting for word to use them. I couldn't let that happen.

I raised my hands in surrender. "I'll go. But you're making a mistake."

"I'll get my lawyer on the phone," Garrett insisted.

My head was spinning. How had this happened? And what in the world was I going to do about it?

I hadn't been able to stop pacing the holding cell where I was being kept. I'd been taken to the police precinct, photographed, fingerprinted and interrogated.

Sure enough, Garrett sent a lawyer who encouraged me to remain quiet. I personally thought being quiet made me look guilty. But I kept my mouth shut, the words "Anything you say can and will be used against you" swishing around in my mind.

When Charlie finally looked exhausted from interrogating me, I was moved to central booking. While a paramedic asked me a million and one questions, I had to also fill out paperwork for my arraignment.

Everything seemed like both a blur and a nightmare.

I was allowed to make a phone call. The fact that no one person stood out in my mind disturbed me and reminded me that I was alone.

No way would I call my dad.

Riley had his own life now.

Sierra had enough on her mind and I didn't want to stress her out.

Chad still wasn't speaking to me.

That meant Garrett was the natural choice. And he was a good choice. I knew he was worried.

I dialed his number and waited as he accepted my collect call. Immense comfort washed through me when I heard his voice. "How are you, Love?"

I glanced around the jail where I was being held and thought of a million sarcastic comments, but decided now wasn't the time to be a smart mouth. "It looks like I'm being charged with a Class 6 felony."

The sickly feeling in my gut sloshed with even more intensity.

"A felony? For vandalism?"

"Something about the damaged items costing more than $1000." All I could think about was the fact that I could be a felon.

Me.

The girl who loved justice. Who believed in the system. Who wanted to be a part of the system.

"I'm sorry, Gabby."

"Yeah, me too."

"I can't believe they would think you'd do this. Did you tell them about your theories? About Arie or Paulette?"

"I mentioned to Charlie that Arie may have plagiarized the musical. Who knows if she'll check her out or not? And Paulette? Even if I'd mentioned my theories about her, no one in their right mind would arrest or even question Paulette."

"Why not?"

"Look at her family. She comes from money and power." *Meanwhile, I'm motherless with a father who's had more DUIs than I can count and a brother who routinely dumpster dives.*

"Money and power aren't everything."

He just couldn't possibly understand. I shook my head. The odds had been stacked against me before and I'd pushed through. I had to do the same thing now. But I also couldn't deny the facts.

"I look guilty, Garrett. I had a key to the school, gasoline cans were found behind my apartment, research about Rose was in my desk, and black spray paint was in my trunk."

"All those things go back to Paulette, don't they? It was her car. She gave you the key. She knows where you live."

His words startled me. He was right, though.

"Nolen is one of the best attorneys I know. He'll look out for you, Gabby."

I leaned against the wall. "He seemed very bright."

My meeting with him was like a blur right now. He'd given me instructions and asked me questions. He was a stern looking man, and if Garrett thought he was smart then he probably was.

"What can I do for you?"

"Pray," I told him. "That's the most important thing."

"I've been praying for you, Gabby." His voice sounded husky.

The phone beeped, and I knew my time was running out. "I need to go. But thank you for believing in me, Garrett."

"Always, Gabby. Always."

When I got back to my cell, it was well past midnight and my body felt tired, but my brain was going at full speed.

Who would do this to me? Why?

All my thoughts of a future career in forensics went down the drain. Being arrested and charged—even if I were found innocent—could do terrible things to my reputation.

Down the cellblock I could hear shouts. Someone seemed to be tapping metal against metal. A prison guard walked the hall.

The dingy, yellowed lights flickered. There was a strange, nauseating stench of urine and body odor in the air. But none of that even began to match the trauma going on in my heart.

I'd felt fear before in my life. Quite often, truth be told. I'd been held captive by a serial killer in a shack in the middle of a swamp. I knew what it was like to be terrified.

But this time it was different. At the hands of a serial killer, I'd feared that my life would end. Here, I feared my life being destroyed while I still had to live it.

In the past, it had been the bad guys after me. People who seemed heartless. Who were selfish. Who wanted life their way without regard for others.

But now the justice system—the very one I believed in, that I wanted to be a part of—had falsely accused me. Betrayal and confusion collided with despair and disappointment in my heart.

Lord, sometimes I really feel like You don't like me. Like You're punishing me. Like You want to drive me away.

Otherwise, how can you explain the trials that keep lining up in my life? Why, Lord? Why?

I hung my head, desperately wishing I'd wake up and discover this was a nightmare. But that would be too easy. If life had taught me anything, it was that grace and mercy came moment by moment, but very rarely did they occur day by day.

In the meantime, I was on the docket to appear before a judge tomorrow. This judge would tell me if I could be released on bail or not.

Now, I had no choice but to wait.

"Bail is set at $20,000." The judge pounded his gavel on his desk.

My mouth gaped open.

"$20,000? It might as well be a million!" I screeched.

"That's enough," the judge warned. He was a fifty-something man who was practically bald, had small eyes, and hadn't cracked a smile since he walked into the room. Based solely on his sour expression, he probably liked to steal lollipops from kids off the street.

Nolen had his hand on my elbow, trying to lead me away. "Because of your history with the medical examiners officer, they think you're a higher risk. You know how to manipulate evidence and that's working against you right now," he whispered.

"But $20,000?" I wanted to cry. I'd been happy to simply pay my bills every month. A savings account wasn't even a possibility for me right now. I didn't own a house. My van was probably worth $10,000 at the most. My net worth was seriously lacking.

"We'll figure out something. In the meantime, just hold tight," Nolen said.

"I have no choice but to do that when I'm sitting in a prison cell." I wouldn't cry. I wouldn't give anyone that pleasure. But I had to fight my tears. This wasn't fair.

An officer led me toward my cell.

I got back to my new home and this time, instead of pacing like a lion, I sat on my bed in the corner with my knees pulled to my chest. I sat like that for what felt like hours. My thoughts turned and turned. My future flashed before my eyes. It was filled with iron bars and orange jumpsuits.

Lord, why?

I guess You know all about being falsely accused. You know about taking punishments You didn't deserve for crimes You didn't commit.

What had happened after Jesus died?

He was resurrected. With His resurrection came hope.

If I got out of here—and even if I didn't—I needed to bring back to life the parts of me that had been withering lately. Maybe this was my scared straight moment when I pulled myself together.

The guard appeared outside my cell. "You have a visitor."

"It's not visiting hours," I mumbled.

"Your lawyer."

Nolen hadn't told me he was coming by again. Maybe he'd discovered something new.

I didn't care. I just wanted to get out of this cell that confined me.

The guard led me down the cellblock, through some gates, down another hallway, and into a contact room—which meant no glass or wall, for that matter, would separate me from my visitor. This space was reserved for meetings with attorneys.

I stepped inside and stopped in my tracks.

Nolen wasn't standing there as I'd expected.

No, Riley was.

THIRTY-TWO

HE SMILED SOLEMNLY. "HEY, GABBY."

I could hardly walk and lost all my words. He met me, took my elbow as if he sensed my knees were weak, and helped me to my seat.

I still felt dazed as I stared across the table at him. Riley was here. Riley.

Finally, some of my senses returned. "What . . . are you doing here?"

"Sierra called and told me what was going on. I knew I had to drive down here and talk to you myself. I found out who your counsel was and asked if I could help. It's your decision, of course. But he agreed that I could meet with you."

"Wow. I had no idea."

"Are you holding up okay?" He leaned on his

elbows across the table, his blue eyes studying my face.

I think I nodded. "As well as can be expected. I could go to prison for one to five years, Riley."

He shook his head. "They won't put you away for that long. I don't think they're going to put you away at all. Even with this so called evidence they have, you have no prior record and you have no motive."

I just stared at Riley, still unable to believe my eyes. For the most part, he looked the same as when I last saw him. He may have buffed up more. His hair was no longer shaggy, but neat and trimmed. He wore a black leather jacket and jeans. Even from where he sat, I could smell his subtle aftershave. Something about the scent brought immense comfort to my heart.

I studied his face, looking for a sign of his injury. He still looked handsome. I didn't see any scars, any indentations on his skull from his surgery.

"You can't even tell by looking at me that they took a bullet out of my brain, can you?" Riley asked, reading my thoughts.

I shook my head, pulling my eyes away. "You're looking good. How are you feeling?"

He shrugged. "A little better every day. Got my license back. I'm trying to engage my brain more. I just took a part-time position in order to do that. Still doing therapy and working out. I'm getting back on track, Gabby."

"I'm really glad to hear that." My throat felt tight as I said the words.

"The job is pretty lame. Lots of paperwork. Too much time behind the desk. But it's a start."

"Starts are good." I attempted to smile.

Something seemed a little edgier about Riley, I realized. I couldn't put my finger on what. But something was different . . . and that wasn't necessarily a bad thing.

"I know we haven't been in touch a lot lately," he started, his voice softening. "My therapist really thinks it's important that I concentrate on one thing at a time. She said relationships after brain injuries hardly ever survive. That's why I want to do this right, Gabby. I want to fix myself before I involve anyone else."

Then who was the girl in the picture? If I asked Riley, he'd know I'd been snooping on him. But if I didn't ask . . . how would I ever know the answer?

"Getting you better is the most important thing here, Riley. I want that more than anything." As soon as my words left my lips, I knew they were true. As much as I desired for things to be back to the way they used to, there were bigger issues at stake. That didn't necessarily help me with decisions about my future, though.

He reached across the table, grabbed my hand, and squeezed. "Thank you, Gabby."

"Should you even be here? I mean, aren't you missing your therapy? Your new job?"

He shrugged. "I suppose. But first things first. I mean, you've been there for me on my darkest days. I couldn't not be here for you."

"That means a lot, Riley." My heart warmed at his words.

"I mean it. Almost dying can put life into perspective. I needed to take this trip. For me and you."

"Sierra and Chad are having a baby," I blurted.

"That's great."

Everyone's life is marching forward while I'm stepping in place. Maybe even backward. Best-case scenario is that I'm moving parallel. What should I do?

I kept those thoughts silent.

"Time's up!" the guard said.

Riley pulled back and straightened. "I'm going to do whatever I can to help you, Gabby."

"Thanks, Riley."

As I was led back to my cell, all I could think was: It's so hard to move forward when your past constantly comes back to haunt you.

I need a resurrection, Lord.

I couldn't bring myself to call Paulette and tell her that I'd been arrested. I was still too unsettled about her role in all of this. But I had to tell someone that I wouldn't make it to play practice tonight.

That's why I called Mrs. Baker.

She answered on the first ring.

"Mrs. Baker, it's Gabby."

"Hey, Gabby. What's wrong?"

I decided not to hold back. "The police think I vandalized the school. I'm in jail."

She gasped. "What?"

"Needless to say, I won't be making it to practice tonight." The words sounded so lame. I might as well have told her I'd been whisked off to Oz.

"Oh, Gabby. You would never do something like that."

Hearing her total faith in me made me feel somewhat better. At least someone believed in me. "Thanks, Mrs. Baker. The police feel differently, however."

"I'm not usually one to encourage people to give up. But I'm wondering if this whole play is a bad idea. So many things have gone wrong, and I'm not just talking about the vandalisms or Scarlet's death. The script and music . . . well, they're not strong. But Paulette is banking so much on this."

I frowned at the mention of Paulette. "I know."

"And without you for a lead . . ."

"Bennie may be able to fill in for me. I've heard her singing and she has a lovely voice."

"I'll keep that in mind. Gabby, I think you should know that we found out how that man in the orchestra pit died."

I held my breath. "Okay."

"It was carbon monoxide poisoning."

"Really?" I tried to put that together in my head, to conjure a theory that made sense. I came up empty.

"Paulette also told me today that the play may have to be delayed."

"Why?"

"The police are questioning Arie about stealing someone else's intellectual property. Apparently, she may have plagiarized *The Music of the Specter*."

Charlie had checked out my story! Maybe there was hope. "I see."

"It's a mess, Gabby. I don't know what's going to happen. Arie, Paulette, and I are going to meet tonight to discuss things."

I realized my talk time allocation was running out. "And one more thing, Mrs. Baker. Could we keep this between us? Could you just tell people I had an emergency? I need to buy myself some time."

"I will, Gabby. For as long as I can. But I won't lie."

"I'd never ask you to do that. Thank you, Mrs. Baker."

"You're welcome. And Gabby? I know this probably sounds strange. But everything does happen for a purpose. It may be hard to see, but there's a blessing in this somewhere. Just keep your eyes open for it."

I'd been arrested. Riley had popped back into my life at either the best or worst time possible—I still wasn't sure which. My business relationship with Chad was quickly disintegrating.

Here I am again, Lord. At the end of my rope. What possible purpose could all of this have?

Three hours later, I had another visitor. A real one, this time. Not a lawyer.

Garrett.

Something clashed in my heart when I spotted him on the other side of the glass. There was so much I liked about him. Yet the fact remained that he wasn't Riley. The fact also remained that I needed to move on.

Just because Riley had visited me didn't mean things were rosy for our future. There may not be any "our" future for the two of us. I had to get out of the state of limbo.

Why was life so complicated?

I picked up a phone so I could hear Garrett's voice.

"I came as soon as I could," he started. "I missed the first set of visiting hours."

"I'm still not sure about all their rules here. It's been a blur."

"I know. What did the judge say?"

I filled him in, ending with, "It looks like I'll be stuck here for a while. I don't even have any assets to liquidate. There's no way I'm getting that money."

"Let me help, Gabby." Garrett's eyes were intense, serious.

"I couldn't do that."

"You know how fond I am of you, Gabby. I couldn't possibly sit on my hands right now and do nothing."

"That's a lot of money. Like, a lot of money."

"It is a good chunk of cash. But I don't want you to have to stay here for a moment longer than neces-sary. This is no place for someone like you."

I wanted to get out of here more than anything. But there was also something holding me back from accepting his offer. Pride maybe? Independence? What would accepting a gift like this mean in the long run?

"I don't know what to say."

"Just a 'thank you' would suffice. But it's going to

take some time to get that money. I may not be able to get you out until tomorrow."

I thought about it a moment. My chances of tracking down the real person responsible for this crime were greater if I wasn't in jail. I had to swallow some pride, let people help—it wasn't something I was good at doing.

I nodded. "I'll repay you, Garrett."

"I'm not worried about it."

And I knew he wasn't. $20,000 to a millionaire wasn't the same as $20,000 to a person who was scraping by month to month. But his offer was still generous and somehow made me feel burdened at the same time.

However, I was in no position to be picky right now.

"Thank you. This means a lot to me."

"What can I say? You mean a lot to me."

My cheeks warmed. "Thanks, Garrett. You mean a lot to me also."

CHAPTER
THIRTY-THREE

SPENDING the night in jail was one of the worst experiences of my life.

A blessing? Why would Mrs. Baker ever think this could be a blessing? I had no idea. Because I just felt like I'd been wrongly accused. I felt helpless.

All I could do was lie on my uncomfortable bed with bars that dug into my back, thinking through all my possible suspects. Their faces circled around and around in my mind, but when the spinning stopped, no one person remained at the forefront.

Arie. She'd stolen someone's play, had her sights on being the lead, and had done everything she could to drum up press attention for herself. She often wandered away from the stage during practice, which would give her means and opportunity.

Paulette's image came to mind next. But why

would she frame me? It made no sense. Of course, she'd hired me, knowing I'd be at the old school, knowing I'd be sneaking around. The evidence had been found in her car, which she had the key to. But I still had no clue as to what her motive might be.

Then there was Roberto. I could see how he might want to ruin Paulette's life. But mine? Why? Unless he'd originally wanted to hurt Paulette but then decided that was a mistake.

Donabell's husband? I really couldn't see him as the guilty party here. He seemed like the type who'd sit back and watch the property fail and then gloat.

I stared at the water stain on the ceiling and tried to keep my thoughts focused. When I got out of here, I needed to talk to Marjorie, Scarlet's roommate again, I decided. She'd overheard a fight with Scarlet and an unknown person. I was certain the answers were somewhere in those details . . . if Marjorie could remember them.

My mind also bounced to Chad. Again, I'd left him shorthanded. It wasn't entirely my doing or my choice at the moment, but still—it had happened.

Was he right? Should we just go our separate ways? Was working together a bad idea?

I sighed and stared at the ceiling.

Finally, my thoughts came to Riley and Garrett. I couldn't believe Riley had visited me. I knew not to read too much into it. The gesture had been one of friendship. Besides, there was still that woman from the pictures. Who was she?

I'd been on the verge of telling Garrett about my decision concerning Africa. But now everything felt like it had been turned upside down.

I closed my eyes. The jail I was in right now was creating a different kind of prison in my mind. It was a mental cell where I couldn't escape my thoughts.

That seemed like the cruelest punishment of all.

The next morning, I was released on bail and given a strict set of rules that included checking in at appointed times, not going within twenty feet of the Cultural Arts Center again, and not engaging in any criminal activities.

Garrett met me with a bag of clothes. I could have worn the ones I was arrested in, but a clean outfit sounded nice. I was pleasantly surprised to see that Garrett had bought me a T-shirt that said, "Survivor," some expensive-looking jeans, and flip-flops made from a yoga mat. Yes, I loved flip-flops whatever the season. He already knew me well because this was my uniform, summer or winter. I changed and escaped from the confines of the jail like a bird flying from a cage.

It had never felt so good to be free.

"I wish I could stay with you, but I've got a board meeting coming up that I can't miss," Garrett said as we climbed into his car.

"Please don't apologize. You've already gone above and beyond. Just take me to my apartment. That will be fine."

"I hate to leave you in a time like this." He sounded so formal, yet endearing all the same.

"Don't worry. I have a plan for my day."

"Why do I have a feeling this plan somehow involves your arrest?" He glanced my way, his eyebrows raised.

"Maybe it's better if you don't know. Then you'll be telling the truth if the police ask you questions."

"Very well then. Just do me a favor and stay safe."

I nodded. "I will."

My cell phone rang, and I saw Paulette's number pop up. I asked Garrett to excuse me for a minute. I hadn't talked to Paulette since I'd been arrested and charged. I wasn't sure how this conversation would go.

"Hey, Paulette. I've been meaning to call you."

"How could you?" Her soft voice cracked.

Tension pulled across my chest. She'd obviously heard about what happened. I knew she would eventually. "What?"

"You're the only person who's never used me.

And now you took advantage of me, too. I thought I could trust you, Gabby."

"Certainly you don't believe that I'm behind any of the vandalisms, Paulette. You know I'd never do that to you. I'm being set up."

"I gave you a key."

"Who else did you give keys to? Several other people, Paulette."

"Just Mrs. Baker. And Peter. And Bennie."

"Bennie has a key?" Hadn't she told me she didn't *want* a key? Had Paulette given her one anyway?

"It doesn't matter."

"Of course it does!" People didn't lie for no reason.

"Paulette—"

"Please don't say anything else." Ice-cold silence stretched for a moment. "This just goes to prove that I have no one in my life to depend on."

She hung up.

I leaned back in the seat, feeling numb. I'd let down the one person who had me on a pedestal—not that I wanted to be there. But I did hate letting down people who looked up to me. It was an awful feeling that made my spirit plummet.

Garrett squeezed my knee. "You okay?"

I nodded, even though I felt anything but okay. "I'll be fine."

"Relationships are messy sometimes, aren't they?"

"Yeah, you could say that."

We pulled up to my apartment building. I started to get out, but he pulled me back. "We're going to get through this, Gabby."

His words warmed me. He'd said "we," which meant he was sticking with me, even through the thick and thin. "That means a lot, Garrett. Thank you."

He leaned forward and planted a slow kiss on my lips, one that made my heart beat double time. "By the way, I thought you might want to see this."

He reached into the back seat and handed me a magazine. *Entertainment Now.*

I stared at Angelina Jolie on the cover. "Is there an article in here pertaining to the play?"

"All about Arie and her supposed comeback." His eyes sparkled.

"You're the best. Thank you!" I kissed him one more time.

"I'll call you later, okay?"

"Sounds great."

I slammed the door and ran to my apartment building, my mind still racing. I didn't have much time to find the real culprit. I had to get busy.

As soon as I stepped foot into the building, Chad and Sierra's door flew open. My heart sunk when Chad stepped out. I'd really been hoping for Sierra.

I braced myself for his reaction. Accusation? Disappointment? Righteous indignation?

Instead, he shoved his hands into his pockets and offered a compassionate smile. "I heard what happened. How are you?"

I swallowed hard. "Feeling a little desperate right now."

He bobbed his head up and down. "Look, don't worry about the jobs. I'll handle them. Besides, I talked Braxton into coming back to work for a few days, at least."

Until I returned, I thought to myself. I kept silent, though. "I really appreciate that, Chad."

"You just take care of yourself."

I wanted to believe his words were sincere, but I just wasn't sure. Part of me couldn't help but think he was faulting me for the same things he'd criticized me for in our earlier conversation.

But right now, I just didn't have time to think about it.

"Oh, and one more thing, Gabby."

I turned on my heel and waited for him to continue.

"I thought you should know that Riley's up in his apartment."

My pulse quickened, though I willed it to slow

down. A tremble of anticipation rushed through me. "Thanks, Chad."

I hurried upstairs, determined to keep my thoughts in check.

At the top landing, I stared at Riley's door. No, I wouldn't go there. I had to keep myself guarded, to protect my heart. That meant I needed to give myself some boundaries.

I rushed into my apartment and froze. Everything was out of place. My books were off the shelf, pictures were turned over, couch cushions were on the floor.

I'd deal with all of this later. Right now, I hopped in the shower, got dressed, made a few phone calls, and started downstairs. I had a long and urgent to-do list.

When I was out the front door, I stopped in my tracks.

My car.

It was still at Oceanside Middle, I realized. Garrett was supposed to send his assistant to pick it up and deliver it. With everything that happened, he must have forgotten. I couldn't blame him.

I threw my head back, realizing this would put a serious crimp in my plans.

The door opened behind me. I twirled around and spotted Riley there. My throat went dry.

"Gabby. I was hoping to catch you. I heard your

door open and you were outside before I could even call for you."

I wiped my hands on my jeans, noticing I was trembling for some reason. "You're still here."

"I told you I was going to help, right?"

My heart warmed. "You did."

"Where you headed?"

"Nowhere. I forgot my car is not here at the moment."

"How about if I drive you?" He tossed his keys in the air.

"Really?"

He smiled. "Yeah, really. Come on. It will be just like old times."

"Thanks for inviting me over," I told Mrs. Baker as she answered the door.

She looked different wearing a sweatshirt and a T-shirt, with her hair pulled into a ponytail. She somehow seemed more human and approachable, less like the woman I'd put on a pedestal.

"I'm glad you could come, Gabby and . . . ." Her gaze traveled beyond me, and confusion spread across her face.

"This is Riley," I explained. It felt surreal to say the words. Like old times. Like something I'd dreamed of happening but that I never thought actually would.

On the entire ride here, I'd updated him on the case. I told him what I'd learned and who my suspects were—everything.

Everything about the play, at least.

I told him nothing about Garrett or Africa or possibly giving up crime scene cleaning.

Mrs. Baker nodded his way. "Nice to meet you."

"You, too."

We stepped inside and out of the cold.

"I know you can't set foot on the property of the Cultural Arts Center, so I thought we could talk here," Mrs. Baker started.

"This has all been like a nightmare."

"I can only imagine. Of course, more than talking about the play, I just wanted to talk to you. Amos is at work and Larissa is working on her homework."

"No school?" I started to slip off my coat when Riley grasped the shoulders and helped tug it off. When our hands touched, a spark raced through me.

I couldn't let myself go to that emotional place. I couldn't get hurt again. But my body seemed to have a mind of its own.

"I homeschool." She pointed to the dining room table. "Please, have a seat."

We lowered ourselves into the wooden chairs there.

"I thought you should know, before we talk too much about other things, that we met to discuss the future of the *The Specter* last night."

"And?" I questioned.

"Arie has agreed to share the credit for the play with Harlot Jenkins. She never conceded to plagiarism, but she thinks she may have inadvertently heard the idea and taken it as her own."

"She said that?"

Mrs. Baker nodded. "She did. Who knows what the truth is?"

"I bet someone paid Harlot off."

"Why would you say that?" Riley asked, looking all lawyer-like with those perceptive eyes and the rigid set of his shoulders.

I frowned. "Paulette apparently paid off Arie to let us keep the play in the first place."

Mrs. Baker's eyes widened. "She didn't."

I nodded. "She did."

"This is all a mess."

I shifted in my seat. "What did you all decide last night?"

"The show will go on. Despite everything that's happened, we've put too much work into this to quit now. We practiced, and Arie stepped into your role, Gabby."

"Arie? Really?" It didn't really surprise me. The

woman was conniving and would do whatever it took to get ahead.

"It's true. It made the most sense. If Bennie took your role, then we'd have no one to replace her." She let out another sigh. "I was so excited to work with three of my former students. Now all of this."

My gaze locked on hers. "Three?"

She nodded. "You, Paulette, and Bennie."

"Bennie is a former student?" Could that be right?

Mrs. Baker nodded. "I thought you knew."

"You quit when Larissa was born."

"I did, but I came back and helped with plays up until the time the school closed. Bennie was in my last production. Of course, her name wasn't Bennie then. It was Bonnie Pratt. Poor girl went through a lot."

"Like what?"

"Her parents went to jail. She was in foster care. But she really turned her life around. Even back in middle school she got involved with the school newspaper and drama. Those creative outlets were better than therapy for her. She's continued to channel all of her hardships into making herself a better person."

That seemed a good reminder that I needed to do the same. But with Riley so close, it was hard. Strangely enough, when I was with Garrett, I felt like

I was being unfaithful to Riley. But now that I was with Riley, I felt like I was cheating on Garrett.

My thoughts drifted back to Bennie. Was the fact that she used to go to Oceanside somehow related to this case? I didn't see how. Sure, she apparently had a key to the building now. But back when the vandalisms started, she wouldn't have had a way to get into the building. Besides, she always seemed so kind.

Mrs. Baker sighed and looked at me for a moment, worry across her face. "Who would do this?"

"Someone desperate to cover up their own crimes?"

"I suppose. I know we need to rehearse, but would you mind telling me about the evidence against you?" Mrs. Baker asked. "Maybe I can help fill in some of the blanks."

A carafe of coffee stood in the middle of the table, and Mrs. Baker began pouring cups for us as I ran through what I knew.

Mrs. Baker shook her head. "Someone actually said they saw you near the vandalisms?"

I nodded. "Someone with curly red hair. Not too many cast members fit that description except me."

"Did you say red hair?"

We all turned our heads to the soft, new voice. It was Larissa. I hadn't even heard her approach.

"You weren't eavesdropping, were you, Honey?" Mrs. Baker asked. "You know that's not polite."

"I just happened to overhear when I was walking past," Larissa said.

"Is there a reason why you're asking?" I chimed in.

She nodded. "I found a red wig the other day. I didn't think much of it, like maybe it was one of the costumes. But what if it wasn't?"

My heart rate increased. "Where?"

"In the maintenance closet."

THIRTY-FOUR

"WHAT IN THE world were you doing in the maintenance closet?" Mrs. Baker asked.

Larissa shrugged, tugging at one of her curls. "I got bored during rehearsal and started walking around. The door was open, so I peeked inside. I saw the wig."

Mrs. Baker shook her head. "I asked you to stay in the auditorium, young lady."

Larissa frowned.

I had other things on my mind, things like proving my innocence. "Did you see anyone else around while the rest of us were in practice?"

She reached into her pocket and pulled out something. "I found this."

My eyes widened. It was a hundred dollar bill. "Wow."

"It was in the hallway."

"Larissa! You can't keep that," her mom said.

She hung her head. "I know. I just kept dreaming about what I'd spend it on."

One hundred dollars that someone had dropped. Where did someone get that money? From doing something illegal—drugs maybe? Stealing items and selling them? I didn't know.

"Mrs. Baker, did Paulette leave your sight on the night when the lights went out and we found the dead body in the orchestra pit?"

Mrs. Baker thought a moment before shaking her head. "No, she was with me the whole time. Why?"

"I noticed she had some dirt on her cheek."

"I remember she dropped one of her rings behind a chair in the choir room. I imagine it was expensive. She must have gotten the smudge when she retrieved it." She paused. "You think Paulette is guilty of murder?"

"Under normal circumstances—no. But she's taking some prescription drugs and she's been drinking. All those things together can be dangerous. Plus, she's desperate for this to succeed."

"Why would she kill people then? How would that help her chances?"

I shook my head. "Maybe those people got in her way somehow. Maybe she thought bad publicity was good publicity. I don't know. But she has possible motive, means, and opportunity."

My eyes locked with Mrs. Baker's. We were thinking the exact same thing. Paulette very well could be guilty.

I had meetings lined up for the rest of the day essentially.

Next, I was meeting Bennie for lunch. She was my inside connection to the cast. Since I couldn't be at practice tonight, I had to use whatever resources I could.

Riley stayed in the car to return some phone calls. His phone had been buzzing all day. Which made me wonder what was going on: His new job? His therapist? His girlfriend?

The last thought made my stomach knot up, made me feel off balance.

Focus, Gabby. Focus.

Thinking about the investigation seemed a lot safer, for my heart, at least.

Which brought me back to my meeting with Bennie.

Of all the people who were associated with the play, the only two I really put any faith in were Mrs. Baker and Bennie. Bennie had been with me and been hit on the head that night we staked out the school. She couldn't have done that to herself, which led me to believe that she was on my side. Or, at least that she was innocent.

We met at the same seafood restaurant Garrett had taken me to last week. Bennie only lived a few blocks away and, honestly, it was the only restaurant I could think of in this direction. However, without Garrett by my side, seating took much longer and my wallet ached when I realized what the bill would be.

I'd just slid into a booth—not by the water this time—when Bennie walked in. I waved her over.

"What's going on?" she asked, depositing her purse in the corner.

"Thanks for coming. I need your help."

"There were all kinds of rumors floating around last night. Someone even had the gall to say you were arrested for the vandalisms at the theater. Can you believe that?" She let out a nervous laugh.

I licked my lips. "It's a really long story. But I have to admit right now that I am desperately trying to find the person who's responsible."

Her face paled. "That means you were arrested."

"Bennie, just try to stay focused right now. I didn't do anything. Besides, we're in a public place. Even if I were guilty, you'd be completely safe right now."

Her shoulders relaxed some. "Okay. What can I do?"

"Tell me about the scuttlebutt behind stage. Is there anyone who's been acting strangely? Specifically about Scarlet?"

She rubbed her throat. I'd obviously made her uncomfortable, which I hated to do. But time wasn't on my side right now.

Bennie had opened her mouth to speak when the waitress appeared. Servers had a knack for showing up at the worst possible times.

I ordered some soup, and Bennie perused the menu for what felt like hours before finally deciding on just French fries and a soda.

Finally, the waitress walked away and Bennie turned back to me. "I don't know, Gabby. Actors are kind of weird sometimes, so it's hard to tell what's normal and what's not."

"Anything would help."

She let out a long breath. "Well, Jerome is always watching people. I don't know why. Maybe he wants to be a character actor? Who knows?"

"Go on."

"Arie thinks she's hot stuff. She's desperate to gain some of her fame back. I have a feeling that she only befriends people if they can do something for her. I don't know if she has a sincere bone in her body."

I'd thought the same thing before. "I can see that."

"I saw her after practice one day. She was talking to Roberto."

"You know Roberto?"

Bennie nodded. "I've seen him around the school a couple of times."

I tilted my head. "Really?"

"Sure. He stops by during the day on occasion to talk with Paulette."

I stored that information away for a rainy day. Why would she be talking to Roberto? I really didn't trust the man.

"This is all very helpful. Is there anything else you can think of? Anyone else?"

"The Shining Twins, as I call them."

"I thought the same thing!"

Bennie smiled. "Something seems off about them, which doesn't make them guilty necessarily. But they do know the backstage better than anyone else, you know?"

I nodded. "I do."

"I can also say that Scarlet and Arie both had strong opinions and they weren't afraid to voice them. They'd had some disagreements about the direction of the play. I overheard Arie saying there was someone else she knew who'd easily fit into the lead role if Scarlet didn't straighten up."

Sure, that person had been Arie herself. She'd wanted to star in the play.

Had they fought over Roberto? What was his connection exactly? He was fast enough and strong enough to be behind the murders.

"Did Arie say anything last night at practice when I didn't show up?" I asked.

"She was gloating because she got to fill in as lead."

So what if Arie blamed everything on me, just so she could be the star of the play? It was a decent theory. But I had no idea how I would prove it.

I finished my lunch with Bennie and gave Riley directions to Peter's place. I was meeting with him before I met with Marjorie. My day was packed, but I didn't have any time to waste. The idea of spending more time in jail had spurred me into action.

As we drove, my mind turned everything over at such a fast pace that a headache began to develop.

"What are you thinking?" Riley asked.

I shook my head. "I'm thinking that everyone could be guilty, but everyone also had a reason why they couldn't have done it."

"What's your gut tell you?"

I drew in a long breath. "That's the thing. My gut

isn't giving me any good indications as to who might be guilty here. No one person stands out. Just when I think I know who's responsible, my mind jerks to someone else."

"Why are you doubting yourself?"

"I'm not. I'm just being honest."

"It sounds like you're questioning your instincts."

I shrugged. "Maybe I am. I guess I'm just saying that this whole case started out seeming relatively simple. I was going to look into people's backgrounds, keep an eye on things behind stage, listen to the scuttlebutt around the cast and crew. Now two people are dead, and I was accused of a crime I didn't commit. If I'm not careful, they'll charge me with the murders, too."

Riley squeezed my shoulder. "Just take some deep breaths. It will come together. What connects all of this? The victim? The play?"

"The school," I muttered. "The school is what all of this has in common."

"Why would two people be killed over an old building?"

"Maybe someone wants the property for themselves. Someone wants the building shut down. Maybe something is going on there that I'm clueless about."

"What could be going on at the school?"

"Drug deals?"

"Couldn't the dealers just move the location? That would be easier than killing people."

"Maybe they're hiding something there."

"Why not just move it?"

I rubbed my temples. "See? This is complicated."

"Who are we going to talk to now?" he asked.

I explained who Peter was.

"Let's see what he has to say then."

"PETER, I'm Gabby St. Claire. I met with you last week about your sister Rose." I waited on the stoop outside his apartment door, realizing this was a cold call and that it might not be productive.

"Of course. Of course." His gaze traveled to Riley.

"And this is my friend Riley."

The two shook hands, and Riley muttered something about it being nice to meet him.

"My mind isn't as good as I thought it was. I thought for certain the young man with you last time had a British accent."

Great. He realized Riley wasn't Garrett. Riley didn't seem bothered, though, and instead he smiled affably.

"What can I do for you, Gabby?" Peter asked. He invited us in out of the cold, and we sat on the couch of his neat little apartment. He perched across from us, his eyes darting back and forth between Riley and me.

"Peter, someone found a red wig in the maintenance closet," I started. "Do you know anything about that?"

He was already nodding. "Sure do. I found it stuffed in a locker. I didn't know what to do with it exactly, so I stored it in the closet and decided to wait until someone reported they'd lost it. Is that a problem?"

"No, not at all. When did you find it?"

He shrugged. "Memory's not that great, but I think it was just a couple of days ago."

"Is there anything else strange you've seen at the school, Peter?"

He sucked in a long breath, his gaze nervously darting about. "Well, I did find some money the other day. I turned it in to that temporary manager lady."

"Paulette?" I questioned.

"No, the other one. Bennie."

"How much did you find?" Riley asked.

"It was a Benjamin Franklin."

Another $100 bill? Who had been losing that amount of money without reporting it? Something fishy was going on.

"One more question, Peter. The gym door. Why do you keep leaving it ajar at night?"

He cringed. "What are you talking about?"

I leaned closer. "Someone keeps leaving doors to the Cultural Arts Center unlocked. Why don't you tell me why you're doing that?"

His hands trembled. "I don't know what you're—"

"Peter, there are a lot of lives hanging in the balance right now. The longer you wait to tell me what's going on, the more trouble you could be in."

He let out a moan. "I knew it was just a matter of time before someone discovered me. I didn't mean any harm."

"Who asked you to leave the door open?"

He shook his head, hanging it down in shame. "You've got to believe me. I have no idea. I got a note with some money. The janitor job doesn't pay that much. It seemed so harmless."

"Then Scarlet died."

"I got another note saying that if I didn't keep leaving the door open they'd report me. Then I'd be out of their hush money and out of a job. Without a job, I'll be out on the streets. I just couldn't face that possibility. I've been there before. I couldn't go back."

I stared at him, trying to gauge the sincerity of his words. His shoulders drooped and his eyes were downcast, as if the guilt were eating him alive.

I decided I believed him. He was desperate. Guilty perhaps, in his own way, but not guilty of murder or vandalisms.

"Is there anything else you can think of?"

"I found some paper." He wandered into his apartment and returned again with something in hand.

"May I?" I reached for it.

He nodded.

I took it from him and studied it. This was the same paper Bennie was using for her scrapbook. I didn't see how this was connected. "Where was this?"

"Outside the gym door one morning."

What? How did that tie in to this? Or did it?

I didn't know, but I had to find out the answers soon.

"I miss this," Riley said as we walked back to his car. With one finger, he pointed back and forth between him and me.

I smiled. "Me too."

He let out a long sigh. "Sometimes it doesn't feel like things are ever going to return to normal, does it?"

I knew exactly what he meant. "No, I guess life is

always about change. Adapt or die. Isn't that what the saying is?"

Just then, my phone chirped. I saw Garrett's number on the screen. "Can you excuse me for a minute?"

"Of course."

I stepped away and answered. "Hey there."

"How's it going, Gabby? I wanted to check on you. Can I swing by tonight?"

I thought of Riley and something twisted in my stomach. He was taken now, I reminded myself. And so was I, I supposed. "Of course. I'd love to see you."

"Great. I'll come by after work."

"Call first, okay? I'm out doing some work. I want to make sure I'm there."

"Of course."

I walked back to the car and smiled at Riley.

"Everything okay?" he asked.

I nodded. "It is. I just have one more person I need to speak with. You want to come along or drop me off at the car?"

"I'm with you, Gabby. All the way."

***

"Hello again," Marjorie said.

Her words sounded dull and monotone, just as

they had before. Was this grief or was this the way she always was?

"Thanks for taking time out of your schedule." I waited for her to invite us inside, but she never did so I remained in the hallway. "This is my friend, Riley."

They nodded at each other.

"I don't have much time between classes. But you said it was urgent. What's going on?" She crossed her arms, apparently content to have this conversation in the hall.

That was fine. I'd just get straight to the point. "Things are getting complicated. I just need to ask you—did you remember anything else strange about Scarlet's final days? Anything at all?"

She stared at me a moment, looking a little dumbfounded. "Not really. Why?"

"It's of the utmost importance. Someone is on the verge of being . . . wrongfully accused in her death. I need to find the real culprit."

"Wrongfully accused? How do you know that? Doesn't everyone claim to be innocent?"

"Well, yes. But I know this for a fact."

She continued to stare. "How?"

She wasn't going to let this drop, was she? "Just trust me."

"Why should I trust you? I don't know you."

I let out a sigh. "This person has actually been

accused of vandalizing the theater, but they're trying to nail her for Scarlet's death, too. That person is me."

Her eyes widened.

"I knew it was better if I didn't tell you."

"Maybe you shouldn't be here." She took a step back.

"I assure you that I didn't kill anyone."

"Like I said, every killer says that."

I sighed again. "But I mean it. I was set up. I have to find the real killer before I go to prison."

"I don't know what you want from me, then."

"I need information. I need to know who didn't like her, who she didn't like, who broke up with her."

"It wasn't me," a deeper voice said.

The door opened farther and I spotted a man there. A Latino man wearing a soccer jersey. My lips parted. "You're not Roberto."

"Who's Roberto?" he asked.

"Scarlet's boyfriend."

"I was Scarlet's boyfriend." He thumped his chest.

"But you're not Roberto." Okay, I was a little dense sometimes, but I'd really thought Scarlet and Roberto were together. This didn't fit the mental image I'd developed. It didn't fit my theory. At all.

"No, I'm Luis."

"Are you Brazilian?" Maybe he was related to Roberto.

"I'm from Venezuela."

"But you play soccer . . ."

"For ODU. What's going on here?" He put his hands on his hips and looked back and forth between Riley and me.

I shook my head, realizing I'd jumped to conclusions a little too quickly. "I was wrong, that's what."

"What's the nature of this visit?"

"I'm trying to figure out who killed Scarlet. I was hoping to find out more information." I wanted to keep shaking my head, shaming myself for assuming things. I should have known better.

"What do you need to know?" Luis asked.

"Why are you here?"

"I miss Scarlet. I wanted to pay my respects."

"How long did you date?"

"Only a few weeks. Then she was cast for this play and seeing her was nearly impossible with both of our schedules. This play was important to her. She'd been taking dance classes and voice lessons since she was three or something. All she wants is to make it on Broadway one day. All she wanted, I should say."

I heard the tenderness in his voice and realized he did care about her. "Luis, what if someone got in Scarlet's way? How do you think she would have reacted?"

His arms moved from his hips to cross over his chest. "What do you mean?"

"What if someone was an obstacle to achieving her dreams? What do you think she would have done?"

"She's the one who died here, so it seems pointless to accuse her of anything." His voice hardened.

"I'm not accusing anyone. I'm just trying to find out some answers. Would she have provoked someone enough that they might kill her? Anything you know would be helpful."

His jaw relaxed slightly. "She had some disagreements with the playwright."

Arie! There she was, coming up again. I couldn't ignore that.

"What did she say?"

He loosened his arms as he shrugged. "She just didn't like Arie that much. Nothing Scarlet did was good enough for her, Arie kept threatening to fire her if she didn't shape up, and she was also critiquing her. I just thought that was Arie's job, not that she was necessarily being hostile. I also remember that Scarlet said Arie was a wannabe actress who had no idea what she was talking about."

"Sounds like she didn't like her very much."

"Scarlet could be a bit snooty sometimes," Marjorie added. She glanced at Luis and tilted her head to the side. "It's true."

"This has all been helpful. Thank you." I stepped toward the door.

"There's one more thing I remembered," Marjorie said.

I paused. "Okay."

"That argument I heard outside of my window a couple of nights before she died? The person Scarlet was talking to had this strange way of emphasizing what seemed like every other word."

Arie! Just what was she up to?

AFTER WE TALKED TO MARJORIE, Riley dropped me off so I could pick up the car. He said he had some business to discuss with Nolen.

I hurried back to the apartment, utterly exhausted and my mind racing a million different directions. Just as I stepped inside, Garrett called and said he was on his way over and bringing dinner.

For some reason, I felt uneasy, but I pushed the impending feeling of awkwardness away. I had no reason to feel off balance. Life was going on.

He arrived fifteen minutes later with some Thai food in hand. We settled at my kitchen table, loaded our plates with pad Thai and spring rolls, and began digging in. As we ate, I told him what I'd learned, strategically leaving out any details concerning Riley.

"Sounds like you've had a busy day."

"I'd say. If there's one thing jail taught me it's that I never want to go back there again. It also taught me that our law system doesn't always work the way it should."

"Life is flawed, Gabby, no matter how much we might want to be idealistic and not believe that."

I squeezed his hand. "Yes, it is. Thanks for sticking by me, even with all the flaws."

He leaned closer. "It's been a pleasure."

I closed my eyes as his lips brushed mine.

I wasn't betraying Riley, I mentally told myself. I couldn't live in limbo forever.

A loud knock sounded at the door. I jumped up, overreacting at the noise. "Who could that be?"

I pulled the door open and saw Nolen and Riley standing there. Riley walked right in and instantly grasped my arms. "Gabby, I've got good news."

"I could use some good news."

Riley's gaze fell on Garrett and then on our leftover plates of food. He dropped his hands and stepped back. "I didn't mean to interrupt anything."

"We're fine," I insisted.

Nolen stepped inside and nodded. "Garrett."

"You're Garrett?" Riley said. He extended his hand. "I'm Riley."

"You're Riley?" Garrett said.

The two men shook hands.

I clapped my hands once. "You stopped by with news?"

All three men turned toward me. Nolen spoke first.

"Good news. The police found witnesses that prove you couldn't have been at the scene of the vandalisms. I guess Paulette Zollin confirmed that she was with you when the gasoline was poured in the hallways. Someone else came forward and said they found a wig in one of the closets that matches the description from the video."

"Does this mean they're dropping the charges?" I glanced at Garrett, hope igniting in me.

"Not yet, but there's a good chance they will," Nolen said.

"That isn't good news. That's great news," Garrett exclaimed.

"Lie low for a while still, just to be on the safe side," Nolen continued. "I guess Mr. Zollin is really pressing the police to figure out who's behind these crimes. He carries a lot of weight around here."

Garrett pulled me into a hug and twirled me around. "You see. I knew this would all work out, Love."

My face flushed. "You did."

I averted my gaze, trying not to look at Riley.

"We didn't mean to interrupt," Riley said. "But we knew you'd want to know. We spent the evening reviewing timelines and evidence. There's no way these charges are going to stick."

"I can't tell you all how much I appreciate this. There's a lot I want to do with my life. I can't do any of it if I'm in jail." I had to get some of my mojo back. Being in jail was a wake up call for me.

Riley shoved his hands in his pockets. "I'm glad to help." He nodded at Garrett. "Good to meet you. Have a good night, you two."

Sadness pressed on my heart. Right or wrong, something about the moment seemed so bittersweet and surreal.

The men went out and Garrett and I were left standing there. I turned to him and saw a new emotion in his eyes.

"Riley's back, huh? The infamous Riley."

"He heard what happened and wanted to help."

"Sounds noble." He pushed my hair behind my ear, something unspoken in his gaze. "I know you've had a long day. I should go and let you rest, okay?"

I nodded, my heart being pulled in two different directions. "Okay."

He kissed my forehead. "Anything at all that you need, you let me know."

I sat on my couch staring vacantly at the wall when yet another knock at the door came. Before I could even get up and answer it, the door started to open.

With everything going on, I wasn't taking any chances. I popped to my feet and assumed a fight position.

Instead, Sierra appeared. Her eyes widened when she saw me, and she raised her hands in surrender.

"Hey, Kung Fu Fighter." She paused in the doorway. "I guess I should have knocked, otherwise I'm risking having you display some of your ninja-tastic moves."

I let out a feeble laugh. "Yeah, when I'm not crime scene cleaning, I'm a ninja. I've been considering the career change for a while now."

I sank back down into the cushions, my muscles feeling like jelly. Just Sierra.

She plopped on the couch beside me. Her belly was starting to show, I realized. Seeing that little swollen bump there made her pregnancy even more real to me. She was going to be a mom!

Sierra pushed her glasses up on her nose. "I've heard about everything going on. I can't stop thinking about you, Gabby. How are you holding up?"

I pulled my knees to my chest, my typical "stressed" position. "My head is spinning."

"Anyone's would be in your situation. And then there's Riley . . ."

"And then there's Riley," I echoed, letting out a long sigh.

"Is he back for good?" Sierra crossed her legs as she sat beside me.

For a moment, it felt like old times. Just me and Sierra having girl talk. About boys, of course. The only thing that would make it any more perfect would be Sierra's world famous acorn brownies.

I shook my head, remembering Sierra's question. "No, Riley's only lending a hand until I'm cleared of the charges."

She squinted at me. "How's that make you feel?"

I nibbled on my bottom lip for a moment before grabbing my cat blanket and pulling it across my legs. "Strange. In one way it's great to have him back. In another way, it just throws my emotions into a tailspin."

"Did he give any indication as to where the both of you stand? Where you stand together, I should say?"

I shrugged and leaned back harder into the couch. I'd kept all these thoughts silent, but it felt good to have Sierra pull the answers from me. Talking about it helped me make sense of my thoughts. "No. I know Riley needs time before making any big decisions. Even then, the answer might be no."

"I see. You're kind of between a rock and a hard pace."

"An all too familiar place. Plus, there's the picture . . ." I winced as I remembered the photo I'd seen in his old apartment.

"What picture?" Sierra rubbed her belly and scrunched her eyebrows together.

"I paid a visit to Olivia across the hall. There's a picture there of Riley with his arm around a woman. A nurse, at that." I told myself not to frown, but I felt my lips pulling downward despite me.

Her eyes widened. "No . . ."

I nodded. "It's true. I saw it with my own eyes."

"Did you ask who she was?" Sierra stopped rubbing her abdomen, her lips slightly apart.

"Olivia said the woman's name was Daniela. Then she had to go. She had class."

"Did you ask Riley about it?"

"Then I'll look neurotic. I mean, every time I see Riley with another woman, I assume the worst. First there was Veronica." His fiancée. They'd called things off, Riley and I had started talking, and then Veronica had shown up again.

"In your defense, they did get back together," Sierra reminded me. "Only temporarily, though."

"That's true. But then there was Veronica again." I remembered that outing to Riley's law school reunion a little too well. Just when I thought that woman was out of my life, she'd realized what she had in Riley and decided she wanted him back.

"And in that instant Veronica was trying to win him back. Your fears weren't unfounded. Of course, Riley wasn't interested because he was engaged to you."

Thank goodness. I remembered that moment when Riley had reaffirmed his love for me. I'd felt so secure and loved.

"And then there was Juliette." I'd discovered information about her when Riley was in a coma and I'd found correspondence between the two of them. Of course I'd assumed the worst. What woman wouldn't?

Sierra scrunched her nose up in an adorable frown. "That was all so complicated. It did look bad, on the surface, at least."

"I have trust issues." Of course, when I looked at my track record with men, I'd practically been programmed to have these issues. Something about me obviously screamed, "Cheat on me!"

Sierra leaned closer, almost as if conspiring. "How about this—I'll visit Olivia and see what I can find out for you. I actually do have a piece of her mail that I need to return."

I sat up straighter. She *was* conspiring and I loved her for it! "You'd do that?"

"Of course I would. That's what friends are for."

As Sierra studied me for a moment, she pressed her lips together in what appeared to be deep thought. "Listen, Gabby. I know Chad has been tightly wound around you lately. Give him some time to cool down."

I raised an eyebrow, wary about how much to share, how much to even let on that I knew. "You know?"

She let out a soft chuckle. "He wants to protect me. Me being pregnant has ignited something in him. In one way, it's cute, I suppose. But in another way, it's grating. He's taking everything entirely too seriously."

"He doesn't want to stress you out."

"That's kind of him, but I'm a big girl." She pushed her glasses up higher on her nose.

"I think I'm majorly stressing him out."

She opened her mouth and then shut it again. She wanted to say something else, I realized. I hesitated a moment, pondering whether or not I really wanted to know. Could I handle the truth?

"What aren't you telling me, Sierra?" I finally said.

Sierra tilted her head, softening her gaze. "Gabby, everyone knows you were made for more than this. I'm not sure if you're hanging on to life the way it is now because you're afraid of letting go, afraid of changes, afraid of disappointing people. But, whatever is, it's okay to look out for yourself."

"Look out for myself?" That concept seemed so foreign sometimes. It seemed like every time I started making progress in my life, something happened to stop me. Someone always needed me—at least, they needed someone. I knew what it was like to have no one watching out for you. Was that why I didn't want anyone else to experience that—because I knew how terribly isolating it was? No one should feel that alone.

Sierra nodded. "Get out there. Apply for more jobs. Don't be afraid to take risks."

"I take risks all the time."

"But you still keep plenty of safety nets. I just want to see you live up to your potential."

I swallowed the lump in my throat. "I'm trying."

She wiped under her eyes. "Everything just makes me so emotional lately!"

I pulled her into a hug. "Oh, Sierra. Thank you so much for caring. It's good to know I've got a friend like you. Everyone should."

"You've got a friend in me."

My lips parted in surprise. "You've been watching *Toy Story*?"

She patted her stomach. "What can I say? I need to familiarize myself with children's movies."

"Good for you. I look forward to watching them

with you." I stood and stretched. "But right now my first order of business is figuring out what's going on at the Cultural Arts Center."

Sierra stood also. "Any leads?"

"A lot of leads. Maybe I just need a good night's rest in my own bed."

She smiled. "That's right. In the morning everything looks better. Unless you're beef cattle."

I couldn't help but chuckle as my friend walked away.

THIRTY-SEVEN

MY PHONE RANG at six a.m. the next morning. I put it to my ear without even looking at the caller ID first. "Hello?" I mumbled.

"Gabby, the show is going on—with you!"

I sat up a little straighter, unsure if I was still dreaming. "Paulette?"

"Yes, it's Paulette. I know you've missed a couple of practices, but opening night is tonight. We need you there."

I blinked a few times, trying to come to my senses. "Last I heard, I wasn't allowed close to the school." *And you were royally ticked at me.*

"I dropped the charges."

"What?" My voice rose in pitch. Had she pressed the charges against me? I had no idea she was actually involved in the process.

"If I don't press charges for the vandalisms at the school, then there's no case. I didn't mean to press them against you specifically. Now, the murders . . . I don't have much say in that. But as far as the vandalisms go, there's nothing. I'm calling them even. I'm done. I don't care. All I care about right now is the show going on."

I had no idea what to think about that. Instead, I said, "If you need me, Paulette, I'll do it."

"We need you. Be there at three so we can run through some things. We have a lot of work to do to get things together."

"Yes, ma'am." I hung up feeling dazed.

Even though the play was plagiarized? Even with everything that had happened? The dead bodies? The lead—me!—being arrested and then released?

This was the moment that someone had been working hard to make sure didn't happen.

I could only imagine what that might mean for tonight's performance.

I peeked out into the audience from behind stage.

I had no idea how this performance would go tonight. Practice had been rough. We'd made some changes and adjustments because of the constraints.

Everyone had been so hurried and stressed that there'd been little time for interaction.

But tonight, of all nights, I needed to really keep my eye on things.

I scanned the audience and spotted Garrett sitting at the front left. I noticed some familiar faces with him and squinted. He really had brought people from his office. A lot of people, for that matter.

I smiled. It was really heartwarming that he'd been that thoughtful, though I would have preferred he not be so kind in this specific circumstance.

I watched as he walked across the room to talk to Chad and Sierra, who sat in midway in the center section. Clarice sat beside them.

My heart relaxed a moment. Maybe Clarice would speak to me again and I hadn't lost her as a friend.

I also saw my dad and his fiancée Teddi, my neighbor Bill McCormick, and even my old friend and first real employee Mr. Harold.

As I watched, Riley walked in and sat on the other side of Chad and Sierra. It was like a big reunion out there.

Wow. They'd all come out just to see me? A strange emotion welled inside me. Gratefulness? Surprise? The tears that popped into my eyes truly made me feel off kilter.

I didn't have time to dwell on the emotion right

now. I'd revel in the supportiveness of my friends later.

My gaze continued to survey the audience. Strangely enough, I didn't see Arie. Where was she? Most likely trying to drum up her press time out front. I could totally see her doing that.

My phone buzzed in my hands, and I looked down to see a text message from Sierra.

I quickly scanned the words. *The woman with Riley is his cousin, who also works at the hospital.*

My chest tightened before all the tension disappeared in an airy laugh. Cousin? *You've got to be kidding me.*

I let my head fall back in exasperation. His cousin.

How many times did I have to come back to this place? It was like I was only capable of taking baby steps forward. Riley had been the man of my dreams and there'd always been a part of me that didn't feel good enough for him. As a result, I always rushed to assume that he liked other women better than me, even when he'd assured me of his love. It had happened time and time again.

It was time to stop living with so much doubt and uncertainty.

"Come and play with us," someone whispered behind me.

"What?" I twirled around.

The Shining Twins stood there, side by side, staring at me.

"I said, 'Come on. Play's starting,'" Karen said.

"Of course." I let out a tense laugh.

"Forever," she whispered.

I looked back and she grinned. I released the breath I held. She was being silly. Thank goodness.

I straightened my costume and looked over at Jerome. "You ready for this?"

"Ready as I'll ever be."

"Paulette had someone come in earlier and double check everything," Sharen told us. "She said she took every safety precaution necessary."

"I know that should make me feel better," I muttered. "But it doesn't."

"At least she cut the scene where you were hoisted into the air," Sharen said.

"Thank goodness." Still, the doubt wouldn't leave me. I couldn't shake the feeling that something was going to happen tonight. Whether I wanted to be or not, I was right in the middle of the danger. There was really no safety net.

As the lights went low, I tucked my cell phone into my costume. There was something about having it near me that made me feel somehow more secure.

The Shining Twins pushed me on stage as the canned music came up. "Knock 'em dead, Gabby!" one of them whispered.

I started the opening number. My voice sounded wobbly at first but, the more I sang, the stronger it became.

For a moment—and just a moment—I actually forgot everything going on and enjoyed being on stage acting and singing.

Until something buzzed against my chest.

My cell phone!

I nearly forgot my line as it continued to buzz.

Who was texting me now? Anyone who might message me was in this room right now.

"Elsa . . ." a voice floated in the background.

I shook my head. This was part of the play. The part where I first realized the Specter was here and that he liked me.

I'd never gotten chills about it in practice. But my blood felt cold right now as warning bells sounded in my head. Something bad was going to happen tonight. It was just a matter of when.

My phone buzzed again.

"Who are you?" I whispered on stage. It was one of my lines, though it could apply to real life as well. "Why are you talking to me?"

"Elsa . . . I have plans for you."

With that last line, the lights went black. End of Act One.

The darkness felt disconcerting. Despite that, I found my way back stage. As The Shining Twins helped change me into my next costume, I pulled out my phone.

Clarice had texted me.

The Specter is Arie's boyfriend. I saw them together in a celebrity magazine.

What? So Jerome, or whatever his real name was, was in all of this with Arie somehow?

He was a gamer. He could have easily set up that swatting episode. Maybe he was trying to help out his girlfriend by drumming up business for the play. It was a possible motive. I didn't know.

What do you know about him? I texted her back.

"You've got to get back out there!" Karen told me.

She pushed me on stage.

I glanced out at the audience, trying to collect myself and remember my next line. My gaze met Garrett's and he gave me a thumbs up.

In the center, I spotted Riley. He grinned brightly.

Something about seeing both men jostled me into action. I made it through the rest of my lines. I sang my heart out. Nothing happened, which only added to my uneasy feeling.

Now it was time for Act Three. Why did I have a feeling things weren't going to remain this calm?

The sense of foreboding remained with me as I geared up for the final act. As The Shining Twins changed my costume, my phone buzzed again. I quickly pulled it out, hoping it was another text from Clarice. I wasn't disappointed.

Jerome was kicked off Cascade Falls *because he had a violent temper.*

All that stuff he said about being an accountant was a lie. I wasn't surprised. But was Jerome behind everything that was happening here?

He and Arie have a turbulent, on-again off-again relationship.

Was Jerome trying to ruin this play so Arie wouldn't be successful? Maybe he'd secretly acted supportive, all the while wanting to humiliate her in public. Murder was a pretty drastic way to embarrass someone, though. Unless Scarlet's death had been an accident. The thoughts collided inside my head until I didn't know what to think.

I didn't know if my theory was correct or not, but I knew something felt off.

"What are you up to?" I whispered to Jerome as we waited for our cue to start.

"What are you talking about?" He looked genuinely confused, just like any good actor might.

"I know who you are," I hissed.

His eyes widened. "I'm Jerome."

"People are going to hear you from the audience," Sharen said.

Jerome and I stared at each other, doing a silent stand off.

"You're on!" Karen pushed us both on stage.

I eyed Jerome before the act started, not breaking my gaze. I needed to show him I was confident, unafraid, and willing to go after him with everything in me. I wasn't satisfied until Jerome looked away, something close to panic racing through his gaze first.

The play continued, feeling both wooden and electrified. I couldn't describe it. The tension between us felt real. It *was* real. Yet, each of my movements felt weighed down as I anticipated what might happen.

I counted down the minutes until the end of the play. Finally, we reached the part where the Specter pulled out a gun, threatening anyone who came closer to me.

I stared at the gun. I remembered my middle school production of *Oklahoma* where someone had switched out the fake gun for a real one. As I gawked at the pistol in Jerome's hands now, my entire body tensed.

What if there were real bullets in that firearm?

Jerome pointed it at Bennie. "Get away from her," he ordered.

I held my breath as I gaped at the barrel.

The guy playing Bennie's boyfriend stepped in front of her. "Over my dead body."

Best original line ever. I mean, really, this play was a knock 'em out of the park, one-of-a-kind masterpiece. I bit my tongue.

My thoughts were quickly distracted as Jerome raised the gun, his finger poised on the trigger.

Everything inside me was screaming that something was wrong. What if someone had swapped out the gun? How could I know for sure?

I knew a lot was riding on this play—right now, my life remained at the top of the list—but aside from safety concerns, I knew Paulette had staked everything on the success of this production.

If I was wrong, I could ruin things for Paulette. But if my suspicions were right and I didn't do anything, I could die.

"No!" I yelled, some kind of primal instinct to survive bursting through me.

Before Jerome pulled the trigger, I tackled him. He fell to the ground, the gun still in his hands.

Please let it be loaded with blanks, I prayed. As we struggled, the barrel jabbed me in the stomach. If there was a real bullet in there . . . it could easily end my life.

"What are you doing? Are you crazy?" Jerome muttered.

"The gun—"

Just then, it fired.

I held my breath.

I waited to feel pain but felt nothing.

As I heard gasps from the audience, I glanced over.

Money rained down from the ceiling.

Money? From the ceiling? Just what was going on?

"I didn't know there was a real bullet. I promise," Jerome whispered.

Based on the fear in his voice, he was telling the truth.

"Who else handled it?" I demanded.

"The twins gave it to me."

Could the twins be behind this? I knew they were strange. That they had an offbeat sense of humor. But what motive would they have?

"This is the best play ever," someone exclaimed from the audience.

"So realistic," someone else said.

"Free money!" yet another voice said.

"Arie's behind this. It has to be her," Bennie whispered. "I bet she's in this with Roberto."

But why would Arie hide money in the eaves above the auditorium?

That's how Scarlet had died, I realized. She'd been up on the catwalk because she knew there was money up there. When she'd said everything would be working itself out soon, it was because she thought she'd be coming into some money. For a young starving artist, having cash could seem like the answers to every problem.

I glanced down as a piece of paper currency floated to my feet. It was a $100 bill.

Just like the ones Larissa and Peter had found.

Someone had been counterfeiting money.

They'd been using the printing press. The machine had sucked up too much power and that was why the lights kept flickering off.

That would explain the strange noises and the electrical problems.

And the man who died, Oliver Cartwright . . . maybe the person behind these crimes used a generator inside to avoid the power going off again. That could explain the death by carbon monoxide.

My pulse spiked.

The most important question remained: Who?

Arie? Roberto? Paulette? Jerome?

No. There was an even better suspect, someone who'd been right in front of my eyes the entire time. It was . . .

I jerked my head up, looking for the culprit.

Bennie crept toward the shadows and out of the spotlight, her eyes as wide as the construction buckets I used. What if her name wasn't like Bennie from Benny and the Jets? What if it was Benjamin, as in money?

She worked the newspaper here. Probably knew about the printing press. She was about my height and, with a wig, she could pass for me. Plus, the paper I'd seen her drop—the one she claimed was for a scrapbook—would have been the perfect size and consistency for a sheet of counterfeit bills.

"It was you," I whispered, even though I knew she couldn't hear me.

She'd gotten the message without hearing a thing. In that moment, I saw the truth in her gaze. She *was* behind this.

I took several steps toward her, and, to her credit, she remained where she was.

"I'm on your side, Gabby," she mumbled when I reached her.

I shook my head. "You gained my trust, only to use our conversations against me."

"Don't be crazy, Gabby. I would never do this." She took a step backward, away from me.

"But why did you leave one-hundred dollar bills lying around the school? Would you have been that careless?" I shook my head again, facts colliding in my head. "Unless you left them out on purpose. Unless you wanted someone else to find them and try to use them for a purchase. It would almost be a test run for you and it would ensure you were less likely to be caught."

"I'm really not that smart." She let out a nervous laugh.

"You're working with someone. You couldn't do all this alone."

"Gabby . . ." Her eyes implored me.

"How could you do this, Bennie?"

"I . . ." Bennie took off in a run toward the exit at the back of the stage.

I couldn't let her get away. "Stop her!" I yelled.

I hiked up my habit and sprinted after her.

The Twins stood there, staring at me with that helpless expression on their faces.

Then, without visible collaboration, they held out their arms in unison and clotheslined Bennie.

Bennie's feet flew in the air before she hit the ground.

"We call that our Wonder Twin move," Sharen informed me.

I grinned. The Shining Twins? The Wonder Twins? I didn't care who they were at the moment. "You two just saved the day. Make sure she doesn't go anywhere."

They nodded and grabbed her arms, even as she struggled against them. When Bennie looked at me, fire blazed in her eyes.

"I overheard you talking to Paulette one night,

and I knew why you were here. If anyone was going to catch us, I knew it would be you. I tried everything to stop you. I didn't want to hurt anyone."

At that moment, Charlie hurried onto the stage and took over. Thank goodness.

I wanted to think this mystery was done. But Bennie hadn't been behind all of these acts herself. Who had helped her? She'd said *us*.

I peered out into the audience in time to see a man wearing all black casually walking toward the back door. I did a double take. I recognized the man's gait. He'd worked as a tekkie and had access to the backstage . . .

I closed my eyes, trying to remember exactly what he looked like. His face flashed into mind. Now that I thought about it, the man had the same pert nose as Bennie did. Her brother maybe? My guess was that this was a family business. As he glanced back, I saw a tattoo snaking up his neck. It was him!

"Someone get him!" I shouted, pointing to the man in the back.

As soon as I said the words, Riley, Garrett and Chad rushed from their seats. They split up to corner the man. When he saw he was surrounded, he stopped. In one fluid motion, he tried to dart over the chairs—and the audience members—but a man stood and grabbed his collar first.

"You owe me money," the man sneered.

He must be the man from the bar! I wasn't totally educated in counterfeiting, but I did know that criminals often tried to sell fake money to other people. Had that man been a client?

As the police rushed into the room, I sat down on the stage. My job was done.

The audience broke into thunderous applause.

Had they all thought this was part of the play?

I decided to roll with it.

I stood up and took my bows.

"THE CAST PARTY wasn't exactly supposed to be like this," Paulette said, her gaze scanning the cafeteria.

"The good news is that I heard several people say how exciting the play was," I told her.

"I have to second that, Gabby," Charlie said, approaching us from outside. "That was the most exciting play I've ever seen. Good work."

"Who was that man in the audience?" I asked her.

"Bennie just spilled everything. He was a potential client who wanted to buy the counterfeit money."

"The other thing I'm not clear about is the man in the orchestra pit. How does he fit?"

"He was a friend of Bennie's. After he died, Bennie's brother—the man with the snake tattoo—panicked. He decided to put him in the orchestra pit in order to make it look like the school really was haunted."

"They were desperate to make a buck, weren't they?"

"Literally." Her smile faded. "And no hard feelings between us, right? Like I said, I just followed the evidence."

"I understand. However, you're officially off any future invite lists. Sorry." I winked.

She let out a soft chuckle. "Parker's back at home, by the way."

I raised my eyebrows. "Is he?"

Charlie nodded. "I guess your friend made him realize what he already had at home." A hint of a smile tugged at her lips. "I've got to run. I'll be in touch."

I watched her walk away before Paulette turned back to me.

"None of this could have happened without you," Paulette told me. "I knew you'd figure out who did this."

"I almost didn't."

"But, the important thing is that you did. I can't believe they were using that printing press the whole time to counterfeit money."

I nodded. "It's true. Bennie's parents were con artists. She told me she 'lost' them four years ago, but what she really meant was that they'd been locked away after being found guilty for fraud, among other things. Bennie confessed to the police that she and her brother found those plates while cleaning out their parents' house. Bennie remembered the press was at the school and knew exactly what they needed to print fake currency. They couldn't move the press from the school—it was too heavy. So the only alternative was to use the press here. The problem was that you'd just purchased the property and started to use part of it for the play."

"So, at first, they were just trying to scare us off?" Paulette blinked as she waited for my response.

I nodded. "That's right. They were trying to make it look like the place was haunted so they could get rid of you. The electricity going out was just an unintentional perk of the whole operation. Bennie and her brother reworked the wiring to run power back to the old newspaper classroom. They accidentally tapped into the same circuit that the auditorium was on, though."

"What about Scarlet?"

"Scarlet caught them in the act of storing the money up in the eaves of the building. It was the perfect place to keep the money because no one would ever think to check there. My guess is that Scarlet wanted part of the cut, and they weren't willing to give it to her."

"So they killed her?"

"Instead, they rigged the railing, knowing she'd try to get some money for herself. When she did, she fell. They changed her clothes to make it look reminiscent of *The Wizard of Oz*, which also helped to play into the ghost rumors. They were really quite clever when you think about it. Everything looked like it could have been accidents. There were enough doubts in everyone's mind to keep people scared."

"The yellow gasoline?"

"Sometimes people dye gas so they can tell it apart from other liquids they're storing. Apparently, that's what they did. The brother was a mechanic on the side. The fact that they brought in a generator that leaked a yellow trail of gas was just an eerie coincidence. The message on the mirror, however, wasn't. They decided to play this up for all it was worth. As soon as they heard about the ghost— which Arie continually mentioned—they knew they had to use the story to their advantage."

"Then they blamed you for everything that happened?"

"Bennie realized I was looking for answers. Because I kept disappearing to investigate, I was the perfect choice. I was acting suspiciously because I was undercover. They used scare tactics like locking Arie and me in the closet, leaving that torn photo in the room, putting a real bullet in the gun, the wet footprints leading to the bathroom, and sending the

SWAT team to Garrett's house. They had a whole bag of tricks and they weren't afraid to use everything inside to try and spook us."

"Speaking of Garrett, how did they know about him?"

I shrugged. "I guess the same way they knew I was a crime scene cleaner. Bennie must have started doing her research. There are some articles about me online. They used everything they found out about me against me. They even planted my business card—I'd guess Bennie took it that night I saw her stumbling from the band room—in the pocket of the man found in the orchestra pit."

She sighed and shook her head. "I was naïve enough to use Bennie's brother to fix your van. She told me he was a mechanic, so I figured I'd give him some business. Little did I know . . . "

"At least it's all over now. The Secret Service is coming in to claim all the money. The investigation is being turned over to them." I studied my friend for a moment. "So, now that all of this is over, will you do another play?"

She hesitated a moment before nodding. "I'd like to."

"If you do I have the perfect person to help you."

"Who's that? Please don't tell me Arie. She's being investigated for plagiarism, fraud, blackmail, extortion. Maybe more. I overheard her moaning about something as some men in suits led her away."

I wanted to say, "Poor Arie," but I couldn't quite bring myself to do it. "No, I wasn't talking about Arie. I was talking about Donabell Bullock."

She blanched. "You're kidding?"

I shrugged. "Not really. I think she could use an outlet."

"I'll think about it then."

I hesitated, but there was something else I had to mention to her. "Paulette, I'm worried about you. All the pills. The drinking."

She drew in a shaky breath. "You knew about that?"

"I put it all together. Paulette, I've seen how substance abuse can ruin a person's life. My father was essentially absent for most of my childhood because he drank so much. He was there physically, but mentally and emotionally, he was gone." I squeezed her hand. "I don't want to see that happen to you, Paulette. Life is too short to waste it."

"I flushed all the pills two days ago, Gabby. I realized they were just making me feel numb, but they weren't really addressing any of my issues. I was so stressed out about disappointing my father and having trouble coping."

I placed my hand on her arm, feeling a speech of "After School Movie of the Week" proportions coming on. "I really think you're going to find your place, Paulette. I know that life can be—"

"If it isn't Gabby St. Claire."

I snapped from my soliloquy and turned toward the deep voice. Paulette's dad approached us, a huge, proud grin stretched across his face. "Mr. Zollin. So good to see you."

He pumped my hand up and down. "You haven't changed a bit. You're still a firecracker. Still doing whatever you set your mind to."

I glanced at Paulette and saw her face fall. "Really, Paulette was the one who made this all happen. I just did what she told me."

Her eyes brightened. Mr. Zollin put an arm around her shoulders. "I'm always proud of my girl. Not so much of a girl anymore. A grown woman who's more than capable of taking on responsibility."

"You mean it, Daddy?" Her eyes were hopeful as she looked at her father. "Even after the dinner cruise fiasco?"

"Of course!" He pulled her into a hug. "In fact, you're now in charge of this whole place. I'm going to make sure you have enough people to help you, though. That was the problem here. I put too much responsibility on your shoulders. Anyone would have been overwhelmed."

Paulette beamed. "Thanks, Dad. You don't know how happy that makes me."

Maybe having her dad's confidence would help occupy her thoughts. Staying busy, having a mission and focus . . . those things could renew a person.

We watched her father disappear to mingle with the other guests here. As soon as he was out of earshot, Paulette turned to me. "I guess this might be a good time to mention that Roberto and I are getting back together."

My lips parted. "What?"

"It's true. I kicked him out because he kept riding my case about the drinking. He was just worried about me, but I became really bitter. I've come to realize that he truly cares about me."

"That's . . . that's great, Paulette. I'm glad you're giving it another try. It sounds like you two can work through a lot of things together."

She nodded. "Plus, I know what Phase Two of the Cultural Arts Center will be. I was going to announce it at the end of the play tonight, but I didn't have the chance."

"Please, don't keep me in suspense!"

She grinned, her whole face lighting. "We're going to use the track and gym for sports programs for students in the area. Roberto is going to head it up. This way, we can work together. I think it will be good for us."

That was why Roberto's Mercedes had been at the school. Everything was starting to make sense.

As if on cue, Roberto showed up and put his arm around Paulette's waist. "Great job tonight, *Pessoa Amada.*"

"Thank you."

He looked at me and nodded. "I told you I wasn't behind any of this."

"What about Arie? Someone saw you talking to her. What's the connection?"

"I was begging Arie to look after Paulette. I was concerned. I needed someone here to keep an eye on her, and I ran into Arie. I promised we'd introduce her as a guest of honor at our next soccer game if she helped me out. She seemed to be willing to do anything for attention."

I bought that part of his story, but . . . "You seemed so angry."

He shrugged. "I'm Latino. What can I say? Full of passion." He thumped his heart and practically growled.

As soon as they walked off to talk to more cast members, Riley and Garrett both approached at the same time. Riley glanced at Garrett. "You mind if I have a moment?"

"Not at all." Garrett raised his glass of water in acquiescence.

Was there uncertainty in his eyes, though?

Riley put his hand on my elbow and led me away

from listening ears. "You did fabulous. I knew you would."

"Thanks so much for being here for me, Riley."

His gaze turned serious. "I have to get back up to D.C."

I nodded. "Of course."

He lowered his voice, his blue eyes imploring me. "I don't know what's going to happen."

"I know."

He squeezed my arm. "Is it okay if I stay in touch?"

"Of course."

"Good. I miss talking to you. I really do." He squeezed my arm again. "Take care of yourself."

Sadness pressed on my heart as I watched him leave. I held my chin up, determined to let the challenges in my life make me a better person. I wouldn't be defeated, and I was slowly learning that my confidence in life had to come from an inner strength.

I could, indeed, climb every steeple and scale every roof.

As Riley walked away, Garrett approached. "Everything okay?"

I put my hand on his chest. "Everything's fine. Just saying goodbye to an old friend."

Garrett's eyes studied mine. "I see."

"I thought you should know that I made a decision about Africa."

"Did you? Do you have your bags packed?" Hope glimmered in his eyes.

A knot formed in my gut. "I can't, Garrett."

He said nothing for a minute before finally nodding. "Okay."

"I want to, Garrett. I really do. But I've got to push ahead with my life. I've got to stop simply taking what life gives me. I need to chase after what I want. I can't just bounce around doing odd jobs or taking international trips with my extremely hand-some boyfriend."

"Boyfriend? I like the sound of that." His eyes sparkled.

I grabbed his hand. "I need to make some big decisions about my future."

"I understand, Gabby." Something changed in his eyes as he stared down at me. "You still love him, don't you?"

My smile slipped. "It's hard, Garrett. I don't know what I feel anymore."

"You went through a lot. You went through a lot together. Why don't we take some steps back and think about things while I'm gone? That will be a good determining factor as to how we should proceed."

I nodded, even though my heart felt heavy and burdened. "That sounds good. Thanks so much,

Garrett. I don't know what I would have done without you these past few months. I mean that."

He kissed my cheek. "The feeling is mutual. You take care of yourself while I'm in Africa, okay? We'll talk when I get back."

"I will," I promised.

As he walked away, my heart panged. Yet despite my conflicted emotions, I knew deep inside that everything would be okay.

I glanced around at everyone else socializing and realized there was nothing else I could do here. It was time for me to go.

Because, as Dorothy in *The Wizard of Oz* said, there really wasn't any place like home.

~~~

Thank you so much for reading ***Foul Play.*** If you enjoyed this book, please consider leaving a review!

Keep reading for a preview of ***Broom and Gloom***.
~~~

NOW AVAILABLE

BROOM AND GLOOM: CHAPTER ONE

I gripped the steering wheel of my economy-sized rental car and veered off the main highway, following the detour sign onto a small road through Oklahoma's backcountry. "On the Road Again" blared on the radio, and the deceitful sun shone brightly in the distance, making the day look much warmer than it actually felt.

A detour seemed a little too appropriate for my life. In fact, my life so far seemed to be defined by a series of setbacks.

Not anymore.

I'd just flown in from Norfolk, Virginia. At the airport, I'd picked up my rental car, and I'd hit the road. Before even checking into my hotel for the forensic conference I was attending, I'd decided to meet with my future stepbrother for dinner. I wasn't sure what my schedule would be like for the rest of the week, so I wanted to meet him now while I could.

His name was Trace Ryan, and he was an up-and-coming country singer. His mom, Teddi, was marrying my dad, and she'd insisted we meet. In an effort to keep the peace, I'd figured why not?

But right now I was in the middle of Nowhere, Oklahoma, hoping for the life of me my GPS wasn't leading me astray.

I looked down at the paper where I'd scribbled some backup directions and stopped at the end of a lane. A large aluminum-sided warehouse stood in front of me, six vehicles parked out front. There was nothing else around. No houses or barns or stores. Just flat land with a few sprigs of dry grass and a dead tree in the distance.

As soon as I stepped from my car, I could hear the whiny tunes of a steel guitar.

I glanced at my paper again. This was the address Trace had given me. I started across the dirt toward the warehouse, the air dry and cold around me. I pulled my canvas jacket closer, wishing I'd brought something heavier. Going out west, somehow I'd expected things to be warmer. They weren't. Of course, it was only March.

When I stepped into the building, a wave of loud

music hit me. I paused and spotted a cowboy onstage with a guitar strapped across his chest. I soaked everything in for a moment. The lights. The fog in the air. The loud music. Two rows of empty chairs in front of the stage.

"Can I help you?" A short man who exuded nervous energy stopped beside me. He had a hipster vibe with his shaved head, trim build, and chunky glasses. His head seemed too large for his body, which only added to his whole offbeat persona.

"I'm here to meet Trace Ryan," I said, nodding toward the stage.

"And you are . . . ?"

"His soon-to-be stepsister."

The man raised his eyebrows, staring at me like I was lying. "Is that right?"

"Talk to Trace. He'll confirm that I'm supposed to be here, Mr. . . . ?"

"I'm Jono, his manager. He would have certainly mentioned this to me." He looked back at the stage and scowled again. "We've had a stressful rehearsal, and I don't want to burden him any more before our big tour starts. This is make-or-break time, if you know what I mean."

"Is that you, Gabby?" Trace said from the stage, shielding his eyes from the spotlights.

"The one and only."

"Fantastic. A few more minutes and I'll be finished here. Jono, behave yourself. She's with me."

"Sorry," Jono murmured. "We get some people coming in here with crazy stories all the time. Can't be too careful."

As he walked away, I settled against the wall and listened to the band as they finished rehearsing. They had a good sound. Trace's voice was deep and not too twangy. Their songs were catchy, and their energy was infectious.

As the guitar and drums finished out a song, Trace pulled his guitar off. "That's a wrap, guys."

He hopped down from the stage and made his way toward me, a bit of Western swagger to his steps. I wondered if his walk reflected his attitude or if it was the boots and tight jeans that made him saunter that way.

As soon as he was close enough to reach me, he pulled me into a hug. "So good to finally meet you, Gabby."

"Same here." I patted his back, not expecting the warm greeting.

I'd never met the man before, nor had we even talked, other than to set up this meeting. I'd figured Trace felt just as obligated as I did to meet. After all, we were both adults. It wasn't like we'd ever live under the same roof or even spend a holiday together.

He turned back to the band. "Let's break for dinner and meet back here in two hours. Sound good?"

They all nodded and began to put away their instruments.

"I promise, I'll introduce you to everyone when we get back. Right now I'm starving." Trace put his hand on my elbow and led me toward the door. "I want to take you to this barbecue place not too far from here. It's Oklahoma dining at its finest. Sound okay?"

I nodded. "Of course."

Up close, Trace had that charisma that seemed necessary for celebrities to have in order to attain success. He had rugged good looks, eyes that were alive with mischief, a trim muscled body, and a voice that made women croon. His hair was light brown, he had a slight cleft in his chin, and he stood at least six feet tall.

After talking to Teddi, I'd formed the impression of him that he was a wannabe country star. He seemed like the real deal, though. He had an aura that garnered attention.

I climbed into his truck, an older-model pickup that looked like it had seen better days. Empty cans of energy drinks clanked at my feet, and dust kicked up behind us as we began traveling down the road.

"So your dad's the lucky man marrying my

mom, huh?" he said, glancing over at me. He had the perfect cowboy profile, especially with his over-sized Stetson on. His shirt was a little too nice, too pressed and unstained to look like a real rancher, but I was sure women loved the image he portrayed.

"My dad's a very lucky man." My dad was a louse, and I still didn't see what Teddi saw in him. But the two of them seemed happy together. I didn't get it, but it wasn't my relationship, so I tried not to think too much about it.

"It's good to hear her happy again. After Dad died, I didn't know if my mom would ever be the same." We bumped down the road, a certain melancholy lingering in the air. "Has your conference started yet?"

"Tomorrow." The conference was my real reason for being here.

"Forensics, right?"

"You know it. It's a highly glamorous field. Just watch CSI sometime," I told him drily.

"Sounds interesting. Especially for a girl."

"What was that?" I jerked my head toward him, certain I'd heard him incorrectly.

A smile spread across his face, and he winked. "Just kidding. I like to give people a hard time. It's my love language. If we're going to be stepsiblings, you might as well get used to that."

"Good to know." I smiled, already liking Trace and glad that I'd come early to meet him.

As quickly as we'd started the journey to the restaurant, we pulled up to a stop at an old lodge-like building named the Tanglefoot Saloon. Trace followed my gaze, hunching to peer through the windshield at the restaurant.

He shrugged. "I know it's not much to look at it, but the barbecue is out of this world. It will have you licking your fingers and begging for more. You'll buy another plane ticket to Oklahoma just to eat here."

"You sound pretty sure of yourself. I never even said I liked barbecue."

"Heresy. Everyone likes barbecue."

As soon as I stepped inside the place, I was drawn back into the Old West. Everyone seemed to wear cowboy boots, drink oversized beers, and have cowboy hats perched atop their heads. The only thing that could have made it more perfect would be a piano man playing "Ragtime" and a group of cow rustlers and hustlers playing poker in the corner.

"A lot of the ranchers around here come in for dinner," Trace said, smiling as he watched my reaction. "It's great. I promise."

"A showdown outside after lunch would make this the perfect experience. Seriously. Even a fight between some farmers and cowmen. I'll take whatever I can get."

"Farmers and cowmen?"

"*Oklahoma*?" I reminded him.

His expression still looked blank.

"The musical? Please tell me you've seen it." It was the first musical I'd ever acted in, all the way back in middle school. It remained one of my favorites to this day.

"I was more into Garth Brooks than I was Andrew Lloyd Webber."

"Rodgers and Hammerstein," I corrected. "Webber did the music for *Phantom*."

"Well, I blame it all on my roots. They're more country and down home than they are cultured and refined."

"I'm sure you get by just fine."

He nodded hello to the voluptuous waitress, whose face instantly lit when she spotted Trace. She sashayed over and grinned. "Hey there, good looking. What brings you in here today?"

"I've got to introduce my sis to some of your barbecue."

"Your sister?" Her eyes turned to me, obviously assessing my worth as she looked me up and down. "I had no idea."

Something subconscious ignited in me, and I found myself hooking my thumbs through my belt loops. What could I say? When in Oklahoma, do as the Oklahomans. "I can't wait to try some of your ribs. They smell fabulous."

She smiled and then giggled. I must have gotten her approval.

"Well, come on back," she said. "I've got the perfect seat for you."

She led us to a corner table by the window. Peanut shells crunched underneath our feet, and the scent of something smoky and spicy lingered in the air, making my stomach growl.

The tables looked like wagon wheels with sheets of tempered glass atop them. The napkins were checkered, and all over the walls were memorabilia of the West—ox yokes, steer heads, black-and-white photos highlighting the past.

I couldn't help but smile. It was how I'd already dreamed Oklahoma would be. I half expected to see Gordon MacRae as Curly pull up in a surrey with fringe on the top. I'd been accused on more than one occasion of living in a musical, and I was okay with that.

After the waitress set down huge jars filled with sweet tea, Trace ordered ribs for both of us. That's when the first moment of silence fell.

"I hope you don't think it's strange that I wanted to meet with you. The truth is, I did have some ulterior motives." He cracked a peanut he'd taken from the silver bucket in the middle of the table.

"Did you?"

He nodded. "My mom likes to talk about you, so I've heard about your past."

Which part? I wondered. There was a long list to choose from—me almost being killed, my ex-fiancé almost being killed, my recent arrest. Take your pick.

Before he could explain, a woman ran up to the table and breathlessly stared at Trace. She was young with wide eyes, big hair, and a low-cut shirt.

"Trace Ryan?" she panted.

Trace grinned that million-dollar smile of his. "The one and only."

"I'm your biggest fan!"

Wow, his celebrity status had grown quickly. This man already had a well-established fan club and supporters who recognized him out in public. Kudos to him.

"I appreciate that. Would you like an autograph?"

"Would I ever!" she squealed. The squeal turned into a pout. "But I don't have any paper."

"Let me see your hand instead."

She happily obliged. He pulled a marker from his pocket—did he always keep one there for moments such as these?—and signed his name on the back of her hand.

The woman screamed again. "You just made my day!"

She continued giggling as she went back to her

gaggle of girlfriends sitting across the restaurant. Trace followed my gaze and winked at the onlookers. He seemed to be a regular Casanova.

Even stranger—either the woman hadn't noticed me at all or she'd chosen ignorant bliss and simply pretended I didn't exist.

Trace turned serious again as he turned back to our conversation. He cracked another peanut, and with the nuts still tucked into the shell, he tossed them back into his mouth like some people downed a shot of alcohol. "Sorry about that. All my fans expect this certain image. It's a lot to live up to sometimes."

"I can only imagine."

He wiped some crumbs into his hand and placed them on a napkin. "So, as I started to say, I need your help."

"What's going on?" I took a sip of my tea, curious now and feeling like I'd been swept up in a world that was entirely different from my own. My life was urban, brisk, and busy. Out here I actually felt like I could breathe. I had the urge to go all Rodgers and Hammerstein and burst into "Oh, What a Beautiful Mornin'."

"It's this lady." He pulled something out of his back pocket and shoved a picture toward me. A woman with hair so blonde it looked white, tanned skin, and a bikini-ready body stared at me from the photo.

"Pretty."

"Looks can be deceiving." He shook his head, a new tension seeming to wash over him. "She's making my life miserable."

"An ex?"

He shook his head. "I feel like a girl saying this, but I suppose she's more of a stalker."

Now this was getting interesting. "Really? Tell me more."

"About six months ago, I started getting fan letters from a woman named Georgia Dalton." He tapped the photo. "She started showing up at all my concerts and sneaking her way backstage to meet me. At first, she seemed like an overzealous fan with boundary issues."

"I have a feeling there's a 'but' in there."

He sighed. "Yes, there is. I quickly realized she was obsessed. I caught her outside of my home once. I still didn't think she was crazy at that point. But I was dating a girl named Caitlyn. One day, Caitlyn found her tires slashed. Then her apartment was broken into and her things ransacked."

"You think this woman is behind those things?" I studied the picture in front of me, wondering if a mentally unstable soul was behind those hazel eyes.

"Yes, I do. The problem is that I could never prove anything. The police could only file reports about the incidents, but there were no fingerprints or video surveillance or anything to point to Georgia."

"What happened to Caitlyn?"

"She couldn't take it anymore. We broke up, and she moved back home to Colorado with her family." His voice sounded earnestly sad as he said the words. "Honestly, I wasn't sure Georgia was behind it. Caitlyn also had an ex-boyfriend who was pretty controlling. I thought it could be him."

"I take it the story doesn't end there?" I took another drink of the sweetest iced tea ever. My teeth started rotting with every sip, yet my taste buds wouldn't let me stop. Maybe it wasn't a bad thing. The sugar was going straight into my bloodstream and making me overly alert.

He shook his head. "Then, two months later, I met Skye."

"Skye?" His life was like a regular soap opera. I was fascinated already.

"A teacher who had just moved here from Arizona for a fresh start. Her parents were killed in a car crash when she was only thirteen, and then her brother died, leaving her without anyone."

"Was she teaching here?"

He shook his head. "No, she said teaching wasn't for her. She was working as a customer service representative for a company. She worked out of her home, doing everything from her office there. It was pretty isolating, I suppose."

"How did the two of you meet?"

A soft smile pulled at his lips. "I was in this old, hole-in-the-wall music store checking out some CDs. The place is old and run down, and no one even knows it's there. Anyway, Skye was in there, and we just started talking about music. We really hit it off."

"Let me guess—that's when everything started going wrong?" I'd been around enough to know how the story usually played out.

"See, I was right. Girls can be good at this detective thing." He flashed a teasing grin that quickly faded. "Skye said she felt like someone was watching her. Then someone wiped her computer clean. Small things in her house kept being rearranged—but nothing that she could prove."

"But she thought someone had been in her home? She thought *Georgia* had been in her home?"

He nodded. "We threw the theory out there."

I shivered at the thought. Unfortunately, I could relate because I'd experienced something similar. "Did she ever call the cops?"

"Again, she couldn't prove anything. It was all a hunch, nothing concrete." He stared off in the distance for a moment. "I got back from a two-week tour. We'd talked several times while I was on the road, but I got back a day earlier than scheduled. I went to her house to surprise her, but she wasn't home."

"Could be a coincidence, especially since she didn't know you were coming."

"True. But I tried to call after that, and she didn't answer. After a day of not being able to get in touch with her, I got worried. Skye was always really good about calling me back in a timely manner."

"What happened next?"

"I managed to find the number for Skye's friend Darcy, but she hadn't heard from Skye in three days. I tried not to panic. I mean, we were at that weird place in our relationship where we'd only gone out a few times. We liked each other, but we didn't have enough time together to be serious. I couldn't say for sure if this was normal or not."

"You mean, maybe she was the type of girl who just liked to take off on a trip without telling anyone?"

"Exactly. She didn't have to answer to me. She's a big girl. Anyway, when I didn't hear anything for two days, I called the police. They got some information from me and did a little investigating. They called the company she worked for, and her boss said that Skye called in and requested time off. The police also said that they'd checked her apartment and there was no evidence of foul play. They came to the conclusion that she left on her own free will."

"But you think Georgia did something?" I leaned back, unsure if it was excitement over the case or my sugar high that made my blood zing.

"I do, but I have no way to prove it." He leaned across the table toward me. "Darcy did say that Skye seemed a bit of a gypsy, that she wasn't the type who wanted to settle down. If she left on her own, I certainly don't want to stalk her. But if something happened to her . . ."

"How long ago did this happen?"

His eyes crinkled with worry. "A month."

"You think every woman you get close to is a target for Georgia. She's some sort of femme fatale?"

"Exactly."

I grabbed a peanut and rubbed it between my fingers, suddenly starving. "What do you want me to do?"

Just in the nick of time, the waitress set our food in front of us and the tantalizing scent of barbecue ribs drifted upward. It wasn't until that moment I realized just how hungry I was, and I instantly wanted to inhale the entire plate of ribs, fries, coleslaw, and beans before me. Of course, I wouldn't, because that would be uncouth.

Trace took his hat off. "You mind if we pray before eating?"

It was refreshing to hear someone else ask that. "Please do."

As soon as he said "amen," I grabbed a fry and got back to the conversation. "So, please continue. I'm curious now."

"I really liked Skye, Gabby. My manager says I shouldn't become attached to anyone. Fans like the illusion that you're single and available to be the 'man of their dreams.'" He said the last four words in a mocking tone. "But I can't stop thinking about her. Not only about her smile but about the possibility that something happened to her."

"Your manager sounds like a pain in the chaps." I picked up a rib, realizing how messy this was going to be. I was willing to chance it.

"He is."

"When was the last time you saw this Georgia woman?"

He raised his fork but still didn't eat a bite. "That's the strange thing. I haven't seen her since Skye disappeared. The day I returned home from my tour, Georgia was waiting for me outside of the recording studio. I tried to brush her off."

"How did she respond?" I bit into the rib, and the meat nearly melted in my mouth.

"Not well. She got angry, and said we were meant to be together and that I'd eventually see it one day."

"Sounds scary."

He nodded. "You can say that again. But then she

left. It's been quiet. Too quiet, you know what I mean?"

I put the bone down and wiped my mouth with a napkin. Trace would never take me seriously with barbecue sauce on my face. I balled up the napkin and tried to look composed before addressing him. "What would you like for me to do, Trace? Find Skye? Track Georgia?"

He scooped up some coleslaw with his fork. "Jono keeps saying I need to let this go and get used to women doing crazy things in the name of having a celebrity crush. But if Georgia did something to Skye, then I feel responsible. I can't live with myself if she was hurt because of me. For a while, I even wondered if Jono might be behind it. I could see him as the type who might pay Skye off in order to ensure I'm single and unattached."

"He'd be a snake if he did that."

"I know. That's why I'd like for you to help me figure out what happened. See if you can locate Georgia and figure out what she's up to. Has she moved on to someone else? Did she have anything to do with Skye's disappearance? I need some answers."

"I understand."

"I know you have classes this week, but I figured you could snoop in the evenings. Maybe you could even stay in Oklahoma a little longer if you needed to? I could compensate you. What do you say?"

I stared at him a moment, at his green eyes as they pleaded with me. "I say, I'm just the girl who can't say no—to mysteries, of course. I'd love to help, but not for pay. We're family. Practically."

He grinned. "Thank you so much, Gabby. Now, eat those ribs. You're going to need your energy for this one."

Click here to continue reading.

ALSO BY CHRISTY BARRITT:

BOOKS IN THE SQUEAKY CLEAN UNIVERSE

On her way to completing a degree in forensic science, Gabby St. Claire drops out of school and starts her own crime-scene cleaning business. When a routine cleaning job uncovers a murder weapon the police overlooked, she realizes that the wrong person is in jail. She also realizes that crime scene cleaning might be the perfect career for utilizing her investigative skills.

SQUEAKY CLEAN MYSTERIES
#1 Hazardous Duty
Half Witted (Squeaky Clean In Between Mysteries
Book 1, novella)
#2 Suspicious Minds
#2.5 It Came Upon a Midnight Crime (novella)
#3 Organized Grime

SQUEAKY CLEAN IN BETWEEN MYSTERIES

Half Witted

Half Truth

THE SIERRA FILES

ABOUT THE AUTHOR

USA Today has called Christy Barritt's books "scary, funny, passionate, and quirky."

Christy writes both mystery and romantic suspense novels that are clean with underlying messages of faith. Her books have sold more than four million copies and have won the Daphne du Maurier Award for Excellence in Suspense and Mystery, have been twice nominated for the Romantic Times Reviewers' Choice Award, and have finaled for both a Carol Award and Foreword Magazine's Book of the Year.

She is married to her Prince Charming, a man who thinks she's hilarious—but only when she's not trying to be. Christy is a self-proclaimed klutz, an avid music lover who's known for spontaneously bursting into song, and a road trip aficionado.

When she's not working or spending time with her family, she enjoys singing, playing the guitar, and exploring small, unsuspecting towns where people have no idea how accident-prone she is.

Find Christy online at:
   www.christybarritt.com
   www.facebook.com/christybarritt
   www.twitter.com/cbarritt

Sign up for Christy's newsletter to get information on all of her latest releases here: **www.christybarritt.com/newsletter-sign-up/**

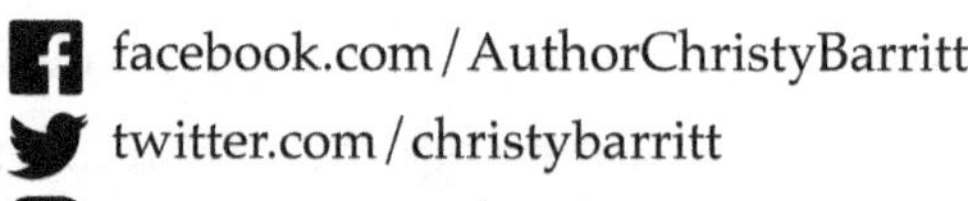

facebook.com/AuthorChristyBarritt
twitter.com/christybarritt
instagram.com/cebarritt